WAS IT
MURDER?

WAS IT MURDER?

by
JAMES HILTON

Dover Publications, Inc.
New York

This Dover edition, first published in 1979, is an
unabridged republication of the work originally published under the title *Murder at School* by Benn, London,
in 1931 under James Hilton's pen-name Glen Trevor.

International Standard Book Number: 0-486-23774-5
Library of Congress Catalog Card Number: 78-74115

Manufactured in the United States of America
Dover Publications, Inc.
180 Varick Street
New York, N.Y. 10014

CONTENTS

WAS IT
MURDER?

CHAPTER I

THE STRANGE AFFAIR IN THE DORMITORY

Pilate might well have added: "What is youth?"—
　And so the modern father too may wonder,
Faintly remembering his own, forsooth,
　But feeling it would be an awful blunder
To tell his sons a tenth part of the truth
　About the sex-temptations *he* came under.
Therefore, in England now, on every hand,
This proper study of mankind is banned.

So, AFTER patient effort, composed Colin Revell in his Islington lodgings on a murky December morning in 1927. You will have rightly deduced that he was young, rather clever, and not hard up enough to have to do any real work. He was, in fact, just as old as the century; had had one of those "brilliant" careers at Oxford that are the despair alike of parents and prospective employers; and enjoyed a private income of a little over four pounds a week. Added to which, he was an only child; his parents were both dead; and his relatives were the usual collection of retired colonels and tea-planters who, from their fastnesses at Cheltenham, eyed him with as little relish as he did them.

His unassuming ground-floor front looked on to a somewhat decayed street within walking distance of the Caledonian Cattle Market. The hour was a trifle short of noon, and the remains of a recent breakfast lay pushed somewhat away from him on the table. His purple dressing-gown and black silk pyjamas contrasted oddly with the landlady's furnishings, which, in an ecstasy of admiration for their Victorian antiquity, he had allowed

9

to remain exactly as when he had first entered into occupation. It was a pose, undoubtedly, but an amusing
one. The landlady, a Mrs. Hewston, thought her
lodger rather "queer," but as he paid her well and regu-
larly and did not appear to mind her stealing his gin,
she was glad enough to keep him.

Gin, indeed, was the sedative with which, having
composed his stanza, Revell restored a somewhat
fatigued mind. His friends were all aware that, besides
writing occasional literary articles for a high-brow
weekly, he was "at work" on a full-length satirical epic
in the manner and metre of *Don Juan*. He had begun it
during his final year at Oxford, and by the date at which
this story opens it had grown to lack only two things—
continuity and a publisher.

A clock somewhere in the neighbourhood began the
chiming of noon. Factory-sirens shrieked; groups of
children straggled out of an elementary-school opposite. And the postman, observing Mrs. Hewston in her
basement kitchen, descended the area steps and handed
her three letters with the remark: "All for your young
gentleman."

A moment later the young gentleman was opening
them. One was a returned article from the *Daily Mail*
(too good for them, of course, he consoled himself);
another was a bill from an Oxford tailor equally famous
for high prices and long credit. And the third was the
following:

The Schoolhouse,
Oakington.
December 15th, 1927.

My Dear Revell,
    I don't think we ever met, but as you are an O.O. and
I am the present Head of Oakington, perhaps we can

do without an introduction. My friend Simmons of Oxford mentioned you to me some time ago as a neat solver of mysteries, and as there seems as if there might be one at Oakington just now, I take the somewhat large liberty of asking your help. Could you spend the coming week-end here? I should be glad to put you up, and there will be the final house-match to watch on Monday, if you are interested.

Yours sincerely,
Robert Roseveare.

P.S.—A good train leaves King's Cross at 2.30 to-morrow afternoon. Dinner-jacket.

Revell digested the communication over a second and more potent gin-and-vermouth. It seemed to him distinctly the sort of thing which (in books) drew from its reader the comment "Whew!" Accustomed and even pleased as he was to receive week-end invitations, the Headmaster of Oakington was hardly a host he would have chosen. He disliked schoolmasters and sentimental revisitings with almost equal degrees of intensity, and the two in conjunction could raise in his mind only the most dismal of prospects.

Yet the letter was curious enough to give him, after his moment of instinctive recoil, the faint beginnings of interest. It was in so many ways the sort of letter one did not quite expect from a schoolmaster. There was a mingling of friendliness and curtness in the wording of it that Revell, as something of a word-fancier himself, could not help but admire. He liked, too, the sentence about the house-match; it was unexpectedly broad-minded of a headmaster to conceive the possibility of an old boy not being interested in house-matches. (And Revell most emphatically wasn't.) And then, too, there was the mystery—whatever it might turn out to be. A mystery always attracted him. Anything attracted him, in fact, that brought with it the possibility of being drawn into some new vortex of interest. His soul yearned with Byronic intensity for something to happen to it. He was almost twenty-eight, and so far he seemed to have done nothing in life except win the Newdigate, give a terrifying study of the Jew in the O.U.D.S. production of *The Merchant of Venice*, publish a novel (of course he had done *that*), be introduced to Mr. T. P. O'Connor, and rake in an unexpected tenner for inventing the last line of a limerick about somebody's chewing-gum.

That little affair at Oxford, as well—it pleased him that it was still remembered and that old Simmons still talked about it. A rather valuable manuscript had disappeared from the College library, and by means of a little amateur detective-work he had succeeded in tracing and recovering it. The whole business, concerning as it did the integrity of one of the dons, had naturally been hushed up, but not without many pleasant compliments to the undergraduate whose versatility could take at a single stride the gulf between Shylock and Sherlock.

But what finally turned the scale in Revell's mind was the last word of the post-script. *Dinner-jacket.* There, he decided, spoke that *rara avis*, the headmaster who was also a man of the world. *Dinner-jacket.* It suggested good food, perhaps even good wine; and Revell delighted in both. For a moment he permitted his imagination to soar; then, having decided definitely to accept the invitation, he packed his bag, dressed with care, sent a wire to the School from the post-office round the corner, and made the necessary arrangements with Mrs. Hewston.

That afternoon, during the rather tedious train-journey, he dallied with further stanza composition, but had not time to do very much before Oakington station intervened. The dingy goods-yard, the gravelled platform, even the faces of one or two of the station staff, were all familiar to him. As he gave up his ticket and stepped into the lane he could glimpse the School buildings directly ahead, surmounting the ancient village with a halo of nineteenth-century Gothic. "The School, sir?" interrogated a cab-driver who evidently recognised him. He nodded with ghastly pride. He was an Old Boy.

Whether Oakington was or was not a pukka public-school might have been aptly debated by a squad of mediaeval theologians raised from the dead. On the one hand, it was included in the Public Schools Year-Book, it ran an O.T.C., it reckoned to send a few scholarship boys to the universities each year, and it had a school-song of unimpeachable mediocrity. Yet, on the other hand . . . there had been a feeling in the scholastic world that Oakington might well be the answer to the question: When is a public-school not quite a public-school? It is only fair to add, however, that this feeling had been diminishing steadily since the advent of Doctor Robert Roseveare. Lately, indeed, in the offices of scholastic agencies and even across the table of the annual Headmasters' Conference, it had begun to be whispered that Roseveare was something of a new broom. And it was generally agreed that after his predecessor's long and easy-going régime there had been a good deal left to sweep up.

Structurally the School was all that gargoyles and crocheted spires could make it. If there were sermons in stones, Revell reflected, as the cab turned into the drive towards the Head's house, then Oakington was a complete ecclesiastical library. He was on the point of mentally elaborating the theme when he perceived through the gathering twilight a newer structure, put up since his schooldays and in a style which he mentally classified as Hampstead Garden Suburb Elizabethan. "That's the new War Memorial 'All, sir," remarked the cabby, glowing with local patriotism. Revell nodded. He had heard of it. More than that, he had even (he recollected) subscribed a guinea towards it. Life was full of such strange ironies.

His spirits rose, however, a few minutes later when a white-haired butler admitted him into a room which, despite the fact that it had not been structurally altered since he had last seen it, looked nevertheless a different room of a different house. Furnished richly yet with taste, it had a touch of masculine severity that was somehow in complete harmony with the butler's words: "The Head is expecting you, sir. He is in the study, if you will follow me."

The study presented another striking change; under the régime of the Reverend Doctor Jury, who had been Head of Oakington in Revell's time, it had been a gloomy, littered apartment, full of dusty folios and sagging bookshelves. Now, however, it looked more like the board-room of a long-established limited company. A thick pile carpet, a large mahogany pedestal-desk, nests of bookshelves in the two alcoves by the side of the fireplace, a very few good etchings on the walls, and several huge armchairs drawn up in front of an open fire, gave an impression that was anything but pedagogic. And Doctor Roseveare himself confirmed the impression. He was tall (well over six feet), upright, and of commanding physique. Bushy, silver-grey hair surmounted a strong, smooth-complexioned face into which, however, as he gave Revell a firm hand-grip, there came a smile both cordial and charming. His voice was melodious, perhaps a little wistful, and in his accent there was just the faintest and most fascinating flavour of something that was not quite Oxford, or even Cambridge. He looked, in fact, rather like a popular preacher (Revell thought of Mr. R. J. Campbell in his spell-binding days), yet with an agreeable and compensating touch of worldliness that his perfectly-cut lounge-suit suggested but in no way emphasised. "Delighted you could come," he remarked, throwing off his gown with a Roman gesture. "Apart from any private reason, it is always a.pleasure for Oakington to receive her old boys. We feel we are in their debt quite as much as some of them feel they are in ours."

Revell nodded politely, guessing that such an adroit remark was bound to have done duty on many previous occasions. As a collector of such felicities, he added it joyfully to his store. A little old-boyishness in response seemed clearly indicated, so he replied, slipping easily into the part, that it would be jolly to look at the old scenes once more.

At which Doctor Roseveare smiled warily, as if rather wondering. For a few minutes they fenced skilfully over such subjects as the weather, house-matches, the coming Christmas holidays, the life of a young man in London, and the new War Memorial Hall. Of this latter Revell diplomatically observed that Oakington had always needed a hall. Roseveare replied: "Oh yes, undoubtedly. Some people like the present structure. The plans, anyhow, were passed before I came here."

The admission, with all its possible implications, drew

them together. Within five minutes Revell had ceased
to be old-boyish and Roseveare had ceased to be—or at
least to appear to be—wary. The two talked easily, intimately, and with that flow of goodwill that always
exists between two people who each know that the
other recognises and appreciates technique in conversation.

By dinner-time Revell had grown accustomed to as-
tonishments. A charmingly-furnished bedroom with the
latest-type of bathroom adjoining, his dinner clothes
laid out on the bed with all their proper creases intact,
an electric warmer already between the sheets—all added
to his sensations of physical, mental and spiritual well-
being. When the second sounding of the gong sum-
moned him downstairs, he found his host reading the
evening-paper with his back to the study-fire. "Ah . . .
no news of any importance. . . . I'm afraid I cannot
offer you a cocktail, but a glass of sherry perhaps? I
usually take one myself."

It was exceedingly good sherry, and the dinner, when
they adjourned to the panelled dining-room, was
worthy of such a handsome beginning. "I have a good
cook," explained the doctor, almost apologetically. The
good cook, however, could hardly claim credit for the
excellent Volnay, or for the Napoleon brandy served
in balloon glasses which, at Roseveare's suggestion, they
took at leisure in the study afterwards.

"You will smoke?" queried Roseveare, offering a box
of Coronas. "I may not do so myself, unfortunately,
but I shall enjoy the scent of yours. Good. . . . And
now, I am sure, you are waiting for me to mention the
little affair I hinted at in my letter to you."

Revell was waiting, it is true, but without any intense eagerness. If life could continue to provide such

agreeable moments of suspense, he at any rate would not be impatient.

"I shall be interested, of course," he answered.

"No doubt my letter surprised you?"

"Well, perhaps I was—a little—puzzled by it."

"Exactly." Roseveare seemed to welcome the reply. "And that, my dear boy, is just my own position in a nutshell—I am *puzzled*."

Revell glanced up with the beginnings of keener interest. There had been in the "dear boy" a suddenly emotional inflection, as if, behind the mask of bland benignity, the elder man were calling out for sympathy from the younger. "I hope I shall be able to help you, sir," Revell said, simply.

"I hope so, too, though I am afraid you may think the whole affair too fantastic even to be considered. Perhaps I had better give you a brief outline—fortunately it will not be very complicated. It concerns an extremely sad and unhappy accident that occurred here at the beginning of this Term."

He waited as if for Revell to make some comment, and then continued: "There was a boy here named Robert Marshall, a younger brother of our head-prefect. A much elder brother—Henry, I think—was here in your time. I don't know if you knew him?"

"Slightly, that's all."

"Ah yes, yes. He was killed during the last days of the War—most tragically, for he was under nineteen and ought not to have been sent out. His death, indeed, was such a blow to his parents that they both died within a couple of years. The two younger boys were left— Robert and Wilbraham. They came on here in the usual way and at the usual ages from a preparatory-school. Pleasant boys—not brilliant, perhaps, but well-liked and altogether a credit to the School. Wilbraham, as I said just now, is our present head-prefect—a boy of sound character, good at games, and very popular. He will leave next summer, no doubt, and enter Oxford—there is, fortunately, plenty of money. But to come to the point. About three months ago his younger brother—Robert, that is to say—was the victim of a most peculiar and distressing accident. A heavy gas-fitting fell on him in the dormitory during the night, killing him instantly."

"Good Lord!" Revell, who till then had been listening rather dreamily, found himself suddenly jerked into attention.

"Some of the London papers had a paragraph about it," Roseveare went on. "I don't know if you noticed it?"

"No, I'm afraid I didn't."

"Then I certainly think it will be best if, before saying any more, I allow you to read the account of the inquest, reported fairly fully in our local paper."

He took out a pocket-wallet and produced therefrom a folded newspaper-cutting. "Take your time," he remarked, handing it over. "And remember—all this happened three months ago."

It was a column and a half in length, and Revell, at a first quick reading, seized its main points as follows. The accident had taken place on the first Sunday-night-Monday-morning of the Autumn Term. It had not been discovered till daylight, when a boy named March, who had chanced to wake early, saw that something had happened, and raised the alarm. The gas-fitting was a heavy, old-fashioned, inverted-T-shaped affair, one of a series that were suspended in a double row along the whole length of the dormitory. Underneath the junction of the horizontal and vertical sections of piping a brass tip had been fitted, apparently for ornamental effect. Marshall, it seemed, had been sleeping with his head exactly under this tip, so that when the whole thing collapsed the effect must have been like a heavy spear falling on him.

Of several witnesses called, none could give much real information. The school doctor, a fellow named Murchiston, described how he had been sent for at seven in the morning to examine the body. Death, he thought, had been instantaneous, the skull and brain having been pierced. The accident might have taken place from five to eight hours before—he would not care to commit himself more than that.

The housemaster, Mr. T. B. Ellington, described the position of his private house, next to the School House block containing the dormitory, but quite separate from it. He was not only Marshall's housemaster, he explained, but the boy's cousin as well. It was his habit to walk through the dormitory and turn off all the gas-jets at ten o'clock every night. He had done so as usual on that particular Sunday night. He had not noticed anything at all peculiar about any of the gas-fittings. After bidding the boys good night he had worked for a time in his own private room adjoining the dormitory and had then returned to his house and gone to bed. That might have been, perhaps, as late as one o'clock, for he had been busy marking terminal examination papers. He had certainly heard nothing unusual during that time. He knew nothing at all about the accident till a boy came to him soon after six o'clock with news of what had happened. He had immediately hastened to the dormitory and had found Marshall dead. The whole gas-fitting, wrenched or broken off at the ceiling, lay across the bed in the position in which, appar-

ently, it had fallen. He had been too much distressed
to examine it minutely. There was a strong smell of
gas in the dormitory, so he had sent a boy to turn off
the supply at the main. Then he had sent another boy
to fetch the Headmaster.

Evidence was then given by several boys, including
the two who slept in the beds on either side of Marshall's. None of them had heard anything during the
night. They agreed that they usually slept well and did
not waken easily.

A "certain liveliness" seemed to have been introduced
into the proceedings by the evidence of a Mr. John
Tunstall, chief-engineer to the local gas company. On
being informed of the accident by telephone, he said, he
had immediately visited the School and made an examination. The gas-fitting was very old, and of a type that
no company would supply or recommend nowadays.
He had found a large fracture in the pipe near the ceil-
ing-rose. This had evidently been the cause of the fitting's suddenly dropping loose. Such fractures did sometimes occur in fittings that had seen many years' service, especially if they had been subjected to any particular sort of strain. Questioned by the Coroner on this
point, he said that he had in mind another and a similar
fitting at the School that had been pulled down as a
result of some of the boys swinging on it.

Doctor Roseveare next gave evidence, if evidence it
could be called. The Coroner allowed him latitude to
make a few kindly remarks concerning the dead boy
and to express sympathy with his relatives. From that
he passed to the more practical announcement that the
governors of the School had already given orders for
the complete electrification of the entire buildings. He
also craved leave to state, since the point had been

raised, that there never had been, to his knowledge, any instance of Oakington boys swinging on the gas-fittings. The incident presumably referred to by one of the witnesses had been that of a window-cleaner who had carelessly broken off one of the fittings with his ladder. As Headmaster he thought it only fair, in the interests of the School, to mention this. . . .

That was all. The jury, without retiring, returned the inevitable verdict of "Accidental Death."

Roseveare waited in silence until he could see that Revell had got to the end. Then, moving forward a little in his chair, he coughed interrogatively. "Well? And what do you think of it?"

Revell handed back the cutting. "It was an odd sort of accident, of course," he commented. "But then, odder ones have happened, I daresay."

"Precisely." Roseveare's grey, deep-set eyes quickened a little. "I naturally regarded it in that light myself. So did the poor boy's guardian, a Colonel Graham, living in India, from whom I received a most courteous and sympathetic letter. And then, just about a week ago . . ." He paused. "You will probably think it was quite a small and insignificant thing. Indeed, I hope you do. Anyhow, let me tell you about it."

Through the haze of cigar-smoke Revell nodded encouragement. Roseveare continued: "Last week I had a letter from Colonel Graham—a second letter. He suggested that Mr. Ellington, as the poor boy's housemaster and cousin, should take charge of his personal belongings until he himself came home from India in about six months' time. I had naturally been expecting instructions of such a kind and had already had everything collected and stored away. I was just looking them over before passing them on to Ellington when—to make a longish story a little shorter—I chanced upon this." He produced a second slip of paper from his wallet. "It was between the pages of the boy's algebra-book."

It was a sheet of notepaper with the Oakington crest and letter-heading. At the top was the date—September 18th, 1927. And underneath, in carefully printed capital letters, the following:

> "IF ANYTHING SHOULD HAPPEN TO ME, I LEAVE EVERYTHING TO MY BROTHER WILBRAHAM, EXCEPT MY THREE-SPEED BICYCLE, WHICH I LEAVE TO JONES TER-TIUS. (SIGNED)—ROBERT MARSHALL."

Revell, after a short pause, handed back the document without remark. Roseveare went on: "You can perhaps imagine my feelings at the discovery of such a thing. It raised—hardly perhaps so much as a suspicion—but a sort of—shall I say a sort of curiosity in my mind. It was rather disconcerting to reflect that on the very evening before the boy died he had been thinking of his own possible death."

Revell nodded. "I suppose there *was* a three-speed bicycle?"

"Oh yes. And he *was* friendly with Jones—I verified all that. I couldn't get hold of another example of his printing to compare with, but the handwriting of the signature seemed authentic enough." He clenched his hands on the arms of the chair and added, with a touch of eagerness: "I daresay the whole thing is just pure coincidence. I certainly don't want you to assume that there is more in it than meets the eye."

Revell nodded once again, but with his glance fixed rather shrewdly on the other. "What is it," he asked, "that you would like me to do?"

"Nothing definite, I assure you—nothing definite at all. Just consider, if I may so express it, that for a few days you hold a watching brief. Here, as I have told them to you, are the facts—presenting a situation that is, shall we agree to say, abnormal enough to be worth a little extra attention if only for its own sake. Just look over it yourself and tell me how you feel about it— that's really all I have in mind."

"But surely, sir, you don't suspect——"

"My dear boy, I suspect nothing and nobody. As a matter of fact—" the emotional inflection was in his voice again— "this terrible business was a great blow to me—far greater than I have allowed people to see. Apart from personal regrets, the publicity that the whole affair received was a great setback to the School. You may or may not know, Revell, the state in which I found things when I first came here. For half a dozen years I have toiled hard to raise and improve, and then —comes *this*. There is no one on my staff in whom I would care to confide. I cannot probe into the matter myself—to do so would draw even greater attention to it. And yet, of course, there may be nothing at all to probe. . . . My nerves, I am aware, are not in the best condition—I need a long holiday which I shall not be able to take until the summer vacation next year. I can see you are tremendously mystified by all this. And no wonder. It is all, I daresay, perfectly absurd."

"I must admit, sir, I don't see a scrap of evidence to suggest anything really wrong."

"Of course not. There isn't any, I don't suppose. And yet—there's that little demon of curiosity in my mind— why *was* the boy thinking of death on that Sunday evening?"

"Who can say? Coincidences like that *do* happen. And

there's nothing very remarkable in the note itself. Just the fatuous sort of thing I might have written myself on a Sunday night after chapel when I'd nothing else to do."

"Probably—you comfort me even by saying so. Nevertheless, you will not decline my vague and probably quite ridiculous commission?"

"Oh, of course not, if you would really like me to look into it."

"Good. You see, no doubt, how well suited you are for the task. As a distinguished Old Boy of the School, you have the best of reasons for being here as my guest. You can talk to both boys and masters without anyone questioning your *bona-fides*. No one, of course, knows or need know why you are really here. You understand?"

"Oh yes."

"Then I leave things in your hands. I have heard splendid accounts, my dear Revell, of your work in connexion with a certain regrettable affair at Oxford. This, I hope, will be less serious. . . . You were in School House, I believe, when you were here?"

"Yes."

"Good—that will give you a convenient excuse for meeting Ellington. I mentioned your visit to him, in fact—he suggested you might care to breakfast with him to-morrow morning."

"I should be delighted."

"Most likely he will drop in later on to-night to meet you. . . . Another cigar? Yes, do, please. Are you interested, by the way, in etchings? I have one or two here that are considered to be rather choice."

Revell perceived that the discussion, for the time being, was over, and he could not but notice and admire the ease with which the other resumed his earlier manner. Nerves or not, he certainly had them well under control. They talked on for over an hour on varied topics; Roseveare showed himself to be a man of remarkably wide interests and obviously enjoyed an exchange of views with the younger generation. Yet there was not a trace of patronage or of condescension in his attitude. He listened sympathetically when Revell told him of his literary work and of the *Don Juan* epic. Revell liked him more and more; it was as if their recent more serious talk had been a strange interlude in a much more real intimacy.

Towards ten o'clock Ellington arrived and was introduced. He was a heavily-built, middle-aged fellow, thick-set of feature and going a little bald. Under his impact the conversation sagged instantly. He appeared cordial enough about the breakfast invitation, but Revell gathered that it was his housemasterly habit to ask School House old boys to breakfast, and that he did it as a sort of routine duty. Revell, in fact, was not greatly attracted to him. When he had gone Roseveare faintly shrugged his shoulders. "A hard worker, Ellington, and a devoted colleague. But not much of a conversationalist, I am afraid. However . . . Perhaps you will take a little whisky before going up to bed? I usually do so myself."

And, since Revell usually did so whenever he had the chance, the ritual was jointly observed.

CHAPTER II

SOLVED!

Sunday at Oakington in Revell's time had always been a depressing day. No cooked foods were served from the kitchens; all newspapers (except religious weeklies) were removed from the School reading-room; no boy could leave the grounds without special permission; games and gramophones were alike forbidden; three chapel services had to be attended; and it was also a day of compulsory black suits, shoes, and ties.

To Revell, comfortably dozing while the chapel-bell importunately rang for the first service, there came the jumbled memories of some hundred or so of such days. Not that he had had an unhappy time at School. But there was an unholy glee to be derived from lying between warm sheets and thinking of the Oakington multitude shivering in its pews on a December morning with the prospect of nothing but cold brawn for breakfast. He wondered also, since Roseveare was not apparently a cleric, who read the lessons. . . .

Roseveare. . . . The name somehow managed to banish his drowsiness; after a little delay he got up, enjoyed the steamiest of hot baths, dressed, and went downstairs. The butler met him with a reminder of his breakfast engagement with Mr. Ellington. He nodded and walked out through the porch into the chill wintry air. From the chapel across the intervening lawn came the sound of a hymn. Ellington's house, viewed from where he was, presented the appearance of a suburban villa leaning coyly against the massive

26

flanks of School House. It was not perhaps very elegant, but it had enabled four generations of pedagogues to combine marriage and housemastership in a manner both effective and discreet.

Revell walked briskly across the quadrangle, climbed the short flight of steps, and rang the door-bell. A woman's voice from the interior called "Come in!" He entered and waited a few seconds in the hall. The voice again cried "Come in!"—whereupon, fired with a little determination, he walked over to the room from which the sound had seemed to proceed and boldly pushed open the door. He found himself immediately in the presence of a dark-haired, bright-eyed little woman, almost pretty, who was frying rashers of bacon at a gas-cooker.

"Oh, I'm so sorry," she stammered, seeing him. "I thought—I thought you might be the boy bringing the milk. . . . Oh, do forgive me. . . . I suppose you are Mr. Revell?"

Revell smiled and admitted that he was.

"I really am most awfully sorry. My husband's in chapel, you know—he'll be here in a few minutes. The servants all go to chapel too, so I have to get the breakfast myself on Sundays. I hope you'll excuse me."

"Rather," answered Revell, gaily, turning on the torrent of chatter he held in reserve for such occasions. "I love cooking and kitchens, as a matter of fact. If I'd been old enough to go to the War, there's only one thing I'd wanted to be—a batman. The morning miracle of ham and eggs——"

"Yes," she interrupted, "cooking is rather fun. And Molly prefers it to going to chapel, I know, but we— or rather, my husband—has to insist on her going to the first service, even if she misses the others. It's an old school custom, I suppose."

"I wonder," said Revell, with that air of slightly cynical abstraction that always or nearly always interested women, "is Oakington really old enough to have any old customs?"

"I don't know." She was, he perceived, out of her depth. But his spirits rose as he contemplated her; she would at least relieve the concentrated boredom of a breakfast with Ellington. Ellington, in fact, appeared on the scene almost at that moment. "Sorry to keep you waiting," he grunted, and to his wife he added, rather sharply: "why didn't you show Mr. Revell into the drawing-room?"

"I'm so glad she didn't," interposed Revell. "A drawing-room in a morning is like—" He paused, trying to think of some epigram, either original or purloined; but as neither the housemaster nor his wife appeared to be listening he gave up his effort and merely smiled. And Mrs. Ellington faintly smiled back.

Eyeing her a little later across the breakfast-table, he guessed her to be anything between twenty and thirty years younger than her husband. Vivacious in a shy, limited kind of way, she talked a good deal about nothing in particular, and Revell, as he had expected, found her animated chatter a pleasant antidote to Ellington's ponderous small-talk. Ellington was, undoubtedly, a prime bore; his conversation consisted almost entirely of house-match anticipations. Once or twice Revell tried to take things in hand himself, but without much success. Even his less subtle witticisms passed unnoticed, though occasionally, a minute or so too late, Mrs. Ellington responded with a scared little laugh, as if she were just beginning to feel her way cautiously into an unfamiliar world.

It began to rain towards the end of the meal. "Bad time of the year for a visit," commented Ellington. "Nothing but rain and fog. Been a pretty bad Term altogether, in fact." Revel waited to see if this were to be a prelude to some remark about the Marshall affair; and so, perhaps, it might have been but for the sudden intrusion, amidst numerous jocund apologies, of a small-statured, red-faced, cheery-looking person whom Ellington introduced as "our padre—Captain Daggat." The two seemed on good terms; Ellington made Daggat take a cup of coffee, although the latter insisted that he had already breakfasted. "Snug little place, this, eh?" he said, winking at Revell. "Not so bad being a married housemaster." He sat down at the table and dominated the talk by sheer fatuousness. He made foolish jokes with Mrs. Ellington, talked shop with Ellington himself, and addressed Revell from time to time with that slangy familiarity which a certain type of parson cultivates in the belief that it makes people feel "at home" with him. Towards ten o'clock, when Ellington had to rush away to take a class in scripture, Revell made polite excuses to go. But Daggat hung on to him mercilessly. "Come along, old chap. You'll enjoy a stroll round the old place, even if it *is* raining. Good-bye, Mrs. Ellington, and many thanks. . . . Seen our War Memorial Hall yet, Revell?"

Despairingly Revell allowed himself to be piloted from place to place. They explored the Memorial Hall, the Museum, the Library, and the new science laboratories. Revell summed up Daggat as that commonest of types, the athletic parson. His slang, his bubbling eagerness to be of service, his frequent references to the War (which he seemed to recollect as a sort of inter-school rugger-match on a large scale)—all would have jarred inexpressibly had not Revell been hoping that in due course, and preferably without prompting, Daggat would talk about the dormitory tragedy. When at length he suggested "a pipe and a pow-wow in my snuggery," Revell agreed willingly enough. The snuggery proved to be on the first floor of the main School House block; it was the usual room affected by such an occupant, with its wide open windows and languishing fire, its sporting trophies, its hackneyed reproductions of too famous paintings, and its mantelpiece full of fixture-cards. Pinned to the wall by the fireplace was the list of preachers in Oakington School Chapel during the current term. Revell glanced at it. "So you're on duty to-day?" he commented.

"Yes. They usually book me for the beginning and end of term."

"I hope I'm not taking up your time when you'd rather be preparing?"

"Oh, not in the least, my dear chap. I always preach extempore. Often I don't even know my subject till I get into the pulpit. It's the only way. Once let the fellows feel that you're not speaking straight from the heart, and you lose grip on them. Don't you think so?"

Revell answered vaguely. He was thinking, as a matter of fact, about Mrs. Ellington, and idly speculating upon how and where she had met Ellington, what in him had attracted her, and whether they had been married long. Daggat roused him from such problems by asking what years he had been at Oakington.

"I was here during the War. 'Fifteen to 'eighteen."

"You were too young, I suppose, to be in the big scrap?"

" 'Fraid so." Revell felt like adding: "Too young to have had any of those stirring adventures which you are going to tell me about now if I give you half a chance." Something of his feeling must have translated itself into a warning glance, for Daggat, after momentary hesitation, twisted the subject to a different angle. "Ten years ago, by God!" he exclaimed. "To think it's all as long ago as that! And yet a pretty good deal's happened in the interval, I must admit—even at Oakington. Almost a complete change of staff, you know. I don't suppose you've seen many familiar faces."

"I caught sight of old Longwell this morning, but he didn't know me—I never took drawing. Some of the servants' faces I seem to remember. But apart from that, everyone's a stranger." He added: "I gather there was something like a clean sweep when the new Head came?"

Daggat nodded. "I came in 'twenty-three—a year after the Head. I heard stories, of course, of what things had been like before . . ."

They chatted on, coming at length to reminiscences of particular boys whom Revell had known in his time, and whose younger relatives were still at Oakington. It was easy in such a connexion, to mention Marshall, and Daggat was only too eager to discuss the tragedy. "I suppose you read about it at the time?" he queried, and Revell allowed him to presume so. "Ah, a terrible business. Queer thing, when you come to think about it, that a gas-thing-umbob should come crashing down just when a boy's head is underneath it. Providence, of course—that's all one can say. As I've told the School in my sermons time and time again—*we never know*. With all our modern science and invention—with all our much-vaunted——"

A sharp tap on the door-panel interrupted a perora-
tion whose conclusion seemed reasonably predictable.
"Come in!" yelled Daggat, in a high-pitched, sing-song
tenor. The door opened a few inches and a man's voice,
deep-toned and rather cultivated, murmured: "Sorry,
Daggat—didn't know you were busy. Any other time'll
do."

Daggat jumped up hastily. "No, don't go, Lambourne—we're only chatting. Come in and meet Mr.
Revell—he's an Old Boy."

The newcomer made his way into the centre of the
room with a sort of nonchalant indifference. He was a
youngish man, rather tall, perhaps in his early thirties,
with dark eyes and hair and a curious half-melancholy
carelessness in the way he nodded and smiled. He was
dressed, if not perhaps definitely unconventionally, at
least in a way that was not quite expected of an Oakington master on a Sunday morning; in fact, Revell decided, liking him a little on sight, there was nothing
about him that was either schoolmasterly or sabbatical.

"We were talking," said Daggat, puffing away at a
huge briar pipe, "about poor Marshall. Revell knew his
brother—the one who was killed in the War."

Lambourne inclined his head, but made no comment.

"I must say I feel dashed sorry for the present Marshall," Daggat continued. "He's here now, you know,
Revell—our head-prefect. The only one left out of three
brothers, and both the others killed. Frightful bad luck,
you know, and his parents both dead, too. The poor fellow was pretty badly cut up, I can tell you. The Head
wanted to give him leave of absence for the rest of
Term, but of course there was nowhere for him to go.
His guardian's in India."

"How about his holidays, then?"

"I think he spends most of them with other fellows' people. He's very popular."

"Once he had a fortnight with Cousin Thomas," put in Lambourne. "Did you know, by the way, that Ellington was his cousin? They toured the Lake District, anyhow, caught terrible colds, and finished up with a very bourgeois week-end at a seaside hydro near Blackpool."

"Yes, he's very popular," Daggat reiterated. "Jolly good at all games, but swimming especially. Quite the best swimmer Oakington ever had, I believe. Different in almost every way from his brother, poor chap."

Revell gathered somehow that Daggat had not greatly cared for the younger Marshall. "You knew *him* quite well too, I suppose?" he queried.

"Oh, fairly well. He was in my junior form for English. Quiet sort of fellow—imaginative, I daresay—read queer kinds of books. Not bad at his work. I expect he'd have taken his School Certificate."

Revell felt that the epitaph on the deceased had, from the schoolmasterly point of view, been fitly and finally pronounced. As if to clinch the matter, Daggat added: "Ah well, the only way to look at these things is to believe that somehow or other they're providential."

Lambourne smiled. "I'm afraid you view Providence a shade too indulgently, Daggat. Even an insurance-company would hardly dare to call a falling gas-fitting an act of God."

Just then the chapel-bell began to ring for morning service. "Must dash away," cried Daggat, picking up his gown. "You two chaps stay here and chin-wag as long as you like."

When he had gone, Lambourne poked up the fire and dragged his chair nearer to it. "I wish Daggat, as a believer in hell-fire, would use a little more coal," he remarked. "It would prevent his vistors from envying the warmth of the lower regions." He dug into the coal-scuttle with the shovel. "Empty, of course. We call him 'the Cherub,' by the way. Decent fellow, except when he's preaching. Then he makes you feel you want to wring his neck. I warn you, you'll have him to-night, if you go."

"I know. He told me."

"You're staying at the Head's, aren't you?"

"Yes."

"Just for the week-end?"

"That's all."

"Pity. You might have come along to dine with me one night at the local pub. I like a change from school dinners now and again." He went on, after a pause, and with disconcerting abruptness: "Like the Head?"

"Pretty well, I think."

"I suppose you mean that you can't quite make him out?"

"No, I wouldn't say that I meant that." Revell was a little resentful of the other's interpretative air.

"You must remember he's been other things besides a schoolmaster. Lived abroad a good deal—America and the Colonies. His degree's a medical one, by the way. Bit of a *bon viveur*, too, and the very devil for being discreet. All things to all men and to nearly all women, you know."

"He makes a good Head, though, I should think."

"Oh, first-rate. Organising ability and all that. Quite a war-time discovery, in fact."

"He was in the War, then?"

"Of it more than in it, though I'm not suggesting he didn't risk his life once or twice. Ran so many hospitals

and things when he took it into his head to want to run
Oakington, the governors snapped him up with joy."

Something in his tone provoked Revell to a question
which, in normal circumstances, he would have been
least likely to ask. "Were you in the War at all?"

"Oh yes. Decidedly. But I didn't organise anything.
I just got gassed and shell-shocked—that was all." He
added, with a faint smile: "I don't quite know why I'm
telling you all this—I don't gossip about my own affairs as a rule. Really, I suppose it's because Daggat put
me in the mood—it always gets on my nerves to hear
him explaining how Providence does this, and that, and
the other in this best of all possible worlds. . . . By the
way, to change the subject, are you the author of a
novel?"

Revell, for whom this was rare and priceless flattery,
admitted that that was so.

"I thought it must be you," Lambourne rejoined. "I
think I read it when it came out. The usual sort of thing
that people do write just after they leave Oxford. Still,
rather better than most, I remember. Done anything
since?"

Damned patronising, Revell thought, yet more in dis-
appointment than anger. And there was undoubtedly
something in Lambourne that appealed to him. "Odd
journalism," he replied, briefly. But he would not confide in him—not yet, at any rate—about the *Don Juan*
epic.

They talked on for a few more minutes, but the
slowly-dying fire made Lambourne less and less happy.
"Really," he said at length, rising from his chair, "I *must*
go and do some work. I think I shall take a hot-water
bottle to bed with me and mark exercise-books until
dinner-time. Midday dinner, you know, on Sundays—

cold meat and beetroot. . . . Come along and have tea
with me one afternoon, if you can spare the time. So
long." It was the pleasantest, politest, and most effective
way of saying: "Don't bother me any more just now";
and Revell, who himself specialised in just such pleasant, polite, and effective methods, appreciated the
other's technique.

Revell found Oakington a rather depressing place, as
he wandered about the familiar corridors amidst silences
unbroken save by the echo of his own footfalls. It was
raining heavily outside; otherwise he would have more
gladly strolled about the grounds. He even half-wished
that he had gone into chapel, except that to attend the
evening service and two chapels in one day seemed
more than could be expected of anyone who was not
still a public-schoolboy.

Things were still pretty much the same, he reflected,
despite Roseveare's uplifting influence. There were the
same spluttering hot-water pipes in the corridors; there
was the same curious smell of dust and ink in the deserted classrooms. From the ground floor he descended
to the basement bathrooms; these, however, had been
considerably modernised since his time. Everywhere, too,
there were new and rather ugly electric light fittings.

He next visited the two dormitories, in each of which
he had slept as a schoolboy. School House had five
floors, including basement and attic; the first and second floors contained the senior and junior dormitories
respectively. Each dormitory was approached by a corridor leading from the staircase landing, and on both
sides of these corridors were the private rooms of the
masters. Ellington had a room on the second floor, immediately above Daggat's.

It was rather melancholy, pacing along the felt matting in between the tiers of beds in the dormitories. In neither of them could Revell feel quite sure which bed he had once occupied—so lightly did sentimental recollections weigh on him. He found, indeed, that his thoughts were far more on the boy Marshall than on his own schooldays. The bright new electric lamp suspended from the ceiling over the central gangway drew his attention to the double row of scars on either side, where formerly had been the gas-fittings. Certainly, as Daggat had said, it was a curious thing that one of them should have fallen directly on to a sleeping boy. And yet such curious things *did* happen. Perhaps the boys *had* been swinging on it previously, despite Roseveare's denial at the inquest. Heads could not know everything that happened.

During lunch, however, he did not mention the matter, nor did Roseveare. After a pleasant meal, punctuated with equally pleasant conversation, the weather improved, and Revell, leaving the other in his study, strolled out into the world of leafless trees and sodden turf. There was really not much that he could do. In his own mind he was quite certain that young Marshall had met his death by an unusual sort of accident, and that the note left in his algebra-book a few hours previously was nothing more significant than a rather remarkable coincidence. What did puzzle him was not so much the Marshall affair itself, as Roseveare's extraordinary fit of nerves over it.

Still, he might as well fill in the time with some sort of inquiry. A chat with Jones Tertius, for instance, was an obvious step, though he did not expect it to yield very much. The junior boys, he knew, usually spent winter Sunday afternoons in the Common Room; so he re-entered School House, put his head in at the familiar door, and asked the nearest occupant if he could tell him Jones's whereabouts. The cry went round, and in a moment or two he found facing him a small, spectacled, rather shy youngster dressed in Oakington's compulsory Sunday blacks.

Revell, when he chose to exert himself, had a distinct way with people. He was young enough, too, to be able to approach a thirteen-year-old without any sign of adult condescension. "Hullo, Jones," he began, with a pleasant smile. "Sorry to drag you away from your friends—" (not "pals" or "chums," as Daggat would have said)—"but I thought you might have a minute or two to spare. Perhaps we could take a turn round the pitch—it's stopped raining."

The boy accompanied him willingly enough but with very natural surprise. "I'm an O.O. up for the week-end, you see," went on Revell, "and when I saw your name on the School list, I thought I'd look you up in case you were the brother of a fellow I knew very well when I was here. Of course I know the name isn't exactly a rare one, but——"

And so on. It turned out that the boy had no brothers, either past or present, but by the time the matter had been fully elucidated, the pair had reached the sports pavilion and were faced with the return walk. And what more natural, therefore, than that Revell should say, as if making conversation: "Awfully bad business about that boy who was killed here at the beginning of Term, wasn't it? Did you know him?"

But beyond the fact that Jones had known him, and had been his particular friend, Revell learned practically nothing. Jones was one of those boys who do not respond to pumping, even by the most expert pumper.

It was evident, though, that he shared none of the Head's curiosity, misgiving, or whatever exactly it was. And as Revell had fully expected this, he bade farewell to the boy at the door of School House with a satisfied smile.

Like some rather preposterous slow-motion film the pageant of an Oakington Sunday tortuously unwound itself. Revell took tea with the Head and dazzlingly propounded his pet theory that Charlotte, Emily, and Anne Brontë were allotropic personalities of the same human or perhaps inhuman being. The Head listened attentively and appeared impressed. In such wise the time passed pleasantly enough until the ringing of the chapel-bell for evening service. The Head, it seemed, was not going to attend. "I have some letters to write," he explained. "But you go, most certainly. Supper will be immediately afterwards. We do not dress on Sundays."

In one of the rear pews of the rather ornate chapel, as the School began to stream in, Revell sought to capture the real, genuine, hundred-per-cent thrill of the Old Boy dreaming of past days. He was far more conscious of a thrill, however, when Mrs. Ellington came to sit in the pew beside him. She smiled cordially, and her husband, next to her on the other side, leaned forward with a nod of reluctant recognition. "I wondered if you would be here," she whispered, "and to tell the truth, I rather hoped you wouldn't."

Of course he asked why.

"Because Captain Daggat is preaching. He really is *awful*."

Revell was thoroughly amused. "So I've been told already to-day."

"Oh yes, by Mr. Lambourne, I know. He said he had met you. He also said you had written a novel. Have you really?"

"England expects," replied Revell, lightly purloining some one else's epigram, "that every young man some day will write a novel."

"But you have, haven't you? Do tell me what it's called—Mr. Lambourne gave me the name, but I'm afraid I've forgotten."

" 'Ancient Lights,' " answered Revell, frowning heavily. (Every time he uttered it, it always sounded sillier, but this was the first time he had ever whispered it to his neighbour in a place of worship.)

" 'Ancient Rights'?"

"No, 'Lights,' " he enunciated, as loudly as he dared.

"How interesting! I must get Mudie's to send it down with their next batch."

The announcement of the opening hymn put an end to further conversation. She was a fool, he thought, as he sang an intermittent and languishing alto. A charming and attractive little fool, no doubt; but a fool for all that. Yet with a half-sideways glance at her dark and sparkling eyes, he felt again the thrill of proximity.

Even apart from his neighbour, he found the chapel service quite interesting, especially as Daggat, within five minutes of beginning his sermon, supplied a perfect clue to the mystery of the note in Marshall's algebra-book.

He would take as his text, began Daggat, in a mournful monotone, part of the eighteenth verse of the twenty-second chapter of Jeremiah. Jeremiah, twenty-two, eighteen. "They shall not lament for him, saying, Ah my brother! or, Ah sister! they shall not lament

for him, saying, Ah Lord! or, Ah his glory!" As it was
the last Sunday before the vacation, he thought it would
not be unfitting to review in retrospect the manifold
blessings and trials of the past Term. It was a good
thing, every now and then, to stop and take a look behind us along the path of life, as it were, and so draw
lessons from the past to help us in the future. There had
been one happening, at least, within the memory of
them all, that had brought them the deepest and most
profound sorrow. Into their midst, unlooked-for and
without warning, there had come the Angel of
Death. . . .

"You may remember," went on Daggat, entering
upon his second half-hour with a preliminary swig of
water from the tumbler on the pulpit-ledge, "you may,
I say, remember words which I addressed to you here,
from this same pulpit, upon the first Sunday of this
Term. How little did I, or any one of us then, imagine
that, so shortly afterwards, my words would appear
prophetic! And yet it should be a lesson to us—a much
needed lesson in this age of boastful science and too-
confident invention—a lesson to us never to forget, even
for a moment, that our health, our happiness, even the
very breath of our life, depend, not upon our own puny
wills, but upon an all-wise and an all-knowing Providence. . . ."

Revell almost laughed. He knew that immediately
after evening service it was the custom for the whole
school to adjourn to the assembly-hall and spend twenty
minutes, presided over by a master, in writing letters,
reading books, or some other silent occupation.

"Wasn't it awful?" whispered Mrs. Ellington, as
they left the pew after the Benediction; and she added,

without waiting for him to reply: "But it was positively cheerful compared with some that we *have* had. By the way, how long are you staying?"

He said that he would most likely be returning to London the next morning.

"Don't forget to visit us when you come again," she said with a smile, and Revell, shaking hands, promised accordingly.

During supper with the Head he could not resist the temptation to be oracular. "I think I've solved your little mystery, sir," he remarked, after preliminary conversation.

But Roseveare, rather to his surprise, showed no eagerness for him to explain. "Revell," he answered, with slow emphasis, "I'm afraid I owe you an apology. There *is* no mystery. I sent for you in a moment of nervous prostration—now, in a more normal condition, I can realise fully what you must have thought of it all. You have disguised your feelings with great politeness, my dear boy, but I can judge of them all the same. And you're right, too. I have allowed myself to be completely foolish, and I apologise to you most sincerely for wasting your time. . . . Do help yourself to some more wine."

Revell did so, rather crestfallen. "All the same," he rejoined, "though I quite agree with you that there isn't any real mystery, I do happen to have found a reason—or at least a theory—to explain the note left in Marshall's algebra-book." He felt rather piqued at Roseveare's latest attitude; having done his job, it was disappointing to be received with apologies instead of congratulations. "You see," he went on, "it was all a matter of the boy's temperament. He was, I gather, the sensitive, imaginative type. Now it so happened that on the first Sunday

evening of Term Captain Daggat preached a rather
doleful sermon—all about sudden death and that sort of
thing. I know, because in his sermon to-night he made a
great point of recalling what he had said then. Well . . .
my theory is that Marshall, over-impressed by it all,
went straight away into the hall afterwards and wrote
out that rather amateurish last will and testament. . . .
Don't you think it possible?"

"More than possible—very probable, I should think.
But the whole thing is, as I said, too foolish to be worried about. . . . Come into the study and let us take a
liqueur and talk of pleasanter things."

Revell was not wholly mollified, even by the excellent old brandy that followed. He could not understand the other's sudden change of mood, and he felt
a little sore at the manner in which his really brilliant
theory had been received. By the morning, however, he
had come to the conclusion that Roseveare perhaps did
suffer from sudden baseless apprehensions, and after
breakfast the two parted with many expressions of
mutual esteem. "You must certainly come and see me
again," urged the Headmaster of Oakington, shaking
hands with him from the porch. "I shall look forward
to it exceedingly." And Revell replied with some sin-
cerity that he would also. Just at the last moment the
other thrust a sealed envelope into his hand. "Don't
open it till you get into the train," he said. "Good-bye
—good-bye."

Revell, of course, opened it in the taxi. It contained
a cheque for ten guineas and a sheet of notepaper on
which were written the words "For Professional Services."

In his private diary (which he vaguely imagined

might some day be published in a number of annotated volumes), Revell wrote: "The Oakington incident is closed. It was all quite pointless, as I thought from the beginning, but it ended in fond farewells and a cheque for ten guineas; which isn't really so bad. I think I rather like Roseveare, nerves or not, but I didn't greatly care for Ellington. The real Oakington mystery, I should think, is why such an attractive woman as Mrs. Ellington ever married him."

CHAPTER III

THE STRANGE AFFAIR IN THE SWIMMING-BATH

MORE DESPERATELY than ever, upon a certain warm June morning in 1928, did Revell long for something to happen to him. And his epic poem in the metre of *Don Juan* was, by a really curious coincidence, about a young man to whom simply all things happened, one after another and again and again—love affairs, adventures, thrills and escapades of every kind, and some of them not a little scandalous.

That very morning he had received a letter from an old Oxford friend asking him to join a proposed scientific and geographical expedition to New Guinea. It was hardly the sort of thing he cared about, even in the rôle of "writer-up" and general publicity manager; but the terms of the invitation had given him a certain inward fretfulness that he could not shake off. "Decadent youth," his friend had written, with what Revell regarded as too ponderous facetiousness, "put away your cocktails and high-brow literary work for two whole years and then go back to them if you feel like it! We hope to leave in September, and, as it happens, we want a man who can turn our adventures into a book. I don't know where this letter will find you, but in case you are in some other part of the world, you can consider the offer open until the middle of August. *Do* come— it is a wonderful chance . . . etc., etc."

No; decidedly the offer did not attract. He hated flies, swamps, pigmies, and the sort of men who put adventures into books—guinea books, as a rule, remaindered at four-and-six. "With Rod and Line in the Sahara, by Major Fitzwallop"—*that* kind of thing— heavens, no—he would not and could not do it. And yet it was, in a way, infernally unsatisfying to long for something to happen and then to have to turn down something quite exciting when it *did* happen.

Fortunately something else happened that morning which took away all thought of the New Guinea proposal. On an inside page of his daily paper Revell's eye caught a small paragraph headed: "Public School Tragedy." It ran:

The swimming instructor at Oakington School made a gruesome discovery yesterday morning when he unlocked the door of the School swimming-bath. On the floor of the bath, which had been emptied for cleaning, lay the dead body of Wilbraham Marshall, the head-prefect of the School, who was to have given a swimming display at the coming Jubilee Speech Day celebrations. It is surmised that Marshall went for a practice swim at night and dived in, unaware that the water had been drawn away. By a curious coincidence, it is only nine months since his brother met with a fatal accident at the School.

This time the decadent youth about town wasted no time in pondering. Almost frantically, and with his mind reacting fiercely to unidentifiable thrills, he consulted a railway-guide and sent off the urgent-sounding telegram—"Roseveare Oakington Arriving this afternoon by one-twenty train Revell." He calmed down a little as he shaved, put on an O.O. tie, packed a handbag, called at the bank to draw some money, made arrangements with his landlady, and taxied to King's Cross. On the train he decided that he had never quite understood why Roseveare had sent for him on that first occasion, and why, having sent for him, he had appeared so eager to dismiss him. He wished he had a Doctor Watson to talk to; he would have liked to recount the whole dormitory incident, concluding with —"Depend upon it, Watson, we have not yet heard the last of this affair."

After the hot morning the weather had grown rapidly stormy, and by the time Oakington came into view the sky was dark, and thunder already rumbled in the distance. There had been nearly a month without rain, and the parched fields and rusty roads seemed to stare hopefully at the clouds massing above them. Revell, as he stepped from the train, felt the first tentative drops of rain upon his face. Ten minutes later, when the white-haired butler ushered him into Roseveare's study, the storm was beginning to break.

Roseveare, standing with his back to the empty fire-grate, welcomed him cordially and apparently without surprise. He was rather pale, and with lines of anxiety about his eyes, looked perhaps more like a popular preacher than ever. "Good of you to come," he began, in a tone of suave melancholy. "It is indeed a terrible affair—terrible altogether."

Revell went directly to the point. "I felt I *had* to be on the spot. . . . I wish you'd give me a few details. I know nothing, I'm afraid, except from a very short paragraph in the *Mail*."

Roseveare eyed him with (so it seemed) wistful admiration of his youthful energy and enthusiasm. "I fear there isn't a great deal to tell. I take it you already know the main facts. Wilson—he's the swimming instructor—opened the door of the baths about eight o'clock yesterday morning—his usual time. He——"

"He *opened* the door? In the paper it said he unlocked it."

"No, the door was merely closed. That was his first surprise. He found the poor boy lying in a pool of blood at the bottom of the bath. Quite dead—skull completely shattered. I was sent for immediately—there was nothing that could be done, of course. A horrible sight —I've seen bad enough things in the War, but somehow this seemed most horrible of all. Murchiston came. He agrees that the boy must have died instantly. From the top diving-platform, too—his wrist-watch was found there. It's awful to think of—and happening just now— only a day before Speech Day!"

Revell inclined his head in sincere sympathy. There really was something rather titanically perturbed about the tall, handsome figure with its crown of silver hair. "I can guess how you must feel about it," he said. "That's why—or one of the reasons why—I came. Do you mind if I ask a few questions?"

"Please do—any you like."

"Thanks. There are just one or two matters. . . . The theory, I suppose, is that Marshall·took a dive without knowing the bath was empty?"

"People are saying that, naturally."

"It must have been dark, then, or he would have seen. Why didn't he switch on the lights?"

"Ah yes, I didn't tell you that. The fuses had gone. We discovered it last night."

"So, presumably, finding that the switches wouldn't work, he decided to swim in the dark?"

"Presumably."

"Was it usual for him to swim late at night?"

"He had done so, I believe, on previous occasions. He was to have organised a swimming display for Speech Day afternoon, you know—that gave him sufficient excuse for any extra visits to the baths. As he was fond of swimming and as it was a particularly hot night, I don't think there is anything intrinsically unusual in his going there at such a time. It is quite against the rules, of course, but rules hardly apply very strictly to the head-prefect. He had a key to the baths, as a matter of fact."

"You say he went on previous occasions?"

"Yes. He went the night before, and on several nights last week."

"But it isn't dark till nearly eleven at this time of the year. Surely he wouldn't go there later than that?"

"It was dark earlier the night before last, owing to heavy clouds. But in any case, we believe that he had been in the habit of going to the baths rather late. As head-prefect, you see, he could let himself in and out of the House whenever he liked."

"Wouldn't he have to be in the dormitory by the usual time?"

"He didn't sleep in a dormitory. He had one of the small rooms."

"Oh indeed? How was that?"

"Well, it was rather an exceptional case, of course. After his brother's accident last year, he was very much distressed and didn't sleep well. He told Murchiston, who had him under treatment, that he thought it would help if he could get up and read for a time whenever he had one of his sleepless nights. Of course he couldn't do that in the dormitory, so Murchiston and I both agreed that he had better have one of the small rooms. We were all of us very sorry for the boy, and anxious to do anything we could to help him, even at the expense of a school rule or two."

"Quite," agreed Revell. "And the result was that he had his own private room and nobody therefore knew exactly when he *did* go to bed?"

"I daresay not. Both Ellington and myself would probably have turned a blind eye to any small irregularities, even if they had come under our notice."

"Yes, I understand. And now about the bath being empty. How was that?"

"It was being cleaned—or rather emptied in readiness for cleaning."

"Isn't it remarkable that Marshall didn't know?"

"I should certainly not have been surprised if he *had* known. Yet, as a matter of fact, the arrangements for emptying and cleaning *were* made rather at the last moment."

"Oh?"

"And I'm afraid that, so far as it may be blameworthy, I must take responsibility for that. I gave the order for the emptying about six in the evening and Wilson stayed late to see to it. It ought to have been done earlier, but in the rush of preparing for Speech Day I had not thought of it until Ellington mentioned it during the afternoon."

"Marshall was not informed about it?"

"Not by me, certainly. If I had chanced to see him,

I should probably have mentioned it in private conversation. So, most likely, would Wilson or Ellington. But it was not exactly anyone's business to tell him. You see what I mean?"

"Where would he have been between six in the evening and dusk?"

"Let me see—from six to half-past there would be chapel. From then until eight I believe he superintended the juniors at preparation. From eight onwards he stayed, I expect, in his study, though he would have to go up to his bedroom to change."

"Did he wear a bathing-suit?"

"Yes. And his slippers and dressing-gown were found by the side of the bath." Roseveare added: "I have willingly answered all your questions and I will just as willingly answer any others that occur to you, but I really don't think there can be much dispute as to what happened."

Revell regarded the other with sudden curiosity.

"Then," he exclaimed, his curiosity turning rapidly into bewilderment, "you don't want me to look into this affair as I did into the other?"

"By all means look into it—I will give you every assistance to do so. The two accidents present a most terrible and remarkable coincidence, and one extremely damaging to the reputation of the School. But I must confess that—on the evidence before us—I cannot feel much doubt as to the way in which poor Wilbraham met his death. . . . The inquest, by the way, is to be held the day after to-morrow—perhaps you might care to attend. Oh—just one other thing—you will stay to-night, of course. I could not think of letting you go back before our Speech Day celebrations. Though,

Heaven knows, they come at a singularly inopportune moment. . . ."

The storm broke in all its fury as Revell left Roseveare's house. He made a dash across the lawn to the School House, barely escaping a complete drenching. The interview had left him with bewilderments and misgivings that did not diminish in retrospect. He felt in a mood for a long solitary walk on freezing roads with a biting east wind in his face, and the almost tropical downpour outside gave him the uncomfortable sensation of being trapped and frustrated. He wondered what on earth he could or should do next. Behind the veneer of blandness and courtesy that Roseveare had offered, it had not been difficult to detect a certain frigidity. Queer that a man afflicted with nervous apprehensions should have worried over the first accident, yet should find (apparently) nothing but "a most terrible and remarkable coincidence" in the second! Queer —yes, decidedly queer. . . . Through the windows he could faintly discern, beyond the mist of falling rain, the cricket pavilion crowded with sheltering youngsters. Suddenly a flash of vivid lightning seemed to explode the whole sky in one immense detonation. By Jove, *that* was near. . . . He felt he must *do* something, visit someone, talk to somebody about something. He thought of Lambourne—perhaps he would be in his room. It was, he knew, on the ground floor, next to the studies. He went to it and tapped on the panel of the door, but there was no answer. After a moment's pause he turned the handle and went in. The room seemed empty at first, but on closer inspection he perceived that a large armchair whose back was towards him was occupied by a huddled figure. He strode into the middle of the room and looked; it was Lambourne.

"Good Lord, man, whatever's the matter?" He saw that the fellow was shivering like a jelly. He put a hand on his shoulder and felt him start sharply.

"Oh, it's you, Revell, is it? I—I didn't know you were up here." It was a brave, rather pitiful attempt at self-composure. "Do sit down. I'm—I'm sorry to—to be like this. I can't help it. It's the storm. Since the War I——"

"That's all right," Revell assured him, as if the whole matter were the most natural thing in the world. "I think we've got the worst over now. Anything I can do? What about a spot of tea or something? I'll put the kettle on, eh? No, no—you needn't show me where everything is—I messed about in these rooms a good deal when I was here."

The casual method succeeded where any more intensely expressed sympathy would probably have made matters worse. While Revell chattered inconsequently and as the storm gradually subsided, Lambourne's condition returned to normal. "I'm afraid I'm not much of a host," he said, as Revell pumped up the primus stove. "I can't stand a din. 'Heaven's artillery,' Daggat calls it in his sermons—he thinks it's a compliment to picture heaven as a sort of super-great-power in a state of perpetual and glorious warfare. . . . There are biscuits in that box. I'll be all right in a minute or two. I suppose you're up here for Speech Day?"

Revell, caught just very slightly unawares, hesitated a second before replying: "Yes, that's it."

"It won't be much of a festival, I'm afraid, with this latest affair hanging over it. Of course you've heard."

"Oh yes. It was in all the papers. Pretty terrible, eh?"

Lambourne raised himself in his chair. "You know, Revell, you do rather give yourself away—to me, at any rate. Why don't you admit that you're here for the same reason as last time—because of the Marshall affair?"

Revel almost dropped the biscuit-tin he was holding. "Really? And—and what makes you think that?"

Lambourne laughed. "Oh, just a suspicious instinct I happen to be blessed with. But I'm proud to say I had my doubts from the first. You overdid it, I'm afraid—or rather, you *under*did it. Anyone would have thought that boys were killed every night in their dormitories, the way *you* talked about it. Even Daggat remarked to me afterwards that he didn't think you'd been very interested in our local gossip. Now if you'd only insisted on visiting the fatal dormitory and sniffing about like a stage Sherlock, I might have believed in you."

Revell shrugged his shoulders hopelessly. "You make me feel I must be a tremendous fool," he said. "Of course your suspicions about me are right—there doesn't seem to be any point in denying it. But I didn't think I was doing things quite so obviously."

"Oh, don't think that—you aren't. It's only my own exceptional acuteness that pierces your otherwise excellent disguise as the Old Boy revisiting his Alma Mater. And you needn't fear I shall breathe a word of it to anyone else. But I really would be interested to know all about the affair from your point of view."

It was just what Revell had been wanting—to tell somebody. He did so, fully, and by the time he had finished the rain had stopped and sunlight was pouring into the room. "I must admit," he said, by way of conclusion, "that there seems just a touch of queerness about it all. Roseveare seemed far more suspicious about the first affair, when he hadn't any real cause, than he does now, when anyone would think he had cause enough."

"Suspicious?" echoed Lambourne, as if weighing the word. "Are *you* suspicious, then?"

"Perhaps I am."

'Of what?"

"That's just the point—I hardly know. It might be almost anything, but I'm pretty certain it's something."

"What evidence have you?"

"None that would stand a moment's examination in a court of law. None at all, really. Just the coincidence of the two accidents, and the Head's puzzling attitude, and my own feeling about it. It's all queer, to say the least."

"As you say, to say the least, Why not say a little more and call it a double murder committed with diabolical ingenuity?"

"*What?*" Revell gasped. "I suppose you're joking——"

"Not at all. As a mere matter of theory, isn't it possible? Isn't the really successful murder not merely the one whose perpetrator never gets found out, but the murder that doesn't even get suspected of being a murder?"

"But, my dear man, as you said to me just now, where's your evidence?"

"Exactly. I haven't got any—I'm in the same boat as you."

"Are you—are you—really quite serious about all this?"

"Perfectly. I suspected it, as a matter of fact, from the moment the news of the first accident reached me. But then I'm afraid I nearly always do suspect things— I have a thoroughly morbid mind. I never hear of a drowning accident but what I wonder if somebody pushed the fellow in. And it's such a dashed clever way of murdering anybody, you know—letting a gas pipe fall on 'em."

"And what about this latest affair?"

"A mistake. No one, however clever, should expect to get away with more than one murder. Tempting Providence, you know. Not that it isn't more than likely that the dear old country Coroner and his twelve good men will swallow this just as willingly as they did the first one. Only, from a purely technical point of view—the only point of view that interests me—the repetition mars the symmetry of the thing."

"But surely, man, if you have suspicions of this sort, you can't be satisfied to leave things as they are?"

"Oh, I don't know. Hardly my business, eh?"

Revell was indignant; he was even (a rare accomplishment) shocked. Lambourne's attitude of cynical indifference was one he had very often adopted himself, yet now he saw it in another he reacted against it instantly. "I don't know how you can say that," he said.

"No? Well, maybe I'm different from you, that's all. After seeing three years of purposeless slaughter backed by all the forces of law and religion, I find it hard to share in the general indignation when somebody tries on a little purposeful though no doubt unofficial slaughter on his own. That's my attitude—maybe a wrong one, but I can't help it. I'll talk things over with you, of course, as much as you like—give you my ideas and all that. Only don't expect me to give any active assistance."

Revell laughed. "You're almost as queer as all the rest of the business. . . . Look here, Lambourne, I do want to get to the bottom of things, if I can. It's building bricks without straw for the present, I know, but that doesn't matter. You suspect a double murder, eh? Well, the first thing to look for, then, is a motive—unless, of course, we're dealing with a homicidal maniac. Do you agree?"

"Quite."

"Well, the only motive I can think of is money. Two schoolboys can hardly have had any personal enemies. But it did occur to me that since all Robert Marshall's money went to his brother Wilbraham, it would be interesting to know where Wilbraham's money goes now?"

"I can tell you that—it's fairly common knowledge, in fact. Ellington gets it."

"Ellington? The devil he does! I say, that's a bit astonishing, isn't it?"

"Oh, I don't know. Ellington's his cousin and next-of-kin. He couldn't very well leave it to anybody else."

"How much—roughly—does it amount to?"

"Matter of a hundred thousand or so."

Revell whistled. "Quite enough to make some people commit a couple of murders."

"Oh, bless you, yes. Some folks would commit twenty murders for a fiver, for that matter. . . . Anyhow, that's one thing settled. We've found the murderer. The only thing left to do now is to find out whether there's really been a murder or not."

"You needn't be so sarcastic," answered Revell, smiling. "After all, in a case like this, doesn't everything depend on personality and motive? Find the murderer, then you know there's been a murder. If you can't find a murderer, then you'll have to believe that the whole thing's been purely accidental."

"Good, Revell—you have, I am delighted to see, an

intricate mind. Ellington's our man, of course. But unfortunately there's not a scrap of evidence against him. All you can say is that he comes into a bit of money through the two successive accidents. Ah, but stay—there *is* just one other little matter. I'd almost forgotten it. Ellington was one of the very few people who knew that Marshall was sleeping in the dormitory on the night of the first accident."

"Good Lord—I never heard anything about that!"

"No, I don't suppose you did," replied Lambourne, relishing his little sensation. "It was a point that didn't come out at the inquest—although, mind you, there was no reason why it should. Young Marshall, you see, had spent the greater part of his summer vacation abroad—he'd been, I think, with his guardian in Italy. Anyhow, owing to time-tables and what not, the Head had given him special permission not to return until the Monday—the rest of the School, you will remember, having re-assembled on the previous Saturday. Did they, by the way, have the system of dormitory-prefects in your time?"

"Yes."

"Ah, then you'll understand how it all came about. Marshall was the dormitory-prefect of the junior dormitory. Now the rule is very strict about having somebody in charge, and as Marshall was to be away on the Saturday and Sunday nights, somebody had to step into the breach, and that somebody was Ellington. I know, because the fellow asked me if I'd oblige, but I made some excuse—I sleep badly enough as it is, without the additional miseries of a dormitory mattress. Besides, as housemaster, it was his job, not mine. Anyhow, he did it on the Saturday night and was doubtless prepared to repeat the performance on the Sunday night as well.

All the staff knew about it—he'd been cursing his luck in the Common Room. But then, quite unexpectedly, about half-past five on the Sunday evening, Marshall turned up."

Certainly, Revell thought, Lambourne had the knack of making things sound devilishly significant, whether they were so or not.

"Yes—he'd caught an earlier cross-Channel boat than he'd reckoned on, or some simple enough reason like that. Anyhow, he went into Chapel and Hall afterwards in the usual way. Daggat may possibly have noticed him—he was preaching that night, which was the reason, as you can guess, why most of the other masters kept away. I did, and so did Ellington. Ellington, as a matter of fact, didn't know that Marshall had come back until nine o'clock, when the boy went to see him in his room next to the dormitory."

"Not in his private house?"

"No. His wife was out visiting, so he was filling in the time marking papers, I believe. He was surprised to see the boy, naturally, though glad enough to discover he could spend the night on his own feather-bed after all. The boy went to bed in the dormitory at the usual time, and Ellington stayed up to finish his marking—at least, that's what he said at the inquest. The point is, you see, that his wife wouldn't be expecting him, and might well be asleep when he *did* go to bed—whenever that may have been."

"Pretty quick work, though, to plan a thing like that at such short notice."

"Oh, I know. I'm not suggesting he did. It may have all been planned beforehand, and he just seized the favourable opportunity as it came."

"Quite. But I'm afraid it all shows how equally well

the whole business *may* have been an accident. Assuming it was, it was pure chance that the boy got killed and not Ellington himself."

"Oh yes. Exactly what Ellington said himself the morning after."

"Which, of course, he *would* say, if he *were* the murderer."

"Naturally."

"Oh Lord, what a lot of assumptions we're making! I wish we had more evidence. Can you connect Ellington with this latest affair in any way?"

"'Fraid I can't, on the spur of the moment. That's your job—you're the detective. If I were you, I should have a look round pretty soon—if there've been any clues left lying about, I don't suppose they'll stay there for ever."

It was a hint, perhaps, and Revell, who felt he would like to be on his own for a while to think things over, was glad enough to take it. "Come and chat with me again as often as you like," was Lambourne's farewell remark, and Revell assured him that he would.

The grounds of Oakington School were roughly circular, and round them ran a pleasant tree-sheltered pathway popularly known as the Ring. Four successive generations of Oakingtonians had found that to make its complete circuit, at strolling pace, was an agreeable way of spending a quarter of an hour when there was nothing else to do, and upon this Wednesday afternoon in June Revell followed almost instinctively the familiar trail. The sunlight blazed bountifully through the washed air; the scents of moist earth and dripping vegetation rose around him in a steamy cloud. From time to time he passed groups of strolling boys who stared at him with that slight and politely-disguised curiosity that is, perhaps, the *fine fleur* of the public-school tradition. He could well guess the chief subject of their conversations. He could imagine the sensation that the double affair of the Marshall brothers would have caused at the Oakington of his day. It was, undoubtedly, the most spectacular of sensations—only less so, perhaps, than Lambourne's theory if it could be proved correct. But *was* it? That, naturally, was the all-engrossing problem that occupied his mind during the half-mile circuit.

The chief trouble, of course, was that it was so fearfully difficult to verify anything that might or might not have taken place nine months before. People so easily forgot details, or even if they didn't, they could easily say so if they were asked awkward questions. He quite saw that there was very little he could hope to discover about that first affair.

He thought a little cynically of the bright new electric fittings that met the eye all over the School. That had been the Head's doing—natural enough, in a way, but a pretty efficient method of clearing up traces if there had been anything wrong. Had the Head, by the way, known of Marshall's sudden and unexpected arrival at the School that night?

He lit a cigarette as he began the second circuit of the Ring. The easiest thing, undoubtedly, was to believe that things were just as they seemed. Two fatal accidents to two brothers—well it was unusual, even remarkable, but was it more so than any conceivable alternative supposition?

Anyhow, as Lambourne had said, he had better tackle the more recent affair, since not only was there a greater chance of discovering things from it, but also his enquiries could be made more openly, as springing from the mere natural curiosity of an Old Oakingtonian about an affair that was for the time being on everybody's lips. And so, as he came round to the School buildings again, he made his way to the low, squat, red-bricked erection, some distance away from the rest, in which, ten years before, he had splashed about on many a summer's afternoon.

His lips tightened irritably as he turned the handle of the door and found it unlocked. The place ought not, he felt, to have been thus left open to any casual sensation-seeker, though of course it suited him well enough to be able to enter so easily. He walked through the small entrance-hall, past the shower-baths and the drying-room, and into the main glass-roofed building. Four elderly charwomen were kneeling on the floor of the bath, busily engaged in scrubbing the white porcelain tiles. At the farther end, by the diving platforms, a rough-looking fellow in grey flannels and a brown cardigan was noisily dismantling an improvised grandstand consisting of several tiers of wooden benches. Revell watched the scene for over a minute before anyone saw him, and even then no one took any particular notice. It was only too obvious that there had been many previous visitors. At length he walked along the edge of the bath and approached the man at the far end. "Busy cleaning up, I see?" he commented, with the air of the fatuous sight-seer.

The man nodded deferentially, noticing the Old Oakingtonian tie. "Yes, sir, and not a pleasant thing to 'ave to clear up, neither." How eager they all were, Revell thought, to discuss the little tit-bit of tragedy that had fallen into their midst! He offered the man a cigarette, which he took with a half-knowing salute. Another of them wanting to be told all about it, Revell fancied him thinking. "Yes, sir, I reckon I don't want to see a thing like that again. Fell right off from the top, and you'd think so, too, if you'd seen what *I* saw. Terrible thing, ain't it? An' 'appenin' just now—right in front of Speech Day. Of course there ain't goin' to be no swimmin' gala —natchrally *that's* been put off."

Revell inclined his head in melancholy agreement. "I suppose the poor chap must have taken a plunge in the dark?" he hazarded.

"Looks like it," replied the other. "The fuses was all gorn. . . . I daresay you 'eard about 'is poor brother larst Autumn Term, sir?" The man's eyes quickened with ghoulish pride.

"Yes, I read about it. By the way, what are you going to do when the cleaning's finished? Fill the bath up again?"

"Yes, sir. Though I don't suppose there'll be any swimmin' till next week. You don't 'ardly feel you'd like to go in it now, some'ow, do you, sir?"

Revell expressed a limited sympathy with this extreme of delicacy and then, with a farewell nod to the man, walked back towards the entrance. The same trick as before, he reflected ruefully—all traces obliterated, and in quite the most natural manner, too. He flung down the stump of his cigarette and ground it under his heel. Really, if there were anything in Lambourne's theory, it had all been managed with devilish ingenuity.

As he descended the outside steps of the swimming-bath a small female figure on a bicycle suddenly dismounted in front of him and greeted him with a bright smile. "Hullo, Mr. Revell—how are you? I didn't know you were up here."

The encounter relieved him momentarily of his load of doubts and apprehensions. "Hullo, Mrs. Ellington— delighted to meet you again. Yes, I thought I'd come up for Speech Day. Not going to be such a joyous festival, though, is it?"

"It's just frightful," she answered, her dark eyes clouding over instantly. "Have you been brave enough to look where it happened? *I* haven't. It was a terrible sight for poor Wilson, I'm afraid. And, you know, I feel particularly awful about it myself, because—in a sort of way—I was responsible. I know it's foolish of me to think so, but really I can't help it."

"But how on earth——"

"You see, Mr. Revell, it was *I* who suggested having the bath cleaned. It wasn't very dirty, but I happened to be looking in on Monday afternoon in connexion with the seating arrangements for the gala display and it just occurred to me then that the bath might be a little bit cleaner. So I mentioned it to my husband and he mentioned it to the Head, and the order was given to Wilson almost immediately. And but for that . . ." She shuddered and stared miserably at the handle-bars of her bicycle.

"But really, Mrs. Ellington, I don't think you can possibly feel responsible—there was no real negligence on your part or anything like that. The whole affair was just a most frightful accident—" He had said it before he realised what he was saying.

"Oh yes, I know, but that doesn't stop me from feeling as I do about it. . . Will you come along to tea, by the way? I'm just putting my bicycle in the shed before I go in. I'm sure my husband will like to see you again."

Revell accepted the invitation and, taking her machine away from her, wheeled it to its allotted space in the covered bicycle-stand. It would not be a bad idea to meet Ellington, he reflected, and to observe him from the standpoint of one who already suspected him of being a double murderer. Apart from which, Mrs. Ellington's company was itself sufficient to make the suggestion attractive.

Ellington was not in when they reached the house, so they prepared the tea themselves, chatting pleasantly meanwhile. She was, he decided once again, a charming little creature—full of elf-like vivacity and so childishly frank as well. "You know," she said, "we come into an awful lot of money through that poor boy being killed. It sounds terrible to be thinking of it even before he's buried, but it's hard not to. Tom's his nearest relative, you see—there was simply nobody else to leave it to. We shall be quite rich."

Revell assumed polite surprise. "Will you leave Oakington, do you think?"

"Oh, I do hope so. The life of a schoolmaster's wife isn't all fun. Have you seen that play *Young Woodley*, by the way, that's on in town?"

"Yes, several times. I liked it immensely."

"Oh, so did I. And I do sympathise so much with the schoolmaster's wife—not so much in connexion with the boy—but just generally. I mean—oh, I don't know quite how to express it in a way that you won't misunderstand, but——"

And as if to illustrate the inexpressible, Ellington himself came in at that moment in an obvious bad temper. Really, thought Revell, for a man who, whether by accident or design, was about to inherit a hundred thousand pounds, he was remarkably peeved. He shook hands perfunctorily with Revell, planked himself down in the most comfortable chair, and told his wife, when she handed him a cup of tea, that it was disgustingly weak.

A boor as well as a bore, Revell reflected. A few mouth-fuls of buttered teacake made the man more talkative, but only to air his grumbles. "Speech Day to-morrow, by Gad!" he muttered. "And the Lord knows what's going to happen—everything either altered or cancelled —no definite plans—no method—and in the meantime the whole discipline of the School going absolutely to pot!" He gulped down a half-cupful of tea. "Boys seem to think that because a fatal accident's happened they can all run riot. I had to thrash several of them to-day for being late, and the excuse they gave me, if you please, was that they'd been in the swimming-bath talk-ing to Wilson!"

"Don't you think it's rather excusable?" Mrs. Elling-ton queried, with an inflection in her voice that Revell thought was slightly acid.

"No, I do not."

Revell interposed tactfully. "I certainly agree," he said, addressing Ellington, "that there's been far too much sight-seeing in the swimming-bath. In my opin-ion the place ought to have been locked up immedi-ately after the accident, and no one ought to have gone near it without special permission. What possibility is there of reconstructing how the accident happened when everybody's been allowed to treat the place like a side-show on a fair-ground?"

Ellington faced him truculently. "*Reconstructing*, eh? What d'you mean? Isn't Murchiston's opinion good enough? And the Head's too? Don't see what need there'll be of any reconstructing, as you call it. Still, you're right about the sight-seeing—there *has* been too much of it. And there's been too much of other things, too. Chattering and gossiping and idle tittle-tattle—the whole School's full of it. I quite expect to have to discuss nothing else from morning till night to-morrow."

"I can quite understand that you must feel heartily sick of it all."

Ellington grunted. "I can't even cycle into the vil-lage without a dozen people stopping me to ask ques-tions. Stupid scandal-mongering, that's all it is."

There was nothing much to be got out of him save repeated grumbles on similar lines, so Revell took an early leave, pitying Mrs. Ellington for having to face the rest of the wrathful outpouring alone. "You must come and see us again before you go," she said, walk-ing with him to the top of the outside steps. And there was (or perhaps he merely imagined it) something in the tone of her voice that added an unspoken—"*Please* come again."

Doctor Roseveare was most charming at dinner. Though his face still bore traces of the strain he was undergoing, he yet managed, with the true courtesy of a host, to entertain his guest without apparent signs of pre-occupation. Revell would have been willing enough to discuss the swimming-bath affair, but he found the other's opinions concerning Oriental china almost equally revealing, at any rate as a proof of his extraor-dinary self-control. Yet this was the man who, nine months before, had been suffering from nerves!

Not till the close of the meal did the conversation approach the narrowed confines of Oakington, and then Revell, seizing the opportunity, asked if he might visit the swimming-bath on his own.

Roseveare seemed more interested in the request than surprised by it. "Why, yes, of course, if you wish. But

I should have thought you would have been there already."

"Oh, I have. But I'd rather like to have a few moments there by myself—and at night."

"Very well—I will lend you my key. I am afraid, though, that you will find very little of interest."

"Still, I'd like a look around. And there's just one other thing, too—I'm sorry to have to bother you about it, but I'm relying on your offer to help me, you know —could I be permitted to see the—er—the body?"

Roseveare smiled rather sadly. "You think it necessary for your—investigations, eh? Well, I won't refuse you, or perhaps you *would* think I was trying to hamper your efforts. But of course you quite understand that nothing must be disturbed in any way. Subject to that condition, I can certainly comply. In fact, I'll take you now—it is almost dark and we shall attract less attention than in the day-time."

At about half-past ten, therefore, on the eve of Oakington Jubilee Speech Day, Revell and Doctor Roseveare made their rather gruesome pilgrimage to the School gymnasium that had been temporarily turned into a mortuary; the doctor unlocked the door and, in the dim illumination of a rather distant electric light, Revell pulled back the linen sheet and looked upon what was left of Wilbraham Marshall, sometime head-prefect of Oakington School. A glance was sufficient—or rather, perhaps, many additional glances would have been no more helpful. The doctor did not look at all.

"And now," said Revell, as they left the gymnasium and relocked it, "I needn't trouble you any further if you will just lend me the swimming-bath key."

Roseveare detached it from his bundle and pressed it into Revell's hand with an almost fatherly gesture.

"Yes, I think I'll leave you to it—I have a number of urgent matters to attend to to-night. You'll help yourself to my whisky if you're back after I've gone to bed, won't you? . . . That's right. Good night."

Revell unlocked the door of the swimming-bath and walked up the entire length of the building as far as the diving-board and platforms. Then he walked back again. That was all. He had seen what he wanted to see, and was rather proud, indeed, of having expected to see it. And also, too, he had heard what he wanted to hear.

CHAPTER IV

A SPEECH DAY AND AN INQUEST

IT WAS surely the most remarkable Speech Day Oakington could ever have experienced. Had the tragedy happened a little earlier, it might have been possible to postpone the Jubilee celebrations, but with less than forty-eight hours' notice, the major proceedings had to remain as planned. Details, of course, were judiciously altered—and yet perhaps not too judiciously, for a little of even manufactured gaiety would have helped to mitigate the sombre melancholy of the affair.

Revell, as a slightly quizzical spectator, watched the curious scene from hour to hour. He saw the reception at the main entrance in the morning—saw Doctor Roseveare, with a mechanical smile and a few mechanical words of welcome, shaking hands mechanically with each one of several hundred guests; he attended the chapel service and listened to an appallingly dull sermon by an Old Oakingtonian whom years and ambitious mediocrity had combined to make a colonial bishop; he sat in one of the rearmost rows in the Hall during the afternoon and heard the lugubrious chanting of the School Song. The guest of honour was Sir Giles Mandrake, a millionaire shipowner; his wife presented the prizes. Roseveare sat conveniently at Lady Mandrake's elbow, ready to give her tactful assistance in any little difficulty that might arise. His massive head ("leonine" was the obvious word), with its crown of silver hair, seemed in a strange way to dominate everything and everybody. A truly remarkable man, as Revell had realised, though never so completely as now. For after the tedious, halting, nerve-racking speech by Sir Giles, Roseveare's cool, exquisitely-chosen words were like healing ointment on a raw wound. He spoke gently of the School's past, wisely of its present, and hopefully of its future. In a single guarded sentence he referred to "events during the past year which we must all deplore and which I, personally, regret more than I can ever say"—but that was all. He made a few half-wistful, half-jesting comments on the School's sporting achievements. He complimented his staff and thanked them for their loyalty. He mentioned one or two scholastic successes. He made, in short, the perfect speech for the somewhat difficult occasion.

In place of the swimming display there was a rapidly improvised concert of appalling badness. Then came a garden-party tea on the quadrangle, during which Revell chatted to several Old Oakingtonians whom he knew and who had brought their families with them. They were all, of course, agog with excitement about the Marshall affair, and the known fact that the body lay in the locked gymnasium awaiting the inquest on

the morrow gave them a particular thrill. "Too bad—
to have happened just now," was a frequent comment,
but Revell imagined that in many cases a more truthful
one would have been—"Too good—to be able to get a
genuine Edgar Wallace thrill out of a school Speech
Day." For already the place was alive with the wildest
and most sinister rumours.

But by seven at night almost the last of the visitors
had departed. Many of the boys whose homes were
within moderate distance had gone back with their
parents for the traditional week-end holiday; the school
servants were busily clearing away the tea-party litter
from the quadrangle; and the whole school, after the
turmoil, seemed lonely and forlorn.

Revell, from sympathy with the Head after the strain
of such a day, would not have mentioned the Marshall
affair on his own account. He could hardly avoid doing
so, however, when Roseveare calmly asked him what
train he intended catching the next day. The question
was put so artlessly and with such apparent casualness
that Revell was for the moment taken aback. Roseveare
seemed to notice this, for he added: "Please don't think
I particularly want you to go—I only imagined you
might have other affairs to attend to, now that Speech
Day is over. There is the inquest to-morrow morning,
which you might care to attend, but no doubt it will
be over by lunch-time."

After a thoughtful pause Revell said: "If you don't
mind, I should rather like to stay on a few days longer."

"You would? Very well, I shall be delighted, of
course. May I take it that your investigations are bearing fruit?"

The question was neither sarcastic nor contemptu-
ous, but perhaps it was just a shade too bland.

"Oh, I wouldn't say that," Revell answered. "Only I just feel I'd like to poke about a bit more, that's all."

Roseveare nodded with complete geniality. "You're a conscientious fellow, Revell, and deserve a far better fate than to be probing a mystery that isn't, I'm afraid, much of a mystery at all. I know the place is full of rumours, but most of them contradict each other, and in any case, the theories of a generation reared on crook dramas and detective novels are hardly worth taking seriously. I do not, of course, expect that even the inquest to-morrow will stop these unpleasant fiction-mongers. They will just go on till they are tired, and we shall have to put up with it."

Revell was silent and the other continued: "I hope you are not forgetting the boy's wrist-watch which was found on the top diving-platform. That, more perhaps than anything else, seems convincing evidence of what happened."

"Possibly, though I don't see why he shouldn't have left it down below, with his dressing-gown and slippers."

"He may have forgotten it until the last minute. It was radium-pointed, so that in the dark its illumination may have attracted his attention just as he was on the point of diving. Would you like to see the watch, by the way? It will be one of the exhibits shown to the jury to-morrow."

"Oh no, don't bother—I don't think it would help me much."

As he exclaimed rather peevishly to Lambourne an hour or so later: "What the hell was the use of looking at the damned watch after it had been mauled about by Wilson and Roseveare himself and God knows who else? Besides, I'm not a finger-print expert, even if the murderer's paw-marks were plastered all over it!"

"Yet you have, I suppose, a theory of your own by this time?" Lambourne queried.

Revell nodded rather gloomily. "Yes, I have, and it would be about as easy to prove to that jury to-morrow as the Einstein theory. Not that I care much about the inquest."

"Don't you? Well, neither do I. Which is why I intend to suppress a little evidence which, even if I took pains to blurt it out, would only be considered highly irrelevant."

"Oh?"

"Yes, it would. If I told them that about midnight on the night before last Ellington was seen walking about the grounds, they'd probably ask me what the devil it had to do with Marshall."

"Good heavens! Who saw him?"

"I did."

"*You?*"

"Myself alone. You see, I happen to be a very bad sleeper and I often go for a stroll late at night. And that night was the hottest of the year—I knew I should find it hard to get a wink, so I thought I'd take a turn round the buildings."

"And you saw Ellington?"

"More than that, I met him and spoke to him. He told me he was doing exactly the same thing—taking a stroll because of the heat. I don't care for his company much, but it seemed churlish not to chat with him, so I did— for perhaps a quarter of an hour or so. In fact, we walked once round the Ring and then went back to our respective habitations. At least, he saw me go into

School House, and I presume he let himself into his own immediately afterwards."

"But, my dear fellow, this seems frightfully important. Why on earth didn't you tell me about it before?"

"Because I didn't want you to know too much against Ellington all at once. It might have biassed you in deciding whether the accident was faked or not. Now that you're pretty certain of that, I don't mind you knowing the lot."

"How do you know I'm pretty certain the accident was faked?"

"Because you had the excellent idea of visiting the swimming-bath in the dark. I was taking another stroll and I saw you—funny what a lot of things I see on my strolls. I saw you go in and I saw you come out again in about half a minute, which is roughly the time it would take any reasonably intelligent person to spot what really happened. Or at any rate, what really couldn't have happened."

"Yes, quite," said Revell eagerly. "I could see the water rippling distinctly. And I noticed, too, that footsteps sound differently when the bath is full."

"You might add that the whole place smells differently—there's nothing quite so unmistakable as the smell of the water in a swimming-bath. . . . Oh yes, the accident theory is hopelessly impossible. Unless, of course, you begin by bringing evidence that three of the boy's senses were deficient."

A silence followed, which Revell broke by the question: "What did you and Ellington talk about when you met that night?"

"Shop, of course. Have you ever heard Ellington talk anything else?"

"It would be amusing if he gave evidence that he met

you at that suspicious hour. And rather clever of him, too."

Lambourne laughed. "You bet he won't. As a matter of fact, he visited me here an hour ago to discuss that very point. And we both agreed that we would not waste the Coroner's valuable time by mentioning such a trivial matter."

"Good Lord! You've got a nerve!"

"Well, it seemed a fairly reasonable arrangement, I must admit. He promised not to say he'd seen me.if I promised not to say I'd seen him. After all, in the eyes of the law, I suppose we should both be equally suspect if there were suspicion at all. Anyhow, the inquest's bound to be the biggest farce you ever saw, so what does it matter?"

And Revell, though he completely agreed with the other's sentiments, could not forbear a slight shudder at the tone of cynical indifference in which they had been expressed.

The inquest was held in the School gymnasium the following morning amidst the gathering heat of a typical midsummer day. It began at ten o'clock and was over within the hour. Revell had never seen anything quite so slickly performed. Doctor Roseveare, calm and weightily sorrowful, brooded over the proceedings like some kindly deity whom it would have been ungenerous and even impious to frustrate. Both Coroner and jury seemed anxious to spare the feelings of such a well-known and valued citizen of Oakington. Indeed, it might almost have appeared that general sympathy was as much with the doctor as with the deceased.

Medical evidence was given by Murchiston in a decorous and hardly audible undertone. The injuries (technically specified) were, he declared emphatically, such as might have arisen through a fall from a considerable height on to a hard surface. Wilson, dressed in his Sunday clothes, described his finding of the body and of his later discovery of the wrist-watch on the top diving-platform. The jury, having previously seen the body, were then conducted into the swimming-bath and shown the place where the body had been found. They also climbed (some of them) and examined the diving-platform. On the return of the entire party to the gymnasium, Roseveare was called upon to give evidence; he explained the boy's habits more or less as he had previously explained them to Revell. No further evidence was called, but one of the jurors insisted on asking at what hour the wrist-watch had stopped. As it had stopped through want of winding and at eleven minutes past three on the afternoon following the boy's death, it was not easy to see the point of the matter, but it served at any rate to prevent the asking of any further and perhaps less foolish questions.

The jury retired and brought in an almost immediate verdict of "Accidental Death." Then the Coroner expressed sympathy all round—with the relatives of the boy, with the Head, with the School, and even with the jury for being called upon to investigate such a distressing affair. "It is only too clear how it happened," he remarked. "Boys will be boys, and we all of us know the temptation of a swim in weather like this."

"And then," as Revell remarked to Lambourne afterwards, "the fatuous idiot wiped the sweat off his thick head. Man, it was awful to have to sit there and listen to it all. Roseveare had 'em absolutely in the hollow of his hand. Of course, I know he's the biggest pot in Oakington and half the jury were tradesmen who depend on the School, but still—even *that* doesn't altogether explain it. Englishmen aren't really corrupt enough to connive at murder. The trouble is, they never *suspected.* They've heard all the queer rumours, but when it came to the point, Roseveare simply hypnotised the lot of 'em!

"*Only too clear how it happened!* God—I nearly laughed when the Coroner said that! Only too clear why a boy should dive into an empty bath in the middle of the night! . . . And I suppose the first inquest was pretty much the same kind of farce?"

"Quite," replied Lambourne calmly. "Yet I wonder you're even surprised at it—it's all so much the sort of thing one has to expect. Most people in this world are incapable of any really critical observation—they won't and can't see anything unless they have a previous hint that it's going to be there. If Scotland Yard men had examined the gas-fittings after the first accident, they might have discovered something rather interesting about them, but as it was, you see, the examiners were merely gas company officials bent on exonerating their own firm. What they may have wondered, among themselves, I've often speculated on—though it's quite possible that they didn't wonder anything at all. That Tunstall fellow, though, seemed to think somebody had been playing the fool with things—only the dear old Head shut him up—reputation of the School at stake and all that sort of thing, don't you know. Mind you, we mustn't blame anyone *too* much, for there *is* a distinct initial improbability about a falling gas-fitting being in reality a diabolically-contrived murder."

"Yet *you* suspected it?"

"Oh yes, but then, as I said before, I suspect everything and everybody."

The attitude, which had been amusing enough at first, only served to irritate Revell now that his thoughts had become further engrossed in the case. That evening, in the privacy of his bedroom, he wrote out a short summary of the whole Marshall affair, concluding with a few supplementary memoranda which might, he felt, help him by being set down logically on paper. Under the heading—"Have there really been murders?" he wrote:

"I think so. The first 'accident' will be hard and perhaps impossible to elucidate, but if the second 'accident' is definitely proved to be murder, then a considerable balance of probability will lie in favour of the first accident having been murder also, especially if there can be found any adequate motive for the double event. And such a motive undoubtedly exists.

"Let us, then, examine the second 'accident.' Clearly, there are only three possibilities—(1) a *bona-fide* accident (2) suicide, and (3) murder. The following points weigh heavily against the first possibility:

"(1) Even on the darkest night any person of normal eyesight can see the water in the swimming-bath—therefore, he would most likely notice the absence of it. If also he were familiar with the bath, as was the deceased, he would probably notice the totally different sound of his own footsteps caused by the emptiness of the bath.

"(2) The wrist-watch discovered on the top diving-platform is a rather suspiciously direct pointer to the theory of the dive.

"(3) The burned-out fuses. Here again we have something by no means intrinsically suspicious, but one must admit that it happened very fortunately or unfortunately upon this particular night out of all other nights.

"We have, then, disposed of the accident theory, though maybe not conclusively enough for a jury—especially a Coroner's jury. There remain the two other possibilities. Suicide seems out of the question; we are thus left with the third—murder—by process of elimination."

Under the heading "Why suspect Ellington?" Revell went on to write:

"(1) He is the only person who apparently benefits by both the accidents together. (Note that he would not have benefited in any way by one of them separately.)

"(2) He is known to have been walking about the School grounds at a time when the murder *may* have been committed."

Lastly, under the heading "Questions to be solved," he wrote:

"(1) In the case of both accidents, how *exactly* was the thing done?

"(2) Why did the Head send for me last December? Why did he appear to have suspicions then? And why hasn't he any (apparently) now? Why does he seem as though he would be glad if I went back and forgot the whole business?

"(3) Is Lambourne entirely trustworthy? Is his pose of indifference sincere?"

And upon these wise and cautious speculations Revell went to bed and to sleep.

Revell stayed on at Oakington, and each morning at breakfast Doctor Roseveare's welcome was just a shade more ironical. The dead boy's body was in the meantime coffined and taken away by motor-hearse for burial in the family grave in Herefordshire; the living boys returned after their Speech Day holiday, full of other and various topics; the swimming-bath again echoed to the shrieks of the junior learners. Oakington, in fact, began to function normally again, and the second Marshall affair seemed as if it might soon sink into impenetrable limbo with the first.

But to Revell, of course, the problem of the two deaths was an ever-insistent reality. He pondered over it night and day, and the readiness of the others to forget only increased his determination. The trouble was, as it had been right from the beginning, that although he had plenty of theories, there was precious little evidence in support of any of them. Nor did his most careful investigations bear much result. He got into diplomatic conversation with various boys who had known the two brothers, but none could tell him anything of importance, and even their "suspicions," when he probed them, turned out to be based on nothing more than the mere coincidence of the double tragedy.

Several times he strolled casually into the swimming-bath, professing a keen interest in the School swimming, but really in the hope of discovering something hitherto overlooked or of surprising Wilson at some suspicious task—one of his theories had included the baths-attendant as an accomplice. But he discovered nothing, and all Wilson's occupations seemed entirely innocent.

In his notebook, naturally, it was all quite simple, for he had written down:

"Assuming that the theory accepted by the Coroner is incorrect, and since the boy's injuries were too severe to have been caused by a mere fall off the side, it follows that his death must have been caused by some object or instrument. It is clear, too, that he must have been struck either (1) while he was standing on the side or (2) he must have been induced to descend into the empty bath and then struck. As there were no blood-stains on the side the second possibility seems more likely. In that case the murderer would have had to be someone who could have made some plausible excuse for inducing the boy to descend into the bath. Ellington, as one interested in swimming, could have done this.

"Question, therefore: What was the weapon or object used to kill the boy, and what was done with it afterwards? What, also, did the murderer do with his clothes, if, as seems likely, they were blood-stained?"

In detective-stories, as Revell well knew, he would only have had to take a few casual walks about the School grounds to discover both the clothes and the weapon, to say nothing of complete sets of finger-prints. Unfortunately, once again, realities were different, and though he kept half an eye on the shrubbery as he strolled round the Ring, it was not with any intense expectation of finding anything. Naturally the murderer would have taken care to destroy or at least to hide his weapon. It was a pity, perhaps, as Lambourne said, that you could not legally prove a thing had existed merely by proving that somebody had had motive and opportunity to destroy it. And it was equally a pity that proof by elimination was not held in such high respect in law-courts as in Euclid.

One thing, however, these few apparently unfruitful days at Oakington did yield, and that was a rich crop of rumours and impressions. The rumours he mainly ignored (they varied from theories of "curses" laid on the Marshall family to reports of masked men searching the School grounds at midnight); but the impressions were valuable. Revell learned, for example, that Ellington was unpopular, being considered somewhat of a bully, and that Roseveare was idolised. Lambourne, he found, was a bad disciplinarian and rather unpopular with the boys on account of his sarcastic manner; Daggat, on the other hand, though laughed at and thought rather a fool, was quite well liked. Murchiston, the School doctor, was also a favourite, chiefly, no doubt, because he was slack and good-natured.

He learned a little more from an afternoon's chance meeting with Mrs. Ellington in the neighbouring village of Patchmere. He had borrowed a bicycle and was pedalling for pleasure about the country lanes he had known years before; she, with her handle-bar basket full of packages, was obviously on business. "I've just been getting butter and eggs from the farms," she explained. "It's really a good excuse for a ride on a day like this, isn't it?"

He agreed. They chatted for a while, standing against the kerb of the sunny village street; then, since she was returning, it occurred to him to accompany her. "I'm only riding about because I've nothing better to do," he said.

She laughed her pretty laugh as she mounted her machine. "All right, then. But why do you come here for a holiday if you are so bored?"

"Oh, I'm not at all bored. On the contrary, I'm enjoying my stay immensely—it's my first long visit, you know, since I left the School."

"And how long *are* you staying?"

"Not—er—not beyond the end of the week, I don't suppose."

She appeared to accept his explanation without any further puzzlement. They gossiped pleasantly along the lane back to the School, and as they turned in at the gateway she said, with a touch of mockery in her voice: "Well, if you've nothing better to do, you might have tea with me, eh? The kettle will be boiling in ten minutes or so."

"Thanks," he answered, laughing. "I'll come."

When he returned after putting away his bicycle he found her alone in the rather conventionally-furnished sitting-room that overlooked the quadrangle. "My husband's away," she said, greeting him with a smile. "He's gone to the funeral of that poor boy—down in Herefordshire, you know." She added: "I'm so glad you're not offended with us—I'm afraid we were rather rude when you came here to tea the other day."

He thought it rather sacrificial of her so say "us" and "we" instead of "him" and "he," and he replied, meaningly: "I'm quite sure *you* weren't in the least rude, Mrs. Ellington."

"Oh well, then, if you really insist on it, I'll say my husband was. I'm afraid he very often is. He's not really happy as a schoolmaster, you know—he's not made for the job. Anyhow, it won't be for much longer—I think I told you we were going to be quite rich. And Tom's decided he'll give up school and go out to Kenya Colony."

"Really?"

"Yes, now that he can afford to buy a decent ranch or whatever you call it."

"But—well—what about you?"

"*Me?* Oh, I don't mind—why should I?"

Yet he felt, somehow, the narrowness of the gulf that separated her from tears. He was thrilled a little, too. For all his man-of-the-worldliness, he could never *quite* escape the feeling that married people, merely by being married, belonged to an older generation than himself; and to that extent he was always rather astonished when they began to tell him their troubles, as they very often did. But Mrs. Ellington was hardly telling him—she was hardly even hinting.

He said, at a venture: "I feel confoundedly sorry for you, anyhow. I don't altogether know why, but it *is* so."

She answered: "I guessed it—right from the time of our first meeting last December. Curious, wasn't it?"

"I say, did you really?"

"Yes. But I hardly thought I should ever have the chance of saying so." She smiled and seemed marvellously on the point of breaking down. "Tell me," she added, in a voice that trembled, "are you writing another book . . . ?"

And the incident, with all its implications and unexplored possibilities, was over.

But, as he had to admit to himself afterwards, he was really no nearer a solution of the Marshall affair. As the days came and went and each morning made it a little harder for him to face the Head's quizzical glance, he came to the reluctant conclusion that his Oxford detecting triumph must have been a fluke. Though, of course, it had been altogether less baffling. Here at

Oakington crookedness and mystery hampered him at every turn; at certain moments the whole place seemed shrouded in an atmosphere of dark malevolence, amidst which Roseveare, Ellington, and even Lambourne strutted about like figures in a nightmare.

" 'Fraid I shall have to give it up," he told the latter on the Friday night that was exactly ten days after the swimming-bath tragedy. "I really can't stay on here for ever, and there doesn't seem much chance of my being able to do anything."

Lambourne nodded sympathetically. "Yes, I rather thought that's what would happen. Ah well, it's not the first time a clever murderer's succeeded in getting away with it. D'you know, I think most people, if they were careful enough, could manage to commit one murder in safety—it's really not so very hard. The temptation is, when you've done it, to repeat yourself with another. Even then you may perhaps carry it through with a bit of luck—the Brides in the Bath murderer did, and Ellington here, we may presume, is having the same good fortune. But the third time is nearly always unlucky—bound to be, by the law of averages, isn't it?"

"The third time? But there aren't any more Marshall brothers, surely?"

"Maybe not, but what does that signify? Once the murderer gets it into his head that he's cleverer than the rest of mankind, he begins to think of murder quite casually as a means of getting rid of anybody he happens to dislike. It's true, Revell—I've made rather a study of the matter. Two successful murders by the same person are very often followed by a third."

"Well, I don't know how he'll manage it. He's not staying on at Oakington after this Term, so his wife says. He's thinking of going out to Kenya Colony."

"Really? That's very interesting, and Ellington as an Empire-Builder is distinctly good. All the same I don't see that my original point needs much altering. I shall await with patience the announcement in the *Daily Mail* that the wife of a wealthy Kenya planter has been mauled to death by a lion or bitten by a poisonous snake or drowned in some river with an unpronounceable name."

"Good God, man, you don't mean that she's going to be the next?"

"Possibly not. Perhaps she'll have an affair with some other chap and *he'll* be the next. Ellington's frightfully jealous, you know."

"It's damnable to think of her living with such a fellow!"

"Yes, isn't it? But then, if you make your bed, you must lie on it, particularly if it's a marriage-bed."

And Revell, making a mental note of the epigram (which he thought might do very well in some novel he might subsequently write), could only agree that it was so.

CHAPTER V

ENTER SECOND DETECTIVE

THAT EVENING Revell informed Doctor Roseveare that he would leave Oakington on the following day. The latter accepted the arrangement without comment, but his conversation at dinner was perhaps a degree more cordial than usual; and over the bedtime whisky he assured Revell that he had greatly enjoyed his company and hoped he would come again. "And I trust," he added, "that the next occasion will not bring you here

with such a melancholy motive." That was all he said
that had the slightest bearing upon the Marshall affair.
He guessed, no doubt, that Revell had failed·to discover anything of importance, and was too considerate
to refer to it openly.

The best train to town left Oakington about eleven in
the morning, and Revell, being in no particular hurry,
decided to wait for it. He bade his host good-bye immediately after breakfast and spent a final odd hour wan-
dering about the School. Vaguely, perhaps, he wondered if he might meet Mrs. Ellington or Lambourne,
though he had paid them both official farewell visits the
previous evening.

Chance took him up the staircase in School House—
chance combined with the knowledge that from the
window of the topmost landing he could see across the
quadrangle and into the cosy domesticities of Mrs. Ellington's sitting-room. But from that topmost landing,
when he reached it, he perceived that the sitting-room
was empty. Ah well, she was probably shopping in the
village—he might meet her on the way to the station.
And, anyhow, it did not greatly matter.

He was just about to descend the stairs again when he
noticed with surprise that the door of the narrower
staircase that led up from the second landing to the disused sick-rooms was standing slightly ajar. Queer. . . .
He had often during the recent trouble wished for an
opportunity to look over those disused sick-rooms, but
the door had always been locked, and he had not cared
to attract attention by asking for a key. Rather pleased
with the chance so simply and casually presented to
him, he pushed open the door and quickly ascended.
Soon he found himself in the apartments in which, ten
years before, he had spent a not unhappy fortnight

with German measles. Since then a new sanatorium had been built at some distance from the School, and these wholly unsuitable and inadequate sick-rooms had been dismantled. Nothing remained but the wooden partitions between the rooms and the worn brown linoleum on which the marks of the bedposts were still visible. In places the linoleum had been pulled up, exposing the bare boards; there were marks, too, of hasty carpentering in taking up some of the boards and replacing them again. That, he surmised, had been the work of the electricians when they had laid cables for the dormitory below.

He tried, mentally, to reconstruct what might have happened on that night at the beginning of the previous Autumn Term. He pictured Ellington, towards midnight, unlocking the door at the foot of the narrow staircase, climbing up, taking up a previously loosened floorboard, and letting drop a previously loosened gas-fitting. That, of course, assumed that the boy's murder had been premeditated and that it would have happened anyhow, some time or other during the Term. The choice of the boy's first night might have arisen from the curious opportunity that had fallen to Ellington of staying up as late as he liked that night without his wife wondering where he was.

Revell was occupied with these and other reflections when suddenly, and to his considerable amazement, he heard footsteps approaching from the head of the staircase towards him. And simultaneously a sharp, rather commanding voice called out: "Well, young man, and what do you think you are doing up here?"

Revell turned and saw facing him a middle-aged man, average in height and physique, moderately well-dressed, and so thoroughly normal in most other respects that he was almost, for that very reason, remarkable. Fresh-complexioned, blue-eyed, and with a small brown moustache, he was the sort of man one usually has a vague feeling of having met somewhere before, though the time and the place escape one's mind. Even his voice had no particular accent or mannerism, and gave no clue to class, profession, or social position. One thing only it did most certainly indicate, and that was a strong and virile character.

Revell, beyond his astonishment, was inclined to resent the stranger's brusqueness. "I think I've as much right to ask you the same question," he said.

"Well, maybe you have. But that's no reason why you shouldn't answer *my* question, is it?"

"Why should I?"

"May I take it, then, that you have a right to be here?"

"Certainly. I am an Old Oakingtonian at present staying here as the guest of the Headmaster."

"And he knows you are exploring these rather gloomy regions?"

Revell flushed angrily. He did not mind abuse, but he never cared for banter. "I really don't see why I should discuss it with you," he retorted, in his best Oxford manner.

The stranger laughed (even his laugh was superbly normal) and took a step forward. "All right, then—no need to get annoyed about it. Queer place to come sightseeing, anyhow—I think you'll have to admit that much. . . .Yes, these boards *have* been loosened, but it was probably done by the electricians when they wired the dormitories. That's what you were thinking, isn't it?"

Revell was too startled to answer. The other continued: "Come now, why don't you be frank about it? You came up here because you remembered that a boy named Marshall had been killed last September by a gas-pipe falling on top of him in the dormitory immediately below. Isn't that correct? No need to mind admitting it—I'm up here for the same reason, as a matter of fact."

"Perhaps you'll tell me who exactly you are," said Revell, guardedly.

"Certainly. My name's Guthrie. Yours is Revell, I believe?"

"Yes."

"I thought so. Well, Mr. Revell, you don't seem inclined to trust me very much. Just tell me this, though—have you definitely formed the opinion that the first of the Marshall boys was murdered? Because I can tell you absolutely that the second boy was. That's quite settled."

"*What!* What do you mean?"

"Steady—don't get excited—we don't want people to hear us talking. I'm prepared to be frank with you if you'll be the same with me. Can we call it a bargain?"

Revell slowly nodded. "You were saying about the second Marshall——"

"Oh yes. He was murdered all right. We dug up his body last night and found a bullet in his brain."

"*Good God!*"

The other made a sign that they should both be as quiet as possible. "In fact," he whispered, "I think we'd better finish this conversation in a more convenient spot. Can I trust you to go down ahead of me, to walk out of the School gates, and meet me in five minutes' time at the corner of the Patchmere lane? And, of course, on no account to mention a word about this to anyone

you happen to meet? Go along then—I'll follow dis-
creetly and lock up—I've got a key."

Five minutes later the two met again in the bright
sunshine of the country cross-roads. Revell by that time
had managed to conquer his amazement; he greeted the
other with a slight smile. "First of all, Mr. Guthrie, I
really would like to know *what* you are and how you
come into all this," he began.

"Soon, Mr. Revell—all in good time. Are you busy
just at present?"

"I was thinking of catching the eleven o'clock train
back to town."

"Were you? Could you possibly make it a later one?"

"Oh yes. What do you want me to do?"

"Well, you might lunch with me at Easthampton, to
begin with. My car's at the pub along the lane here—
we can be at Easthampton in half an hour."

Easthampton, the busy market-town fifteen miles
away, had several pretty good hotels, and at one of
them, the *Greyhound*, Guthrie appeared to be staying.
"There's too much gossip in a little place like Oakington," he said, as he left his car in the hotel-yard. "Come
on—there's not a great crowd here, so we shall be able
to talk."

He chatted about unimportant matters till the wait-
ress had left them alone after their meal; then, offering
Revell a cigarette from his case, he went on, as if there
had hardly been any interruption since the conversation in the Oakington sick-rooms: "Yes, it was a bullet
all right—found it in the first five minutes. That old
darling Murchiston's too old for his job—don't believe
he'd have found a cannon-ball even. Still, we mustn't
blame him, since he served our purpose pretty well."

"The Coroner seemed just as big a fool."

"Oh, the Coroner? Mustn't blame him, either, I'm afraid—he only did as he was told. Privately he suspected something was wrong, but we suggested to him that a verdict of Accidental Death would be a good thing if it could be managed. And it was. Oh, he's smart enough—make no mistake about it."

"*You* suggested to him about the verdict?"

"*We*, yes—Scotland Yard, I mean, though perhaps I oughtn't to tell you. Oh yes, we're not so blind as people often suppose. What *I* want to know now is how *you* came to have suspicions?"

"It's rather a complicated story, I'm afraid."

"Never mind, I'll listen. I've been pretty frank with you—now it's your turn. Go ahead."

Revell, after a doubtful pause, began at the beginning and told the whole history of his connexion with the Marshall affair. Guthrie did not question him during the narration, but when he had finished, the good-humoured, rather nondescript face took on a sudden look of alertness. "So you're what might be termed an amateur detective, eh, Mr. Revell?"

"I don't claim the title, I assure you. I came in, at the beginning, because of Roseveare's invitation, and when the second affair happened I think it was rather natural that I should take an interest in it."

"Oh, quite. And for an amateur you really haven't done so very badly. The point is that we professionals have all the cards in our hands. Inevitable, isn't it? You've no credentials—no police force to back you up. The only thing an amateur can do—and that, very often, quite easily—is to scare the criminal and give him a good chance of getting away."

"I don't think I've done that."

"Did I say so? Personally I think the Oakington murderer is very far from being scared. The inquest verdict must, as we intended, have reassured him considerably."

"There have been all sorts of rumours about, though."

"Oh, I daresay. Most likely some of my plain-clothes fellows have been seen—I put them on to keep an eye on things at night."

"Do you mean that you've been searching the place already?"

"Hardly that—though by pure luck my men *did* find something—but this weather's the very devil—gives everybody such a reasonable excuse for taking a stroll in the middle of the night. . . . However, most of that's by the bye. What I was just going to tell you was that a few days ago a man named Graham arrived in town. He also had noticed the rather remarkable accidents that had happened to two boys at a public-school. He was the boys' guardian, in fact, so he had every right to be interested. But instead of trying to solve the mystery, if any, on his own, he very wisely—yes, *very* wisely, if I may say so, Mr. Revell—came to us at the Yard for a little talk about it."

Revell accepted the implied rebuke with a faint smile.

"Not that he had definite evidence, of course," continued the other. "One very often hasn't, at the beginning of a case. But he told us enough for the Yard to send me to Oakington—just for a little unofficial look around. I hope I didn't make myself too conspicuous, though I did have a chat with the local Coroner and police. Like you, Mr. Revell, I very soon came to the tentative conclusion that the second boy, and possibly the first as well, had been murdered. Then, quite by chance, one of the constables on patrol duty found something that definitely gave us a clue. On the strength of it we were able to approach the Home Office with a request for the exhumation of the body. That's how it all happened. . . . Now don't ask me what it was that my men found, for a detective has to keep a few secrets to himself. Tell me now, if it doesn't happen to be one of *your* secrets, whom do you suspect?"

"The obvious person seems to be Ellington—the housemaster of School House."

"Yes, yes, I daresay. And what are the reasons that make you think he is so very obvious?"

"Well, to begin with . . . but, as a matter of fact, I tabled them all in my notebook—perhaps you'd care to have a look?"

"Yes, I certainly should."

Revell produced his notebook, opened it at the proper page, and handed it across to the other. Guthrie studied it intently for a moment or two. "I suppose you took a First in Greats at Oxford, eh?" he remarked, as he handed it back.

"Well yes, I did, as it happens, but——"

"So did I, too—but I've had twenty years of hard experience since, which make up for it. You've made some clever and quite valuable points, but you should beware of theorising too much. However, there's one little minor mystery that we ought to be able to clear up within the next few hours. And that is the very queer attitude of the celebrated Doctor Roseveare. Will you undertake that little job for me?"

"I'll try, of course. But how do you suggest I should set about it?"

"In the directest manner possible. Tell him that the boy's body has been exhumed and that Scotland Yard is investigating the murder—watch the fellow's face and don't give him time to make up a yarn. Ask him for a full explanation of all that puzzles you. I'm giving you the job because it occurs to me that he might be franker with you than he would be with me—that's the sort of sly fellow I am. Anyhow, we shall see if it works." And he added: "By the way, I wouldn't chatter too much about all this to Lambourne. You may perhaps have been a shade too free with that young man."

Guthrie motored Revell back to Oakington towards tea-time, and arranged to meet him again later on in the evening. When or how Revell was to get back to town afterwards was not even discussed.

He felt rather bewildered when he was left alone. So much seemed to have happened during those few hours since the morning. He had been caught up, as it were, in the swift maelstrom of great events, and though it was just the sort of thing he had always longed to have happen to him, he was not altogether sure that it was as pleasant as he had expected. Now that he knew beyond all doubt that the affair in the swimming-bath *had* been murder, he felt, more than he had ever felt before, a certain overlying horror in the atmosphere of Oakington. Strolling round the Ring on that lovely mid-summer afternoon, with the song of birds and the plick-plock of cricket in his ears, he felt with awe that some-where thereabouts, perhaps in one of the rooms whose windows glittered in the sunlight, or perhaps even on the pavilion-roof watching the game, was someone who had carefully and callously schemed the deaths of one and perhaps of two persons. Over the entire School there seemed to hang the dark and spectral shadow of such a deed, and all the more terribly because it was still invisible to so many.

He thought of Guthrie with grudging admiration mingled with astonishment that any Oxford man could contrive to look as he did at the age of forty or so. There was a queer forcefulness about the fellow—a personality, undoubtedly, that hid behind the deliberately average manner. Guthrie, too, had been very confidential, and Revell felt more than a little proud to think that his own deductions, even without much background of evidence, had proved so largely correct. Theory, even with the recent stamp of Oxford upon it, had its place if it could so intelligently anticipate the findings of practical research.

Towards six o'clock he walked up the drive leading to the Head's house. He was perhaps just the least bit nervous, but apart from that it was a relief, after so much speculating and theorising, to know that at last he was about to tackle something straightforwardly.

Roseveare, busy with correspondence in his study, was naturally astonished to see him again. "Missed your train, eh? There's another good one at seven, I think—you can verify it from my time-table here. . . ."

Revell flushed under the scarcely veiled hint. "I came back, sir," he began, slowly, "because I wanted to have a few words with you—confidentially."

"Confidentially? Dear me, that sounds very interesting. Please sit down—these letters, I hope, will not keep me very long."

Revell would have quickly resented such treatment in more normal circumstances; as it was, he merely interposed: "I think, sir, you would rather I gave you my message without delay. I really came to tell you that yesterday the body of Wilbraham Marshall was exhumed and it was found that he had been shot."

The effect upon Roseveare was electric; he looked up with suddenly piercing eyes that were like the gleaming tips of a pair of foils. But after the first be-

wildered second there came to him, as from immense
reserves of hidden strength, a sort of defensive blandness which might have concealed anything or everything behind its ramparts. Revell, who had expected a
good deal from the suddenness of his announcement,
was not altogether satisfied with its results.

"But, my dear boy, you're not serious, are you? All
sorts of rumours, I know, are still in circulation——"

"This isn't a rumour," Revell cut in. "I heard it from
a Scotland Yard man who has been in Oakington to-day
and who attended the exhumation yesterday."

"Scotland Yard? And in Oakington? But surely—
surely—if that were so—he would come to me with his
information?"

"Apparently not."

"And you say it was discovered that the boy had been
shot?"

"Yes. They found the bullet in his head."

"That is dreadful—very dreadful." A look of horror
entered his eyes for a moment, before giving way to
renewed astonishment. "But really, you must tell me
more about this. It was good of you to miss your train
and bring me the terrible news. Yes, very good of you
—and—I thank you sincerely." There was an ample gra-
ciousness in his voice. "Now tell me—how did you come
into possession of this appalling information? Where
did you meet your informant? Why did he tell you?"

Revell, who had come to cross-examine rather than
to be cross-examined, was somewhat taken aback by
this string of inquiries. Nevertheless he answered: "I
met him—er—quite accidentally. As for why he told me,
I don't know, unless he thought I might be able to help
him. Anyhow, it's established now that the boy was
murdered and that the accident was a mere fake. And

naturally, sir, I'm a little puzzled over one or two small matters that concern you and me in this affair."

"Such as?"

"Well, in the first place, why did you *really* send for me here to begin with? I daresay you can quite understand that this recent affair rather opens up the earlier one. You obviously had suspicions of some kind when you sent for me originally, and the reason you gave was —if you don't mind my being perfectly frank about it— paltry. I put it down to the state of your nerves at the time—but I really can't understand how and why your nerves have been so totally unaffected by this second affair. This was far more suspicious, on the face of it; yet you didn't seem to have any suspicions; you didn't send for me; and when I did come, you gave me the impression that nothing was or could be wrong and that I was altogether wasting my time. Rather a puzzling change of front, sir, it seems to me."

"Yes, I'm sure it must have been puzzling."

"I wish you could explain it to me, anyhow," Revell went on. "In a serious affair like this, every little mystery cleared up is so much to the good. Besides, I'm sure you must be anxious that the person who murdered one and perhaps two of your boys shall be discovered as soon as possible."

The simplicity of the appeal seemed to bring Roseveare nearer to emotion than hitherto; after a pause, and in a rather different voice, he replied: "I don't quite see how my explanation can help towards the discovery of the criminal, but still, I recognise your right, in the circumstances, to be told rather more than you know already. I will give you the explanation, therefore, though I doubt if it will do any good. It concerns other persons besides myself, unfortunately, so you must allow me to mention no names. I wish I could prevent you from guessing, but I may hope, at least, that you will try to respect as many privacies as you can."

It was an easy promise to make, and Revell made it.

"You will believe me, I am sure," Roseveare went on, "when I tell you that I had not the slightest suspicion at first that the dormitory accident was anything but what it appeared to be. There was nothing to suspect; there was nobody to be suspected; it seemed just one of those tragic, almost pointless mishaps that do happen from time to time. The inquest returned what appeared to me and to everyone else the only possible verdict. Not for two months—till the end of November, in fact —did I harbour the very least misgiving. Then, one afternoon, the wife of one of my staff visited me alone in this room and unfolded an exceedingly remarkable story. She gave me to understand that her husband had done several things that seemed to connect rather curiously with the death of the boy."

"Good heavens! You mean that she suspected her husband of having murdered him?"

"Nothing nearly so definite as that, I am afraid. She was far too incoherent and hysterical to frame her suspicions into anything so tangible. I did not, as a matter of fact, believe her or take much notice of what she said, which is perhaps a pity. I remember she mentioned the sick-rooms over the dormitory and said that her husband had been there several times during the vacation, and without apparent reason. She also said that on the night of the accident he had not come to bed until very late. Anyhow, as I said, I regarded her case as rather pathological—she seemed to me to be in a highly hysterical condition and I packed her off as quickly as I could and tried to think no more of the matter."

"Yet you did, I suppose?"

"I did. I confess it. It's curious how a suspicion, dismissed at first as utterly preposterous, improves its status after a time. Not, of course, that I really came to believe her. But I did, perhaps, come to feel that the matter was just worth probing a little. After all, there are queer things in this world, and I knew that as well as anyone. The trouble was, of course, that I was not in a position to do any of the probing myself. To have attempted even the most casual investigation would have attracted notice—you would be surprised how hard it is for a headmaster to find out what is going on in his own school. So, to come to the point, I recollected a chance conversation I had some years ago with the Master of your college at Oxford, and I sent for you.

"Well now, consider my position when you came. I did not feel justified in telling you the truth—to have done so, I judged, would have prejudiced the impartiality of your investigation, apart from being an atrocious slander upon a colleague for whom I had and still have every respect. On the other hand, it was clearly necessary that I should give you some reason for having sent for you. I therefore concocted the little note which I told you had been left between the pages of the boy's algebra-book." He half-smiled. "It sounds, I daresay, a childish thing to have done, but it was really the only thing I could think of. And I was, I confess, rather amused when you discovered a plausible and an altogether satisfactory reason why the boy should have left the note which, in fact, he did not write at all. The moral, perhaps, is that it is easy for an ingenious person to find reasons for anything."

He continued, after a pause: "That week-end you were here, however, something happened that removed all my misgivings completely. The lady in question visited me again, but in very different circumstances. She came, in fact, to apologise for her previous visit, and to tell me that all her suspicions were really quite groundless and merely the result of nerves. This tallied, of course, with my own theory of the incident, and I was very glad to take her word about it."

"Although really you had no more reason to suppose she was speaking the truth then than before?"

"Well, perhaps not, according to the strictest logic. But you must remember that, as something of a doctor myself, I could see the immense improvement in her condition—she was calm and rational upon this second visit and gave every evidence of being bitterly ashamed of her previous one. Anyhow, I *did* believe her. And so, by the time you made your report to me, the matter was already settled in my mind and I was thinking that I had sent for you on somewhat of a fool's errand. It was not, of course, your fault, but I was naturally anxious for you not to waste any more of your time."

"And what about this second accident? Didn't it awaken any of the old suspicions?"

"Why should it have done? It was, I admit, a most remarkable coincidence, but in the face of Murchiston's evidence, to say nothing of the evidence of my own eyes, how could I have thought of anything but accident? Your attitude, of course, was bound to be different, for you could not know the whole truth about the first affair. I wasn't in the least surprised that you came along, but you can hardly have expected me to invite you."

"You really thought it possible that the boy did dive into the empty bath?"

"Certainly. It was unlikely, but perfectly possible. It

seemed far more possible to me than any theory of murder. In fact, but for the bullet which you say has been discovered, I doubt if murder could or would have been thought of. What puzzles me is why the Home Office so readily permitted the exhumation. They must have been given reasons beyond mere local tittle-tattle."

"The detective told me his men had found something —some piece of evidence—he didn't tell me what."

"Found something? Where?"

"Here. On the premises, somewhere or other."

"Do you mean to tell me that policemen have been searching the School?"

"Not searching, I think, so much as watching."

"Watching or searching, it is all equally scandalous." His voice lost, for the first time, its smooth precision. "Common courtesy, I should have thought, would have made even a detective ask for the permission which he might know I should have to give. You may tell your detective friend, Revell, if you see him again, that I should like very much to know by whose authority he sets his spies to trespass on private property! A disgraceful infringement of all public and personal rights!"

And so the interview closed on that note of anger. It was something to have found out that trespass, if not murder, could raise the ire of the Headmaster of Oakington.

CHAPTER VI
LAMBOURNE'S STORY

REVELL WAS determined not to sacrifice his entire independence in the investigation. Greatly as he respected Guthrie, he had no desire to be merely his assistant, or to give up his own rather interesting position in an affair that was certainly becoming more interesting at every moment. When he met the detective that evening in one of the country lanes near the School, he gave him a fairly full account of his interview with Roseveare. Guthrie nodded complimentarily when he had finished.

"So you got it out of him, then? The question is, of course—is it the truth?"

Revell had wondered the same thing himself, but he was a little astonished by Guthrie's calm suspicion. "Do you mean that you suspect him?" he queried.

"Oh, I wouldn't go so far as that. It's rather that I always suspect a queer yarn. And his, you'll admit, is pretty queer. Who's this woman he was talking about—I suppose you *did* make a guess?"

Revell paused uncomfortably. "I don't know whether I ought——"

"Of course you ought," interrupted Guthrie with a laugh. "It's all informal—betwen ourselves, you know. Anyhow, if you prefer it, I'll have a shot myself and say she's Ellington's wife. Impudent-looking piece, with black hair and a turned-up nose—that's the lady, isn't it?"

The description astonished Revell so much that he

did not reply; but Guthrie evidently took his silence for an affirmative.

"Why should she go to the Head with such a yarn, I wonder? If she *did* go, that is. We must remember that either or both of them may be complete liars. By the way, Roseveare wasn't Head in your time here, was he?"

"No. He came a few years after the end of the War. I daresay you know all about his War record and so on?"

"Oh yes, I gathered he was rather a mandarin in those days. I even went a bit further back and looked up his record before the War. That was quite exciting, too." Guthrie stopped to light his pipe in the gathering dusk. "Thought so—these hedges are full of young lovers, and young lovers, contrary to the popular idea, are not so intent on their own affairs that they won't listen to two strangers chattering in high-pitched voices about a local big pot. We must talk more quietly. . . . Now let me tell you a few things about our friend the Headmaster of Oakington. To begin with, he hasn't any ordinary schoolmaster's degree—the 'doctor' before his name is a medical title."

"I knew that."

"Oh, you did? Well, it's unusual, rather, isn't it? Then again, he had no scholastic experience before he came to Oakington. He's been many things in his time— doctor, politician, business man, even a sort of gentleman farmer—but till a few years ago he never ran a school." Guthrie paused and puffed reflectively. "Of course, you know why Oakington took him? The place was in a bit of a bad way under the previous fellow— Jury, wasn't his name?—and they—the School governors—imagined Roseveare would pull the show out of the mire. Which, to a large extent, I believe he has done."

"He has a wonderful personality, I think."

"Oh yes—no doubt about that. Don't think I'm attacking the fellow at all. I'm merely pointing out that we're not dealing with the average Eton and Oxford headmaster who composes Greek epigrams and wears a parson's collar. Roseveare's a man of wider experience altogether. Twice at least he made a fortune and lost it—once in America and again in New Zealand. He had and still has an extraordinarily persuasive way with him. In America he made a great hit as a company-promoter."

"Really? That reminds me that I've very often seen him poring over the stock-market reports in the papers."

Guthrie smiled. "That, by itself, isn't very remarkable, I'm afraid. There's hardly a headmaster in England who hasn't dabbled in shares—generally to his loss. . . . Roseveare, however, really was a sort of financier at one time in his career. Oh, quite honest, yes—or at least as honest as a financier can be. He was unlucky, though, in the end—lost all his money and crossed to New Zealand. There he set up as a local doctor in a small town where the schoolmaster's name was Ellington."

"Good Lord—you mean the Ellington who's here at Oakington now?"

"Yes. What's more, when Roseveare became successful and took a practice in a larger town, Ellington soon afterwards followed him there as a schoolmaster. They were obviously very close friends. The only place Ellington didn't follow Roseveare to was the War. He stayed in New Zealand, where there wasn't conscription, and became rather unpopular. Later, in 1921, when Roseveare was appointed to Oakington, Ellington came hopping over from the other side of the world to become a housemaster here. Curious, don't you think?"

"Very curious. I say, don't you think it looks rather like blackmail? Supposing Ellington knew something a little bit discreditable about Roseveare's past—after all, a man with all those different careers may well have done something or other——"

"He may, of coure, but there's absolutely not a shadow of evidence."

"Well, just for the moment assuming that he had done something a little bit over the line in one way or another——"

"That's all very well, but I fail to see what possible connexion it can have with the murder of the boy Marshall. After all, that's what we're investigating."

Suddenly Revell was attacked, conquered, and completely overwhelmed by an idea. "Yes, I know, and see how it fits in. Do you remember me telling you that the boy came back unexpectedly that night and that very few people knew he was in the dormitory? Roseveare didn't—at least, I don't think he did. Well, supposing Roseveare, having been blackmailed by Ellington till he was desperate, had decided to get rid of his oppressor once and for all! He knew that Ellington had to sleep in Marshall's bed in the dormitory until the boy came back. He didn't expect the boy back until Monday. Isn't it just possible, then, that the death of the first Marshall was that somewhat rare combination—a murder *and* an accident?"

Guthrie broke into a gust of laughter. "Now that's really clever of you, Revell, and if there were only the least little bit of evidence in support of it, I'd say it was worth looking into. Even so, I don't know how you'd fit in the second affair. What possible motive could the

respected Headmaster have had for murdering the second boy?"

"Exactly." Revell's voice was sharp with excitement.
"And have I ever suggested that he murdered them
both? Mayn't there just as easily have been two murderers as two murders?"

"Oh, get away with you—you're too clever for a poor
old honest plodder like me. Besides, I think we've done
enough theorising for the time being. What we want is
facts, and the sooner we set about getting them the better. Now let's turn back for a final drink before bedtime."

Nor would he say another word about the case except, just before they separated, to mention that it might
be just as well, in the circumstances, if Revell were to
stay on for a time as the guest of Doctor Roseveare.

Revell accordingly spent another night in the Head's
comfortable house. Roseveare had already gone to bed
when he came in, but it was clear that he was expected
to stay, since his bag had been unpacked again and
whisky and sandwiches left hospitably on the dining-
room sideboard.

In the morning, when he went down to breakfast,
the butler told him that Doctor Roseveare presented
his apologies but was breakfasting that morning in the
Master's Common Room.

The reason for that became apparent an hour later,
when Revell met Lambourne in the corridor of School
House. "Hullo, Revell!" cried the latter, with a jaunty
air. "Still here? I guess you'll stay on now, won't you?
Such a sensation, isn't it? Come along into my room and
I'll tell you all about it."

As soon as the door had closed upon them, Lambourne continued breathlessly: "We've just been accorded the rarest of honours. The Head breakfasted with us in the Common Room. You've no idea, Revell, not being a poor devil of an usher, what that means. Of course we knew immediately that something had happened or was going to happen—the last time we had him to share our Quaker Oats was when five prefects made a dash to the Wembley Exhibition with five barmaids. But that was years and years ago. This time the news was even more serious. Unfortuntely the surprise part of it was rather ruined by the fact that we'd all just been reading the thrilling news in the *Daily Mail*. Journalistic enterprise in these days, my boy, is a horse that wants some beating."

"I wish you'd tell me what on earth you're talking about," said Revell, a trifle peevishly. He had slept badly and was in none too good a humour.

"Is it possible that you haven't yet seen the morning papers?"

"I haven't, no."

"Then you aren't aware that Wilbraham Marshall's body has been exhumed and that the authorities suspect what the Sunday press will delight to call 'foul play'?"

Revell's surprise needed no assuming, for he had had no idea that the matter would already have come to the notice of the newspapers. Lambourne continued, well satisfied with the sensation he was creating: "That's a pretty sort of scandal to happen to a school whose clientele is just struggling on to the border-line that separates Golder's Green from Kensington! Naturally our learned and respected chief was fairly rattled about it. Told us, in so many words, that detectives were about and that any one of us, at any time, might be suspected of murder. Advised us all to keep calm and 'endeavour to reconcile our duty to the School with our duty to society.' I suppose he means we're not to be too helpful when the detectives come to cross-examine us."

"I expect you were all pretty staggered, eh?"

"*Staggered?* Wouldn't you have been?"

"Did anybody—anybody in particular—appear concerned?"

"Ellington went rather pale, if that's what you're angling after. As a matter of fact, the person most affected was quite probably myself—I fainted. Never could stand the little touch of drama."

"Well, well," said Revell, with a sigh, "I suppose we must resign ourselves to events."

"The Head isn't exactly in a mood of resignation, I can tell you. He's put servants at all the gates to act as pickets and stop newspaper men from coming in. No one is to enter the grounds without authority—no one is to answer any questions put by strangers—all town-leave is stopped for the whole school, prefects included, until further notice. We're a beleaguered garrison, rallying under our gallant Captain Roseveare against the expected onslaughts of the Fleet Street Fusiliers." The bell began to ring for morning school. "That means I must hurry away to inject a little English literature into the fourth form. They won't do any work, of course—and do you blame them?"

Revell laughed and left him. Since Guthrie's cautionary remark, he had taken care not to confide too much in Lambourne; indeed, he was now definitely on his guard against him.

The Head was just leaving his study when Revell entered it a little while later. He greeted Revell with his customary urbanity; and never, in some sense, had

Revell felt his charm more hypnotically. In such a presence the theory that postulated him as a murderer melted into absurdity.

"Sorry to have left you alone for breakfast," Roseveare began, "but I thought it best to make an announcement to the staff at the earliest possible moment. Even so, I find I have been forestalled by the newspapers. I do wish your detective acquaintance would hurry up with his enquiries—I am afraid the work of the School will be sadly affected until the whole thing is cleared up. Have you any idea what he intends to do and when?"

Revell confessed that he knew nothing. "I should think, though, that he'll get to work pretty quickly—he seems that sort of man."

"I'm glad to hear it. In spite of his discourtesy I shall be very willing to give him all the help I can. Do you yet know, by the way, what it was that his men found here while they were searching—or, as you put it, watching—the place?"

"I'm afraid I don't."

"I only wondered if it might have been a revolver. Because Mr. Ellington told me this morning that he had missed his from the place where he usually keeps it."

Revell fought back his excitement. "Really? I didn't know he had a revolver, even."

"Neither did I, till he told me. It's a relic, apparently, of more strenuous days in the colonies before he came to Oakington. Anyhow, he discovered last night that it was missing. Naturally, it occurred to me that perhaps it was that which the police had discovered."

"It may have been. In any case, the missing revolver seems an important clue."

"Very, I should think. Mr. Ellington was most distressed about it, as you can imagine."

"I suppose he felt that it—er—in a way—threw a certain amount of suspicion on himself?"

Roseveare appeared utterly shocked and astonished. "Good God, no—I don't suppose such a preposterous notion ever entered his head—or anyone else's, either! What distressed him was the thought that by his own slackness in leaving his drawer unlocked the tragedy may have been enabled to take place."

"You mean that the murderer may have taken Ellington's revolver?"

"Murderer? Why are you and your detective-friend so persistent in assuming murder? All that is known is that the boy was shot. Far be it from me to teach Scotland Yard its job, but I really do feel convinced, in my own mind, that suicide is a far likelier supposition. It is horrible enough, but it is by no means impossible. Ellington, I may say, tells me that ever since the death of the boy's brother last year, Wilbraham suffered from moods of extreme depression. He confided in Ellington a good deal, it appears, and had free access to his rooms at all times—which would have given him ample opportunity to take the revolver."

"But why on earth should he shoot himself in the swimming-bath, of all places?"

"How can I tell you? It might occur to him as a place where he would be likely to cause least disturbance."

"And why should he climb to the top diving-platform?"

"Again, how can I tell you? But, in any case, are you sure that he did?"

Revell looked his astonishment, and Roseveare, tak-

ing his chance, resumed: "My dear boy, don't be so bewildered. In a case like this it is really our duty to consider all possibilities, however remote. I may as well tell
you that I have given a good deal of careful consideration to the matter, and I have already evolved a theory
—tentatively, of course—which seems to me at least as
reasonable as any other. I believe, briefly, that the boy
did commit suicide."

"From the top diving-platform?"

"Not necessarily. The bath is ten feet deep and the
boy was nearly six feet tall—the extent of his injuries
seemed to me quite consistent with a fall from the edge.
And I speak, remember, with some medical knowledge
and experience."

"And the wrist-watch?"

"Ah, now we come to a different point. Clearly the
wrist-watch was placed on the top platform by somebody, and if not by the boy himself, then by whom?
And, even more important, why? The only reason I
can think of is that someone entered the bath after
poor Wilbraham had shot himself, discovered the tragedy, and tried to make a suicide look like an accident."

"Why?"

"The obvious reason would be consideration for the
boy's family—for the School's reputation—for, indeed,
everybody concerned. Accident is bad enough, but suicide, you will agree, is much worse."

"And murder worst of all?"

"Oh, undoubtedly, but I really must decline to consider such a possibility until every other avenue has been
thoroughly explored."

"Well, according to your theory, the thoughtful visitor, whoever he was, placed the boy's wrist-watch on

the top platform, removed his dressing-gown and slippers, if he had them on, and also took away the revolver."

"Those are undoubtedly matters that would naturally occur to anyone who wished to produce the impression of an accident."

"But he would hardly leave the revolver lying about for the police to discover afterwards?"

"Pardon me, but how do we know that the police have discovered it? I understood just now that you yourself were not certain about it. All that seems definitely established is that Ellington's revolver is missing, and since Ellington reported the loss himself, it would seem obvious that he, at any rate, was *not* the person who visited the scene of the tragedy that night."

"Then whom do you suspect?"

"My dear boy, that is hardly my province. I am merely putting forward a theory which, for all its excessive complication and intricacy, seems to me infinitely less improbable than to suppose that one of my colleagues, whom I have known and respected for many years, should suddenly and for no conceivable reason commit the cold-blooded murder of his own cousin. As a matter of fact, I do happen to know, on very good authority, that someone did visit the swimming-bath a short time after it may be supposed that the tragedy took place. Now, now, don't cross-examine me—I am not, at the moment, prepared to say more than that."

With which altogether cryptic remark he gathered up his papers and gown and left Revell to think things over.

He thought things over, and two hours later, having received a message from a uniformed policeman (there was not much pretence of secrecy about things now), met Guthrie outside the school entrance. He had his car with him, and the two drove rapidly to Easthampton. "I've got to fetch my things across," he explained. "I've taken lodgings for the present at the house of the local police-sergeant—it's on the spot and Oakington gossip doesn't matter so much now. You don't mind the ride to Easthampton and back, I suppose?"

Revell assured him that he would positively enjoy it, and further went on to describe his recent interview with Dr. Roseveare. Guthrie listened attentively. At the end he offered no comment of his own, but asked Revell for his.

Revell hastened to oblige. "Well, it seemed to me pretty obvious that Roseveare and Ellington had had a confidential chat together. Roseveare never hinted at suicide yesterday when I talked to him, but he had it all very pat to-day."

"It's an ingenious theory, anyhow. We mustn't ignore it."

"It looks to me as if it were made specially to fit in with the possibility that the police have discovered Ellington's revolver. I wish you'd tell me whether they really have or not."

Guthrie half-smiled. "I think once again I must plead the Official Secrets' Acts," he answered, jocularly.

"But why? I've been pretty frank with you, and you said it was a bargain between us——"

"All right," Guthrie interrupted, with that imperturbable good humour that was perhaps his most annoying trait. "Tell you what—if you really are devoured with curiosity, you can listen in to a couple of interviews I shall be having this evening. It'll be a bit stagey, but that can't be helped. I shall be in Ellington's room in School House, and you can hide in the little room next door. The partition's only match-board—you'll be able to hear through it. By Jove, yes, it's an idea—and you might be really useful, too, apart from enjoying yourself. Do you happen to know shorthand, by the way?"

"I'm afraid I don't."

"Pity. I've never yet met an Oxford graduate who did, but I've met dozens who'd be twice as efficient *if* they did. Take my tip, Revell, and learn it as soon as ever you get back to town—join a class and work till you can do at least a hundred and fifty words a minute. . . . Anyhow, if you can't take shorthand notes, you can keep your ears wide open, I daresay. It might be handy to have you as a witness afterwards."

"I'll do my best, I assure you. Who are the two persons you intend to see?"

"You'll know in good time."

He was, Revell felt, being merely provoking, but there was nothing for it but to accept the situation as it stood. They lunched at Easthampton and then, after the detective had settled his account at the hotel, drove back to Oakington and deposited his luggage at the police-sergeant's cottage on the outskirts of the village. The sergeant was on duty, but his buxom wife offered tea, which they took in a parlour which, in less strenuous days, Revell would have lauded as a masterpiece of Victorianism. As it was, he allowed Guthrie to talk football and politics to his heart's content (the detective was almost equally ardent as a Twickenham rugger "fan" and as a Liberal). Not till the village clock struck five did Guthrie suggest a move, and then, with a sudden return to business, he gave instructions. "I don't want us to be seen together too much," he said, "so you had better walk to the School from here and go straight up to Ellington's room in School House. I shall take the car—I'll be ahead of you by ten minutes or so, I should reckon. Anyhow, a minute or so either way won't matter."

Revell agreed, and within a quarter of an hour, after a warm walk over the meadows, was turning the handle of Ellington's door. Guthrie was there, reading a newspaper by the window, and gave him a nod and a signal to be quiet. "Ah, that's right, Revell, you're in plenty of time." Following the detective's further instructions, Revell settled himself in the small adjoining apartment which had at one time been the bedroom of an unmarried master. There were cracks here and there in the matchboard partition, and he arranged his chair so that he could see a good deal of what went on in the main room. Guthrie cautiously approved. "All right so long as you're not seen yourself," he whispered. "I expect our first visitor along in a few minutes. Just wait patiently, and for the Lord's sake don't want to sneeze."

Revell waited, and after a few moments heard the School bell ringing for the end of afternoon school. A few seconds later came the sound of heavy footsteps ascending the stairs and marching along the corridor; then the door was suddenly flung open and Ellington, in cap and gown, and with books under his arm, strode into the room.

"Good evening, Mr. Ellington," said Guthrie instantly.

Ellington stopped sharply as he heard his name spoken. "Hullo!" he barked, seeing the trespasser. Then he added: "I don't think I know you. What the devil are you doing in my room, anyway?"

"Oh, merely waiting to have a little chat with you, Mr. Ellington."

"Chat be damned! What I want to know is what right you have to be here!"

"But surely, Mr. Ellington, you don't object to people waiting in your room when they call on you and you happen to be out, do you?"

"It's not that. It's—it's—the circumstances. I suppose you're the detective that's been prowling about here lately?"

"Yes, you've guessed it."

Ellington raised his eyes to the ceiling as if in mute protest to the powers above. "All I can say," he retorted, at length, "is that if *I* were Head *I* wouldn't put up with you interfering with the whole routine of the School in this infernal way! It's scandalous, and I've told the Head so! There seems to be a conspiracy on the part of officialdom to ruin the School altogether!"

"Now that's an interesting idea, Mr. Ellington," said Guthrie, with exquisite blandness. "I wonder if there could possibly be anything in it? The Home Secretary, shall we say, murders a boy in order that the resulting hullabaloo shall make Oakington a less dangerous rival of Eton and Harrow! By Jove, I don't think the idea had ever struck me before!"

"It's no joking matter, I should think."

"You're quite right. It isn't." Guthrie's voice became suddenly serious. "Look here, Mr. Ellington, I'm only the servant of authority—I have to do these things. There's been a murder committed—it's my job to investigate it. Don't you see?"

"I don't see, because in the first place I don't agree that there *has* been a murder committed," retorted Ellington, but his manner was certainly a shade less truculent. He went on: "Ever since Robert's accident last year there's been a positive epidemic of unpleasant rumours going about the School. No proof, no evidence —merely suspicion, insinuation, and scandal. I've done my best to trace it all to its source, but without success. Now comes the second affair, and I find the Home Office and police taking all these ugly rumours for evidence and framing a murder theory quite vaguely and off-hand, without the slightest foundation that would stand up in a court of law——"

"I'm afraid the murder is a little more than a theory by now, Mr. Ellington. You know, of course, that a bullet was discovered in the boy's head."

"So I understand. But I still say that to deduce murder from such evidence is the most fatuous thing I ever heard of! Who would or could have shot the boy? On the one hand you have absolutely no reason at all why the boy could have been murdered, and on the other hand you have a very likely reason why the boy could have taken his own life!"

"Really?" Guthrie leaned forward with as much interest as if the idea were absolutely new to him. "Yet another theory, Mr. Ellington? Come now, you must give us details."

And Ellington proceeded, with a fluency rather unexpected in a man of his type, to outline the identical theory that Roseveare had previously outlined to Revell, and that the latter had recapitulated for Guthrie's benefit. Guthrie listened with every appearance of respectful attention and nodded gravely when Ellington had finished. "A highly ingenious theory, Mr. Ellington," he commented. "Is it impertinent to ask if you thought of it yourself?"

Ellington looked for a moment on the edge of a complete explosion of temper. Guthrie continued: "I'm really not meaning to be offensive at all. Only I happen to know that Doctor Roseveare has given his support to the same theory, and I should like to know whether he suggested it to you or you to him. It doesn't very much matter, of course."

"It was his idea, first of all," said Ellington gruffly, after a pause. "I'm not the sort of person who could have thought of such a thing, and I won't pretend I am. But I do entirely endorse it—every word of it."

"Quite," agreed Guthrie. "And thanks for being so confidential. You really are helping me tremendously. . . . By the way, I understand you missed a revolver of yours quite recently?"

"Yes." Ellington's face went a little pale, though he had obviously been prepared for the question.

"I wish you'd tell me how it happened."

"I missed it yesterday—I opened the drawer where it usually was and found it gone. The drawer was un-locked—I'm afraid that must have been due to my own slackness some time or other, but I can't remember when."

"When did you last see your revolver?"

"Months ago—perhaps six months. I keep it in the bottom drawer of an old bureau, along with a lot of old examination papers. I just happened to want to refer to them yesterday—otherwise I might not have missed the thing at all. It's no use here, of course."

"Was it loaded?"

"No, but there were cartridges in the drawer along with it."

"Were any of these missing?"

"I really couldn't say. I can't remember exactly how many there were to begin with."

Guthrie nodded as if in complete satisfaction and understanding. After a pause he continued: "Oh, by

the way, Mr. Ellington, you don't happen to have
missed anything else lately, do you? Not a weapon—
but just—well, anything?"

Ellington seemed puzzled. "No—at least, I don't think
I have. Why?"

"Oh, I only wondered. I thought perhaps you might
have lost, say, a cricket-bat."

"A cricket-bat?" A curious look of astonishment
came into his eyes. "That's really very extraordinary,
you know. For I do believe I have lost one—now you
come to remind me of it. I was looking for it in the
sports pavilion the other day, though of course I didn't
bother very much when I couldn't find it—I had too
many other things to think about. And besides, I wasn't
sure if I hadn't put it somewhere else."

"You have a locker in the pavilion, I suppose?"

"Yes, but I'm afraid it's a locker that doesn't lock." A
touch of his earlier and perhaps more normal truculence returned to him. "People here borrow one's possessions in a most disgraceful way—it's quite possible
that one of the boys took my bat and has it still. I'll
make enquiries, if you like."

"Oh no, I wouldn't bother."

The truculence blazed up suddenly. "Indeed I shall! I
have a right to investigate the loss of my own property,
surely? Ah, but I see . . . are you suggesting that the
cricket-bat and the revolver are connected in any way?"

"My dear Mr. Ellington, I'm suggesting nothing at
all. But I really am most grateful to you for answering
my questions, and before you go there's only one other
thing I want to say. And that is, do you mind if I stay
here for half an hour or so and talk to someone else
whom I have asked to meet me here?"

"Stay here as long as you like," said Ellington. "I

can't stop you, can I?" He took up his cap and gown and made towards the door.

"I'm afraid, if it comes to the point, you can't," Guthrie called after him through the already opening door. "But I always like to be polite whenever I can, that's all."

Some seconds after Ellington's footsteps had ceased to echo down the corridor and staircase, Revell cautiously peered round the edge of the partition. Guthrie was relighting his pipe and grinning. "What an unfortunate man, Revell!" he exclaimed. "And still more, what an unfortunate manner! Do you think I ought to have arrested him?"

"It depends whether you think him guilty. Do you?"

"Well, there's rather a good deal against him, you know. Motive, of course, to begin with. And then the missing revolver."

"He gave us that information himself, remember."

"Oh yes. But not until Roseveare had told him that my men had found something. He may have thought it good tactics to come forward with a voluntary statement. As it happens, what my men found wasn't the revolver, so our friend Ellington has thoughtfully made us a free gift of valuable evidence."

"It wasn't the revolver?"

" 'Fraid not."

"I suppose you're waiting for me to ask again what it really was."

"Not at all. And in any case, I don't propose to tell you—not yet, anyhow. Perhaps it won't be long before you find out, though."

Conversation soon wilted under the strain of the detective's irritatingly vague responses, and for the final ten minutes before the arrival of the second visitor

Revell and Guthrie hardly spoke at all. At last came the sound of slower, quieter footsteps along the outside corridor; the door opened cautiously; and Lambourne entered.

His face was exceedingly pale, Revell noticed; he was obviously very nervous. "You wished to see me?" he began, approaching Guthrie.

"Yes, that's right, Mr. Lambourne. Please sit down. I'm glad it wasn't inconvenient for you to come at this hour."

"Oh no, I managed it all right."

"Good. Smoke if you care to."

Lambourne sat in the easy chair facing Guthrie and quakingly lit a cigarette. Guthrie did not speak for at least a minute; then, with a manner very much more direct than he had adopted with Ellington, he plunged straight into the midst of things. "I would like you, Mr. Lambourne," he said, quietly, "to tell me exactly where you were and what you were doing between the hours of eight-thirty p.m. and two a.m. on the night of Wilbraham Marshall's murder. I choose eight-thirty as a beginning, because I know that until then you were making preparation in the Hall. Now tell me just what happened after that."

Lambourne inhaled vigorously before replying, as if struggling for some sort of control over himself. "I think," he answered, at length, "I was in my study most of the time until midnight. It was terribly hot—the hottest night of the year, I believe. I knew I should have difficulty in sleeping, so about midnight or so I thought I would go for a walk outside—I have often found that a good way of bringing on drowsiness. I therefore went out, took a stroll round the Ring, and came back. I might have been out perhaps a quarter of an hour alto-

gether. Then I went to bed and fell asleep fairly quickly
—probably long before two a.m. That's about all I can
tell you, I think."

"You met someone while you were out, didn't you?"

"Oh, yes. I thought your enquiry concerned merely
my own movements, or I would have mentioned it. I
met Ellington, as a matter of fact."

"I see. And that is really all you have to tell me?"

"Yes. I think it is."

"Would you like time to think a little more?"

Lambourne's hands twitched nervously as he jerkily
shook his head. Guthrie, nevertheless, allowed considerable time to elapse before he spoke again; but he was
watching the other continuously. At last, and with a
sharpness that was rather like the bark of a dog, he said:
"I'm sorry you should think it worth while to lie to me,
Mr. Lambourne."

"*Lie?* But I'm—I'm not lying!"

"*You are!*" Again the bark. "You were seen entering
the swimming-bath at half-past ten!"

The effect of this was not quite what Revell had
expected. Lambourne did not break down, but by
a mighty effort he managed to appear amused. He
laughed, even—rather hysterically, it is true—and threw
his half-smoked cigarette almost jauntily into the fireplace. "The game's up, I see," he remarked, with an air
of nonchalance. "You're a cleverer sleuth than I took
you for, Mr. Guthrie. May I ask how you found out?"

"No, you mayn't. You're here to answer questions,
not to ask them. You admit that you were in the swimming-bath at ten-thirty?"

"I suppose I must."

"Did you see Marshall?"

"Yes, I saw him." The note of hysteria almost dominated his voice.

"Then you were probably the last person to see him alive. Do you know that?"

"Not at all." Lambourne's voice rose to a high-pitched declamation. "Oh no, not at all. On the contrary, I was far more probably the second person—counting the murderer—to see him dead. Don't you believe me? No, of course you don't—I don't expect you to—that's why I never told you or anyone else. And besides . . . Oh God, what a muddle it all is!" He dropped his head into his hands and began to sob.

"Calm yourself and let's have the whole story. You went to the swimming-bath. Why?"

Lambourne, when he looked up, was again laughing hysterically. "Why did I go? Because, my dear Sherlock Holmes—oh, you'd never guess unless I told you. I went because I wanted a swim!" And his face worked with uncanny merriment.

Guthrie took no notice. "Go on. You went to the swimming-bath because you fancied a swim. Did you meet anyone on the way?"

"No."

"What happened when you got there?"

"First of all, I found the door unlocked. That surprised me, to begin with. Then I was surprised again to find that the switches wouldn't work. But it wasn't quite dark, so I went through into the main building. I saw then that the bath was empty."

"So what did you do?"

"As I looked down into the empty bath I could see something at one end that showed faintly against the white tiles—some dark heap of something, it looked. I—

I climbed down the steps at the end to see what it was
—I struck a match—and—and—" He shuddered. "I don't
want to have to describe it—don't ask me—please don't
ask me! But I'll tell you this much—the blood was still
warm!"

"Well, go on. What did you do?"

Lambourne prepared himself for an obvious ordeal.
"I'll tell you," he cried, "though I know you won't believe me. I hardly believe myself, when I think of it. I
stood perfectly still by the side of the body for about a
quarter of an hour and thought things out. And by that
time I had come to the conclusion that seems to be fairly
generally accepted now—that the affair wasn't an accident at all, but a murder. More than that, I had made up
my own mind as to who had done it. I saw the whole
diabolical plot—this second affair as the perfect coun-
terpart of the first one—murder of an amazingly clever
and subtle kind. And I decided, at that same moment, to
accept the murderer's challenge, as it were, and do
something that would bring his marvellous and intricate
scheme to ruin!"

"Go on," repeated Guthrie impatiently. "Let's have
less of what you decided and more of what you did."

"I'm coming to what I did. My aim was to ruin the
accident theory, and—more than that—to incriminate
the murderer. The murderer I knew to be Ellington. So
I thought out a scheme as neat as his own, and, having
thought it out, I put it into operation immediately. I
left the swimming-bath and walked over to the sports
pavilion. In Ellington's locker, as I had guessed, there
was a cricket-bat. I took it back with me to the bath; I
smeared it in the blood that was lying about; and then
I left the bath finally, closing, but not of course locking,
the door behind me. Last of all, I hid the bat in some

bushes near the rifle-range, where I knew it would be found sooner or later."

"You provided us, that is to say, with a faked clue?"

"Yes."

"Why didn't it occur to you to come straight to us and tell us the truth about it all?"

"Because I never thought you'd believe it was murder unless you had a clue of some kind."

"Did you have any idea that the boy had been shot?"

"Not the slightest. My theory was that he had been killed by bashing on the head—that was why I thought of the cricket-bat."

"Did you tell anyone of your suspicions about Ellington?"

"There was—and is still—a young fellow here named Revell who took an interest in the case—I told him."

"But no one else?"

"No."

"Why not?"

"I—I didn't want to be—personally—connected with the affair at all. I—I hate inquests and law-courts and all that sort of thing."

Guthrie's face, already hard, appeared to harden. Slowly his cross-examination was becoming keener and more hostile. "Now let's turn to another aspect of the matter. What were your relations with the boy?"

"With Marshall? I had hardly any at all. I didn't tutor him in anything."

"I know enough of public-school life to know how little that may count. You were both in School House— you must have been fairly often in contact. How did you get on together?"

"Fairly well, I think."

"Wasn't there some kind of trouble at the beginning of this Term?"

"There was a bit of an incident—I should hardly call it 'trouble.'"

"Never mind what you'd call it—we're not here to split hairs. Do you feel inclined to give us your version of the incident or the trouble or whatever name you think it ought to have?"

"It was really quite a trifling matter. The boy had been speaking of me—rather openly—in a way that tended to undermine my discipline."

"And you lost your temper with him?"

"I'm afraid I did."

"You threatened him?"

"I—I may have done. I lost my temper—and—and when I do that I—I—probably—say things I don't mean."

"Now, Mr. Lambourne, will you tell me——"

But just then two things took place almost simultaneously. Lambourne, his nerves strained to breaking-point, gave a little cry and plunged forward in a state of collapse, while, at the same moment, the door opened and Mrs. Ellington appeared, halted for a second on the threshold, and then rushed forward.

She took in the situation with her usual alertness; nor was she doubtful as to whose side she favoured. "Oh, what a shame!" she exclaimed, turning on Guthrie sharply. "I suppose this is what they call the third de-gree—to bully someone weaker than yourself! You couldn't try any of your games on my husband, so you thought you'd have better luck with a poor fellow who was shell-shocked in the War and has suffered from neurasthenia ever since! You coward!"

In any other circumstances Revell would have been amused at such a gallant attack. Yet Guthrie faced it stolidly enough. "I'm sorry you think so hardly of me, Mrs. Ellington," he said, quite calmly, "but I'm afraid it can't be helped. People have to be questioned, you know—especially if they have things to hide. Anyhow, I suppose there's nothing more can be done just now. Have you any brandy you could get me for him?"

"If you'll help him along to my house," she answered with cold dignity, "I think I can manage all the rest myself. I used to be a nurse, and I've helped Mr. Lambourne before when he's been ill."

Lambourne had by this time recovered somewhat, and with Guthrie and Mrs. Ellington on either side, he managed to stagger out of the room.

CHAPTER VII

THE THIRD OAKINGTON TRAGEDY

REVELL DID not see Guthrie again that evening. After the detective had left with Mrs. Ellington and Lambourne, Revell followed the party at a discreet distance and saw them enter Ellington's house. He rather expected Guthrie would seek him out afterwards, but as time passed he grew tired of pacing about the quadrangle in anticipation. Then, while the school were in evening chapel, he suddenly saw Mrs. Ellington and Lambourne walking over to School House. He could only conclude that Guthrie had gone back to his lodgings in the village—perhaps by the side-door that communicated directly with the lane.

On the whole, he was not too pleased with Guthrie. He rather inclined to agree with Mrs. Ellington that the cross-examination of Lambourne had been harsh, if not positively cruel. He had to admit, however, that Lambourne's story in some sense justified it; the man, on his own confession, had lied, suppressed evidence, manufactured false clues—committed almost every crime to rouse the ire of a detective.

Presumably, of course, it was the cricket-bat that Guthrie's men had discovered, though Guthrie had not definitely said so. Lambourne's story exculpated Ellington to that extent, but in other ways it seemed only to strengthen the probability of the housemaster's guilt. The motive, combined with the missing revolver, certainly made strong evidence. But what had been the make and calibre of Ellington's revolver, and did it tally with the bullet found in the body? Surely Guthrie must already have pursued such obvious lines of enquiry. The trouble was that the detective, after his first confidential outburst, had seemed to disclose less and less of his routine procedure.

It was another hot night, and Revell slept badly. Soon after dawn the twittering of the birds awoke him—a sound which ought to have been soothing, but somehow on this occasion missed being so. On the contrary, after a few minutes of it, he was so restless that he got up, had a cold bath, dressed, and went downstairs. Till about seven o'clock he idly read the previous day's evening papers; then, as the servants began to be heard, he let himself out at the front door into the cool, sunny air of early morning. For several minutes he walked about with aimless vigour, wondering why he didn't get up as early every morning of his life (though it was quite obvious why not). Soon, however, his meditations were interrupted by the realisation that someone was running towards him and trying to attract his attention. It was Daggat. With hair unkempt and a dressing-gown wrapped round his fat little body, he looked more like a cherub than ever. (Though a cherub would not, Revell decided as the man came nearer, have smelt so aggressively of soap and bath salts.)

"Thank God somebody's awake and up!" he cried, panting with excitement. "Revell, the most frightful thing has happened—oh, the most frightful ——"

Here his breath gave way and he leaned limply on Revell's arm till he recovered. Revell was almost equally astonished and excited. "Good heavens, Daggat—what's the matter? What on earth's happened?"

"It's—it's another of these frightful tragedies. There's a curse laid on the School—I've heard people say it before—and I'm beginning to believe it. I was having my morning tub when Brownley came for me. He'd been to Lambourne's room to call him and couldn't get an answer. Then when he went in he found—oh, it's terrible—on top of all these other affairs——"

"Come on, man, get it out! You mean that Lambourne's *dead?*"

"Yes. Died in his sleep apparently. I've already sent for Murchiston. I told Brownley to send for the Head, too. No need for anyone else to know just yet. But I'm dashed glad to find you about the place—one feels the need of a pal in an affair like this. Come back with me now to his room, will you?"

If only Daggat wouldn't be so provokingly sentimental, Revell thought; but he allowed the man to cling to his arm affectionately during the hurried walk. "It's pretty awful, Daggat, but you must keep calm about it," he said. "I wonder—" He was wondering what Guthrie would think about it, but he checked himself in time and merely added: "I wonder how soon the papers will get hold of it. Tremendous sensation, of course.

Third tragedy at Oakington—can't you just picture it all?"

When they reached the familiar room at the end of the ground-floor corridor, they found Doctor Roseveare already there, partially dressed, and talking in a hushed voice to Brownley, the School House butler. "A terrible business, gentlemen," he said, in a voice that seemed to Revell the most perfect example of correct and appropriate feeling in the circumstances. Not that he imagined Roseveare to be at all insincere. On the contrary, the bitter anxiety in his face and eyes was only too visible. But it was all done with such perfect technique, and Revell admired technique.

He moved a little forward and looked at the bed. Lambourne was lying on it quite normally; but for a little extra pallor and curious rigidity of feature, it would not have been hard to think him merely asleep. There was no sign of a struggle or of any suffering before the end. Roseveare seemed to be reading Revell's thoughts, for he remarked: "A peaceful finish, don't you think? Poor fellow—one can almost feel glad, in a way. Few people ever knew how much he suffered." He half-glanced at Brownley, as if he might have said more had not the servant been present.

But the arrival of Murchiston put an end to such observations. The seventy-year-old doctor, whose house lay just across the road from the School main entrance, had evidently made no delay in answering the summons. Yet even at such short notice he had attired himself in the conventional frock coat and striped trousers of an earlier generation of practitioners. Carrying his tall hat and gloves, he looked rather grotesque by the side of Daggat and the Head. "Dear me, this is very sad!" he murmured, almost mechanically, as he shuffled into the centre of the little group. Revell felt that Murchiston had arrived at an age when nothing could or would very much surprise him. Nevertheless, he approached the bedside with a briskness rather startling in such an obvious antique, and for several moments gazed steadfastly and without speaking at the dead man. Perhaps he was thinking, Revell speculated; or perhaps he was merely wondering what to think. At length he pulled down the bedclothes and gave the body a business-like though necessarily perfunctory examination. When he turned round he addressed Roseveare. "Sudden heart attack, I should imagine," he said. "But I'd better not give it you as a certainty. Have a look yourself if you like."

"I had already come to the same opinion, doctor," replied Roseveare, without moving. "In fact, I should hardly think myself there is any doubt about it. I always understood that the poor fellow was liable to drop dead at any moment."

"Yes, but I haven't been attending him for several months and—and—" Murchiston coughed gruffly and added: "In the ordinary course of things I would have given a certificate, but after recent affairs—with all these damnable insinuations going about—one can't be overcautious."

"Yes, of course. I quite appreciate your position. So you think there will have to be a post-mortem?"

"If anybody wants to do it. *I* won't."

Revell could not but feel a certain grudging sympathy with the downright old fellow. The newspapers had been none too kind to him about his evidence at the Marshall inquests, and their innuendoes had evidently stung him pretty deeply. And, after all, as Revell had to admit, who could have expected him to probe the boy's shattered head in search of a bullet? Anyhow, he was clearly determined not to make any more blunders, and Revell did not blame him for his attitude.

While Roseveare was discussing with Murchiston and Brownley the arrangements to be made about the body, Revell, struck with a sudden idea, slipped away from them and hastened to the Head's house. There, at the study telephone, he rang up the local police-station and asked if a message could be sent to Detective Guthrie. There had been an important development at the School, was all he said, and could the detective come over as quickly as possible? The voice at the other end gave a promise that such a message should be delivered immediately; after which Revell put down the instrument and hurried away to breakfast. Roseveare did not make an appearance, and from the butler's face Revell knew that the news had already spread.

A quarter of an hour later he saw the detective's car entering the drive. He rushed out and in a few short sentences told him what had happened. Guthrie nodded. "All right—thanks for sending for me. Let's go and see things." They hastened together into School House.

Brownley, on guard outside the locked door of Lambourne's room, barred their admission. "I'm sorry, sir, but I have orders from the Headmaster not to—" he began, but Guthrie cut him short. "You'll open that door, my man, or you'll find yourself under arrest," he snapped, with outrageous exaggeration of his own powers. "I'm a detective and I don't intend to waste any time over you." He whipped out his official card with a gesture that Revell had seen before, but only at the cinema. Brownley caved in and admitted them.

In the little room where Lambourne's body still lay,

Guthrie continued to behave more like a stage or screen detective than Revell would ever have imagined. He pranced about the room, examining books, papers, crockery—anything, it seemed, that came under his roving notice. Revell half-expected him to produce at any moment an insufflator or a magnifying-glass or some other implement of the more sensational modern Sherlock. He did seize a small bottle with evident triumph and put it in his pocket, but Revell, having glanced at it before, had noticed that it contained only aspirin tablets.

The examination was still proceeding when the door opened and Doctor Roseveare entered. (Revell guessed that the faithful Brownley had been to tell him of the invasion.) At any rate, Roseveare betrayed no great surprise at what was in progress; Guthrie's at seeing him appeared far greater. "Doctor Roseveare?" he queried, unnecessarily, and the other bowed slightly.

The two men faced each other in silence for several seconds, as if sizing each other up. They were certainly well-matched, both physically and intellectually. Guthrie, with a shrug of the shoulders, began at last: "You must forgive my taking the law into my own hands, Doctor Roseveare."

The Headmaster of Oakington was at his suavest.

"Most certainly, Mr. Guthrie, since the law already *is* in your hands. In fact everything is in your hands entirely—including, I fear, our own personal rights and liberties. But of course it has to be endured."

"I can assure you that my only aim is to get at the truth. Perhaps you can tell me something about this tragic affair?"

"I am perfectly ready, as I always have been, to tell

you anything that is in my power. Mr. Lambourne, as
perhaps you know, had very bad health—his heart was
weak——"

"Thanks, but as there will be an autopsy, we need
not argue about that. Tell me—when did you last see
Mr. Lambourne?" (As an obvious crib from the famous
question addressed to Doctor Crippen, Revell thought
this distinctly second-rate.)

"Last night. About nine o'clock, I should think. I had
been dining out, and visited him immediately on my
return."

"Alone?"

"He *was* alone, when I arrived here. I stayed for
about an hour or so, talking and trying to cheer the
fellow up a little. I gathered that you, sir, were to a
large extent responsible for his condition."

"Never mind that. Who told you, in the first place,
that he was ill?"

"He missed taking his lessons, and the fact was reported to me in the usual way."

"Did you visit him at all before the evening?"

"No. I caused enquiries to be made, but I had not
time for a personal visit until after dinner."

"You were on good terms with him?"

"I am on good terms, I am glad to say, with every
member of my staff."

"Were you satisfied with his work?"

"Is that question really necessary?"

"If you don't answer it, I shall draw my own conclusions."

"Perhaps I had better say, then, that while Mr. Lambourne was not the best or most successful of teachers,
I knew that he worked hard and I was very willing for
him to remain at the School."

"All right. . . . Now you said he was alone when you arrived here—in this room—last evening. What about when you left?"

"Mrs. Ellington arrived about ten o'clock with some invalid food that she had prepared for Mr. Lambourne. I thought I should perhaps be somewhat in the way if I remained, so I left them almost immediately."

"Mrs. Ellington, I believe, was formerly a nurse. Do you know if she was in the habit of looking after Mr. Lambourne when he has been ill?"

"Very likely. She had—and I had also—a very deep sympathy with Mr. Lambourne."

"Have you any idea about what time she left him last night?"

"Not the slightest. Why not ask her yourself?"

Guthrie allowed the questioning to cease. He had been, if not exactly worsted, at any rate met on equal ground by one of his own mettle. "All in good time," he said, with a return to his usual imperturbability. "I think we'll leave things here just as they are for the present, if you don't mind." He manœuvred Roseveare out of the room and locked the door on the outside. "Of course you'll have to give evidence at the inquest," he added, putting the key in his pocket.

"I had imagined so."

The two men gave each other a final stare, half-hostile, half-respectful; after which Roseveare strode away with immense dignity.

Guthrie turned to Revell. "Can't help rather liking the fellow, can you? Such dignity—such pride—such a marvelous way of quibbling all round the question. What a K.C. he'd have made!"

"You seemed pretty doubtful about him?"

"Did I? Oh, I think it was all fairly plausible. But we

must have a little chat with the Lady with the Lamp, of course. And by Jove—here she is!" This final exclamation was whispered, for Mrs. Ellington was hastening towards them along the corridor. She was ashen pale, and her eyes showed signs of recent weeping, but there was a calm eagerness in her voice as she addressed Guthrie. "I've been looking for you," she began, abruptly. "I want to see you—to speak to you. It is most important. Will you—both of you—come up to my husband's room just above?"

"Certainly, Mrs. Ellington, if you wish."

No more was said till they were all three of them seated in the room next to the dormitory in which the first of the tragedies had occurred. Revell was glad to note that Guthrie's attitude toward Mrs. Ellington was both courteous and kindly. He seemed to have entirely forgiven her for her outburst of the previous day. (And no wonder, Revell thought, since by his death Lambourne had given the most convincing proof of his unfitness to stand the ordeal of a detective's hostile cross-examination.) "There now," Guthrie said, as he settled himself in the easy chair opposite hers. "We shan't be disturbed here and you can tell me anything you like. Do you mind if I smoke?"

She signified impatient permission. "I feel I *must* tell you," she went on, agitatedly. "I hate doing so—more perhaps than I have ever hated anything—but I think it is only fair to so many others. And—I suppose—really, I owe you an apology."

"I can't think what for," replied Guthrie, gallantly. "And anyhow, don't let that bother you at all."

"It's because of my attitude yesterday," she insisted. "I hated to see you bullying Mr. Lambourne—if you *were* bullying him, that is. And yet I can see now how right you were—from your own point of view."

"What makes you think so, Mrs. Ellington?"

She paused before answering, and when she did answer, it was hardly to the point. "I wouldn't like to be a detective, Mr. Guthrie. It must be so terrible to find people guilty."

"Ah, but there are compensations. You often find people innocent as well."

Her face brightened. "Yes—and that is why—one reason why—I must tell you. It has all been so frightful for everybody here lately—so much doubt and suspicion. . . ." She nearly broke down, but managed to save herself by a last effort. "Do you know, when I heard that Mr. Lambourne had died during the night, I was glad?"

"You were?"

"Yes—glad. Can't you guess why? Shall I have to put it all into words for you?"

"Well, I daresay I *can* make a guess. I suppose it was because you think Lambourne's guilty?"

Revell started in astonishment, but a slight glance from Guthrie quelled him. Mrs. Ellington slowly nodded. "I not only think he is," she said. "I *know* it. It was he who killed Wilbraham Marshall. And Robert as well." She buried her face in her hands and was silent for a while.

"Both of them, eh?" Guthrie seemed hardly surprised. "And how do you know that?"

"Because, Mr. Guthrie, he told me."

She gathered courage now that her secret was out. "Yes. He told me last night. He was terribly ill—ill in mind, I mean—and I tried to comfort him. Then he told me. He thought you were on his track and he felt he must tell somebody about it. I seemed to freeze up—I didn't know what to say to him. Oh, what *could* I have said to him? I believe I told him he must confess to you —and he said he would in the morning—this morning, that would have been. I think he was quite out of his mind when he did it—he was often out of his mind for short spells. I was sorry for him—I couldn't help it— even after he had told me. Was that wrong of me? He was almost raving at first, but I calmed him and made him give his promise. He said—they were almost his last words—'I'll tell Guthrie to-morrow.' Then he went to sleep and I left him."

She looked first at Guthrie and then at Revell as if in pathetic challenge. It was Revell who first spoke. "But, Mrs. Ellington," he exclaimed, "why on earth should Lambourne have done it?"

She shook her head despairingly. "I know—that was just the question I kept on asking him. And his reasons were so strange. That's why I think he must have been out of his mind. He said—it's such an awful thing to have to repeat—but he said he hadn't meant to kill the boy at all in the first place—it was my husband he wanted to kill. And he thought my husband would have been sleeping in the dormitory that night."

"Yes, I understand how that could have arisen. Go on, please," interposed Guthrie. "Did he tell you why he had wanted to kill your husband?"

She smiled a wan half-smile. "It was because of me, he said. That's what makes it so terrible for me to think of. But for me . . . You see, Mr. Lambourne and I have always been friendly—we have tastes in common— books, plays, music, and so on. And because my husband doesn't care for such things, Mr. Lambourne imagined I was unhappy."

"And have you been unhappy, if I may ask the question?"

She returned him a glance of tranquil sadness. "If you want a really truthful answer, Mr. Guthrie, I could not say 'no.' But I assure you that Mr. Lambourne exaggerated, and in any case, I never complained to him or discussed my private affairs with him at all."

"I see. But all the same, you think his reason for wishing to kill your husband was to free you from a partner he thought you disliked?"

"Perhaps. It looks like it. But he had nothing to hope for from me—I mean—I want to be quite clear about this—there was nothing whatever between us. We were simply friends, and I had never given him the slightest encouragement to imagine anything else."

"The trouble is, of course, that some men don't need any encouragement. Anyhow, what about the second murder?"

"I'm coming to that. He said that when he found out that the person in the dormitory bed had been the boy and not my husband, he was at first overwhelmed with remorse. And I do remember, as it happens, how ill he was at the time. Then—so he said—his hatred of my husband grew in him until it gave him no rest at all. And, as time went on, he began to think of an extraordinary way in which his original murder, which had been, as one might call it, a mistake, might be turned to good account."

"Yes, I understand. This is all very interesting and you are putting it very clearly."

"The motive was always, you see, the same—hatred of my husband. And the plan that came into his head was—briefly—to murder the other brother so that suspicion should fall on the man he hated. He reasoned that no one could have any apparent motive for murdering the two boys except my husband (who inherited their money, as you know), and that two such suspicious accidents would undoubtedly cause enquiries to be made."

"Did he give you any details as to how each of the murders was done?"

"Yes, he told me everything. The first one was done by letting the gas-pipe drop down on to the bed. He had previously loosened it. He went up into the sick-rooms above the dormitory and staged the whole thing."

"Yes. And the second murder?"

"He went to my husband's room one day when he was out and took away his revolver and cartridges. He knew that the boy used to take a swim in the evenings during the hot weather. On that particular night he went down to the swimming-bath himself. He found the boy already there, cursing his luck because the water had been drawn out. Mr. Lambourne was in his dressing-gown and pyjamas, as if ready for a swim—it was his excuse, of course, for going there. He chatted with the boy for a time, gradually leading him along the edge of the bath as far as the diving-platforms. He waited till the boy was standing on the edge facing the empty bath with the platforms just above him; then he sprang back suddenly, whipped out his revolver, and shot up at the boy from behind." She trembled as she spoke the words. "Oh, he *must* have been out of his mind to do such a thing—he *must* have been. Don't you think so, Mr. Guthrie?"

"Very possibly, Mrs. Ellington. Most murderers, at the moment of their murder, must be very near the border-line of insanity."

"*He* was, I am sure."

Guthrie nodded. "And I suppose, after shooting the boy, he staged the affair to look like an accident?"

"Yes."

"Did he give you any details of how he did that?"

"He took off the boy's wrist-watch that he was wearing and climbed up to the top diving-platform with it."

"Yes. Anything else?"

"He . . . Oh, it's too terrible—he went down into the bath and hit the boy over the head—but the boy was already dead——"

"Did he tell you what he hit the boy with?"

She looked dazed. "No—or at least he may have done, but I don't remember. It's so hard to remember every detail of it all."

"Yes, of course. And it isn't, perhaps, so very important, so long as we know he hit the boy with something. After that, I suppose, he just went back to his room and to bed?"

"No—he was flurried and took a walk to calm himself. My husband can vouch for that, because they met. My husband was having a stroll before going to bed."

"Yes, I think I know about that." He paused thoughtfully and added: "Perhaps, Mrs. Ellington, as you knew Lambourne rather well, you can tell us a little more about him—about the man personally, I mean?"

She responded eagerly, as if relieved to talk of less tragic matters. "He was a charming man, Mr. Guthrie, in his ordinary moods—one of the cleverest and most interesting men I ever knew. He was very badly hurt in the War—that's what began the trouble, I daresay. He had the most awful pains in his head, and sometimes deep depression would come over him like a cloud—that was how he described it. He told me once that he hadn't had more than a dozen happy moments during the whole of the past ten years—and all the dozen, he said, had been when he was with me. I felt sorry for him when he spoke like that. He had no relatives in England and he wasn't the sort to make friends—he had too sharp a tongue. He wasn't very popular either with the boys or the masters—he found teaching rather hard, but it was the only way he could possibly earn a living. Doctor Roseveare befriended him—*he* understood how he suffered, too, I think. Then his heart went wrong and he was told by the doctors that he might drop dead at any moment. Do you wonder I pitied him?"

"Not at all. I should have been surprised if you hadn't. Now don't distress yourself, Mrs. Ellington—" she had begun to cry softly—"you have really done all that you could possibly do, I think. It has been very good of you to come and tell me all this." She was still crying, and Guthrie, with a little gesture of kindliness, rose from his chair and touched her lightly on the shoulder. "Well now, I don't think we need trouble you any more for the time being. If I should want to ask you a few more questions later on, you won't mind, I know—but I don't suppose I shall. Your statement seems to clear up an exceedingly distressing and unhappy affair. There's only one thing I want to ask you —and that is, not to mention to anyone else what you have just told us."

"I won't," she promised.

"Have you told anyone so far?"

"No. Not even my husband. He would have—have misunderstood how—how Mr. Lambourne could have come to be so confidential with me."

"Ah yes, I understand. Well, remember, now—not a word to anyone. Good-bye for the time being, and once again—many thanks."

She gave him a sad farewell smile as he held open the door for her to escape. "Escape" was indeed the word that occurred to Revell; it was as if she were some wild thing that had been trapped in a cage and was now, by gracious permission of the snarer, allowed to fly stumblingly away.

"Whew!" exclaimed Guthrie, after she had gone. "That puts the lid on it, doesn't it? Revell, without asking me any questions (though I know you are bursting to), will you kindly go downstairs and make an appointment for me to see Doctor Roseveare as soon as possible? And then, after that, unless he can see me immediately, you might go down to the tobacconist's shop in the lane and get me an ounce of shag. Yes, shag, my boy—it's what I feel like."

Revell obeyed. There was really nothing else to be done.

CHAPTER VIII

THE DETECTIVE GIVES IT UP

THE BODY of Max Lambourne had been taken to the local Drill Hall, and there the inquest was held a couple of days later. It was a far more public affair than the two previous ones; the accommodation for the press was much larger, since the newspapers had featured the third Oakington tragedy on the grandest scale.

Revell sat in the public gallery, an interested watcher

of the proceedings; he had been informed beforehand that he would not be wanted to give evidence.

Everyone seemed to have learned a lesson from the two earlier inquests, and to have made up their minds that this one, at any rate, should stand out as a model of correct inquest procedure in every possible way. The Coroner was careful to the point of being punctilious, and even the merely formal matter of identification was treated as if there might be some doubt about it.

After the jury had viewed the body (which naturally conveyed very little to them), witnesses were called. The first was the School House butler, Brownley. He described how and when he had found Lambourne dead. The Coroner questioned him a little, mainly (so far as Revell could judge) to give the court an impression of his own shrewdness.

"It was your usual time for calling him?"

"Yes, sir."

"Did you touch him at all?"

"I shook him a little to try to wake him, sir, but not really enough to move him in any way."

"What did you do after that?"

"I went to fetch help, sir. The first person I saw was Captain Daggat—he was just leaving his bath, sir. He told me to fetch the Headmaster, while he telephoned for Doctor Murchiston."

"So you went to the Headmaster's house?"

"Yes, sir, and the Head came at once."

Brownley was then permitted to stand down. Daggat gave evidence next, merely amplifying the butler's account of the discovery. The third witness was Murchiston, who made as usual a somewhat striking figure in his frock-coat and cravat. He testified to having been sum-moned by telephone, to arriving at the School, and to making a cursory examination of Lambourne's body.

"What do you mean by a cursory examination?"

"A rapid one—such as could be made on the spot."

"Very well. Please tell us what opinions you came to."

Murchiston had evidently prepared a careful answer to such a question. He replied, slowly and with deliberation: "My examination was not such as enabled me to come to any definite opinions, especially as it was several months since I had last attended Mr. Lambourne professionally. His condition seemed consistent with a sudden heart attack, to which I knew him to be liable, but in the circumstances, I thought it best to leave the matter to be decided by a post-mortem."

"You did not perform the post-mortem?"

"No, but I was in consultation with the doctor who did."

"Do you agree with his findings?"

"Certainly."

The next witness, obviously, was the doctor who *had* performed the post-mortem. He was Hanslake, the police-surgeon. A brisk, brusque, younger man, he had no time for the old-fashioned niceties of a Murchiston. With commendable brevity he testified to his examination of the body and to the cause of death, which he declared outright and without any emotion whatever to have been an overdose of veronal.

This, as might have been expected, caused something of a sensation in the court. When it had subsided, the Coroner turned to Murchiston again.

"Was Mr. Lambourne, to your knowledge, in the habit of taking veronal?"

"I knew that he had done so on some occasions. He

took it for sleeplessness and headaches, I believe. I warned him strongly against it, but he told me that it was the only thing that gave him peace."

"What exactly was the matter with him, Doctor Murchiston?"

"It would almost be easier to say what wasn't the matter with him. He had been gassed and blown up during the War, I understand. Apart from a bad heart, there was nothing organically very wrong, perhaps, but the whole state of his mind and body was extremely low."

"Would you call him a neurasthenic?"

"The term was not invented when I studied medicine, but so far as I know the meaning of it, I should say he was one."

"Would such a condition be likely to give him suicidal impulses?"

"Possibly. I could not say more than that."

The Coroner returned to Hanslake.

"You said it was an overdose of veronal. Was it a heavy overdose?"

"Heavy enough for anyone who wasn't an out-and-out addict."

"Is there, then, any possibility that it could have been taken accidentally? I mean—supposing the deceased had felt particularly unwell, might he have taken so much without suicidal intent?"

"It is possible, of course."

"Is it possible that anyone could have taken a similar amount and not have died?"

"My experience, I'm afraid, isn't wide enough to give a definite answer."

"You see what I am trying to get at?"

"Oh yes, you want to know whether it could have

been an accidental overdose and not suicide. I think in a case of this sort there is always the possibility."

"You said just now that the dose was heavy enough for anyone who wasn't an out-and-out addict. Did you mean that such an addict might take it harmlessly?"

"Not necessarily. Most addicts die from an overdose."

"But the deceased was not what you would call an addict?"

"I should say not."

"Thank you."

Mrs. Ellington was next called. She gave her evidence in a calm clear voice and answered all questions unhesitatingly. She had been friendly with the deceased, she said, for some years, and had sympathised with him a great deal in his afflictions. She was a trained nurse and had sometimes visited him when he had been ill. She had visited him on the night before he died, and had found him then in a very troubled condition.

"What was the cause of his trouble?"

"Nothing very definite. I think it was just one of his periodic attacks of depression."

"What time did you leave him?"

"Soon after eleven. I waited till he was asleep."

"Did you know he took veronal?"

"I had guessed that he sometimes took something. I did not know it was veronal or anything dangerous."

"Did you see him take anything while you were with him?"

"No."

"Had he ever said anything to you about taking his own life?"

"No. He was often despondent about things, but that was all."

"Thank you."

The last witness was Doctor Roseveare. In suave and mellow tones he testified to Lambourne's unhappy existence. "He worked hard, he was conscientious, and we all felt very sorry for him. He was as much and as clearly a victim of the War as if he had died on the battlefield, except that his suffering had been infinitely more protracted." And Doctor Roseveare paused, aware that his words would be headlined throughout England the following day, and would probably be the theme for articles in all the next Sunday's papers.

"You visited him on the night before he died?"

"Yes. Like Mrs. Ellington, I tried to cheer him, but, I fear, with less success."

"Do you know if he had anything to worry about?"

"Nothing at all connected with his work here, I am quite certain. I was perfectly satisfied with him."

"Did you know that he took veronal?"

"I had not the slightest idea."

"Did he ever talk to you about taking his life?"

"Never."

"Thank you. I think that will be all, unless any of the jury would care to put a question?"

One of the jurymen, a local saddler, stood up and said: "Can Doctor Roseveare tell us if the deceased was at all worried by the Marshall affair?"

The Coroner glared furiously at the questioner, as if he had committed the grossest of blunders, to say nothing of the most deplorable breach of good taste. But Doctor Roseveare was perfectly unperturbed. "I am afraid," he answered, "that the Marshall affair, as you call it, has been a worrying thing for all of us at Oakington recently, but I cannot see any reason why it should have affected Mr. Lambourne any more than the rest of us."

The juryman wriggled as he stood. "I was only meanin', sir, that if the deceased was in a low state of mind, like what the doctor said, it was the sort of thing 'e might 'ave worried about."

"Oh, quite—quite." The Head was most affable. "I see your point, and in a general way, I think it very possible."

But everyone somehow knew that the saddler had made a fool of himself.

The Coroner, before the jury retired, said it was one of the saddest cases he had ever come across. The deceased, as Doctor Roseveare had said, had died a soldier's death in the sense that the real cause, undoubtedly, had been the injuries honourably received in the service of his country. (Roseveare had not said anything of the kind, but there was no one to contradict.) Unfortunately, perhaps, it was their task, as a court, to enquire into the more immediate cause of death, which two medical men had agreed was an overdose of veronal. There seemed no doubt that the deceased had acquired the habit of taking the drug to relieve his sufferings, both physical and mental. The dose that killed him was heavy, but there was nothing at all to show that he had taken it with the intention of ending his life.

After that, of course, an open verdict was almost inevitable. The jury deliberated for less than five minutes before deciding upon it; in less than ten the court had dispersed, the newspaper-men were hurrying to the local post-office, the Head was entering a taxi on the way back to the School, and the Coroner was enjoying a smutty story with the police-surgeon. The third Oakington tragedy had been accounted for.

It was during lunch with Roseveare at the School that Revell learned where Guthrie had been. "He said there was no need for him to attend the inquest, so he spent the morning packing. He's going back to town this afternoon. I suppose you know that he's giving up the case?"

"*Really?*"

"I had a long talk with him yesterday about it. He was frank enough to admit that he had no evidence against anyone, so there was nothing for it but to accept the situation. A likeable man, Revell, apart from his detestable occupation."

Revell smiled, though he was rather bewildered by Roseveare's information. He had guessed that Lambourne's confession must inevitably end the matter, but he had not quite realised that the end would come so soon and so tamely.

Roseveare continued: "By the way, Revell, what exactly are your intentions, now that this unhappy business seems to have worked itself out? Do you particularly wish to go back to London?"

Revell hesitated, and the other went on: "Because, if you aren't keen to return, you are very welcome to stay on here until the end of Term, which is only four weeks away. As a matter of fact, I would rather you did so. I don't think your real position here has yet been guessed by anyone, and that, you will agree, is a good thing." (Lambourne had guessed it, though, Revell remembered.) "I fear that if you were now suddenly to disappear, the circumstance might only add another to the monstrous cloud of suspicions that we are now hoping to disperse. My staff, I trust, feel that so far I have done my best to protect them and their interests, but their attitude might change were they to discover that

I had imported an Old Boy of this School to act as amateur detective and spy on them."

"The description of my job isn't exactly flattering," replied Revell with a laugh, "but still, I see your point." He was thinking, as a matter of fact, of sunny afternoons with Mrs. Ellington by his side as the two of them cycled along country lanes, of cool tea-times with Mrs. Ellington ministering to him in her little chintz drawing-room, of restful Sabbath evenings with Mrs. Ellington beside him in the visitor's pew in chapel. "I'll stay on if you like," he added. After all there was nothing else to do, and the thought of his sooty little *pied-à-terre* in Islington was far from attractive. "But you must let me do some work for you, or something like that. Otherwise it will seem just as strange as if I were to go."

"Quite. I had already decided, in fact, to offer you a temporary post as my secretary. And at a salary which you will discover for yourself at the end of the Term."

"You are really too generous, sir."

But it was difficult not to be put in a good humour by such jovial and beneficent methods.

Yet, for all that, Revell was slightly annoyed, and his annoyance centered upon Guthrie. It was unmannerly of the fellow, to say the least, to clear off without a word of explanation or thanks to one who had undoubtedly assisted him to the best of a perhaps more than average ability. Then an idea struck him; if he were going to stay on at Oakington for the rest of the Term, he must first go back to his rooms and make arrangements with his landlady, pack a few extra things, and so on. Why not go that very afternoon and travel on the same train as the detective?

Thus it came about that the two of them met in a compartment of the 3.20 train to King's Cross. Guthrie seemed not in the least surprised, and welcomed Revell quite cordially. "Another deserter, eh, Revell? Given up the Oakington case as hopeless even to the amateur?"

"I'm staying on at Oakington till the end of Term," Revell explained. "The Head asked me to. But I'm just going back to pick up a few things."

"Oh, so you've taken the secretary's job, then? He told me he was going to ask you."

"I'm trying it till the end of the Term, anyhow," replied Revell, cautiously.

"Congratulations." And Guthrie laughed. "Not at all a bad job, I should think. Precious little work, and plenty of time to flirt with the charming Florence Nightingale, eh?"

Revell found himself, to his intense annoyance, flushing like a schoolboy.

"Oh come now, no need to look shocked! She's a pretty little piece for those who like their *multum in parvo*. Can't say I do, myself, but tastes differ, don't they?" He added: "I'm glad we're to travel together—it will save me writing you a very nice letter of thanks."

"What I'd like as much as thanks," said Revell, "is to know a little bit more about what exactly happened."

"Oh? You want me to go over the ground like the fiction detective, do you, and explain every point? The trouble is there's not much to explain, I'm afraid. Lambourne's confession closes the affair, of course, and neither the professional nor the amateur branch of the service can really claim to have covered itself with glory. It's rather an annoying thing, to get a confession at second-hand. Legally, you see, it doesn't count. It's a particularly vicious example of what the soldier said."

"You mean that you can't even announce it to the public?"

"Advisable not to—so they tell me at headquarters. Can't be proved, you see. Some relative of Lambourne's, if he has any, might up and sue me for slandering the family name. Dashed queer thing, the law, isn't it?"

"So the Oakington murders will go down into history as unsolved crimes?"

"If they go down to history at all, I suppose they will. Of course I've had to tell my superiors the truth about it. But nobody else. And I should advise *you* not to, either."

"Haven't you told Roseveare?"

"No. Why should I? Let the poor man stick to his suicide theory—it's less unpleasant for the School's reputation, and that's all he cares about."

He leaned back amongst the cushions and puffed contentedly as the train gathered speed out of the station. "It's been a disappointing case altogether—there's no doubt about it. By the way, I understand the inquest went off all right? Were you there?"

"Yes. They brought in an open verdict."

"Good. Mrs. Ellington and Roseveare and I were anxious that that should happen. No use bringing more scandal on the School, was there?"

"Yet you think it was suicide?"

"I'm positive of it. Suicide to escape a murder charge. But I could hardly have said that in the court, could I?"

Revell thought for a moment. At last he said: "It's a queer business, the whole thing. What sort of a man do you think Lambourne really was?"

"You want a character study, eh? Well, I'm not particularly good at that sort of thing, but I'll do my best. I should say his chief characteristic was cowardice."

"Cowardice?"

"Yes. You know, Revell, behind all the sentimental stuff, there isn't very much to be said for the coward. And Lambourne, I'm afraid, *was* one—utterly. During the War, for instance—I wonder why nobody beside me ever thought of looking up his record. Oh yes, I know he was shell-shocked—and I'm not talking of anything he did after that—it may have been excusable then, but it wasn't before. Anyhow, he narrowly escaped a court-martial death-sentence."

"For cowardice?"

"Yes. It's on the record. That sarcastic manner of his, too—it's very often the mark of the coward, especially in dealing with boys. Then again, if he had a passion for Mrs. Ellington, why on earth didn't he have an affair with her if he could persuade her to it? That's what a normal man does in such circumstances. He doesn't plan a complicated system of murders to bring her husband to the scaffold. Finally, of course, there was the suicide. Perfectly in character—a last act of cowardice rather than face the music."

"Would you have got him, do you think, if he hadn't confessed?"

Guthrie smiled. "That's tempting me, isn't it? To be perfectly frank, I don't know. His brains were so much better than his nerves."

"What puzzles me is that he should have bothered to make the murder look like an accident at all. Why not leave all the clues pointing straightforwardly to Ellington if his object was merely to get Ellington hanged?"

"Because, my dear boy, he was far too clever for that. Murderers don't leave clues pointing straightforwardly to themselves. Don't you see that by making the thing look like an accident he was really making the case blacker than ever against Ellington? It was clever, damnably clever, I admit. But even cleverness can't circumvent fate. And it was fate that made Brownley see him that night as he left the swimming-bath with the cricket-bat under his arm."

"Oh, it was Brownley, then, who saw him? But he had a pretty marvellous explanation of it all, didn't he?"

"Marvellous, as you say. To twist it round to make things look blacker than ever against Ellington was sheer genius—nothing less. Perhaps he *was* a genius, in his way. Ah well, the case is over and done with, and perhaps it's as well he did take his own life—it's saved the world a lot of trouble. Even if we'd got a full confession written out and signed by him, a clever lawyer might easily have cast doubts upon it. The law never likes too much to depend on the word of the man in the dock—whether it's for or against him." He yawned for the second time. "Let's forget it, Revell, if we can. Always a mistake to think too much about these things. That was the trouble with Lambourne—he *studied* crime —read all the high-brow books about it—got 'em locked up in a little bookcase in his bedroom—ever see it, by the way? . . . Ah well, if the Oakington affair's done nothing else, it's made us acquainted—maybe we shall meet again some day."

"I hope so," answered Revell sincerely enough.

They chatted on until King's Cross was reached, and then, at the entrance of the tube station, shook hands with great cordiality.

Four hours later, having done all he wished, Revell was again at the station on his way back to Oakington.

CHAPTER IX

THEORIES

HE WAS glad to be back. He realised it as he stepped out of the train at Oakington station; the sham Gothic towers and buttresses no longer repelled as formerly, but lured with a sinister fascination that grew as he walked along the lane towards them. Two boys—two brothers—had been killed within those grotesque precincts. The murderer had then killed himself. Yet somehow, instead of the apathy that usually follows the final closure of an unsavoury incident, Revell was conscious of a widening and deepening interest in the whole affair. It was closed, finished, wound up—yet he was still a little curious; there were still things that he wanted to know about it.

That evening the Head talked to him of the harm that the affair had done to the School's reputation. Revell sincerely sympathised; Roseveare, as always exercised a queer personal fascination over him. "It's been pretty awful, I know," he said, "but it's over and done with now, and people soon forget." (He did not really think so, but it was the thing to say.)

"They never forget a name," Roseveare answered. "Long after I am dead—perhaps long after you are dead, even—people will still say, when they hear 'Oakington' mentioned—'Why, isn't that the school where those two boys were killed?' Don't you think they will? Don't people still remember Rugeley as the town where Palmer poisoned his victims?"

It was true, Revell admitted to himself. Merely dur-

ing his hasty visit to London he had been able to esti-
mate the extent to which the Oakington tragedies had
impressed themselves on the popular imagination. In
Oakington village it was only to be expected that the
School's affairs would loom largely, but it had been
rather a shock to see the word "Oakington" on half the
newspaper placards in London. His landlady, even, had
added the name to the small list of notorieties that
formed the currency of her street-door and garden-
wall chatter. And she had shown him proudly an article
she had cut from one of the cheaper and more lurid
weeklies; it was headed—"Dormitory Death-Drama and
Swimming-Bath Shooting Shambles; Oakington's Two
Mystery Tragedies Now Capped by Schoolmaster's
Sudden Death."

Revell recollected all this as Roseveare talked. The
smooth and rolling periods followed each other ma-
jestically; Roseveare had acquired the rare knack of
talking like a book without sounding like one. "For
weeks, Revell, we have lived in a state of siege; we have
had forced upon us such indignities and espionage as
no community can endure without contamination. The
good feeling between master and master has been sadly
affected—how, indeed, could it have been otherwise,
when each one of us has had an eye on someone else as
a possible murderer? Discipline—*esprit de corps*—the
tonic life-blood of the School—has almost ceased to
exist. A deplorable state of affairs, but now, perhaps,
we may feel that the worst is over, and may begin the
task of restoration. And the first step, since this terrible
chapter of mysteries has been left unsolved by the
authorities, is to establish some basis of hypothesis on
which the matter may conveniently be discarded. It
was with this in mind that this afternoon, while you

were away, I allowed myself to be interviewed by a group of newspaper-men."

"Oh? I'll bet they were pleased."

"They were. I made them a short statement which will doubtless appear in the papers to-morrow. A judicious statement, I hope, which will do good, whether it is true or not. But," he added, "it is just as likely to be true as any other supposition. When one is faced with so many theories, all without tangible foundation, one has surely a right to choose the least objectionable?"

"Surely," agreed Revell.

The next morning, therefore, in common with some millions of others throughout the United Kingdom, he was able to read "the first authentic interview with the Headmaster of Oakington." It was amusing to learn that "Doctor Roseveare is a tall, handsome man with a charming smile and a quiet, forceful personality. He greeted our representative most affably, and begged to be excused for not having received him before. 'I felt,' he explained, 'that while the case was as it was, it had better not be discussed. Now, however, that circumstances have altered, I am glad to be able to make a statement.'" (All of which, as Revell perceived, meant exactly nothing at all.)

"'First,'" continued the statement, "'I think I may tell you definitely that the police have retired from the case. They have discontinued the quest for the murderer, which they would hardly do if they still believed he existed. I conclude, then, that they do not now believe that any murder was committed at all. As this corresponds with the personal opinion I have myself held all along, I cannot pretend to be surprised.

"'The first death—that of poor Robert Marshall—

was, I think, undoubtedly an accident. There has never appeared, at any rate, the slightest scrap of definite evidence to the contrary.

" 'The second of the unfortunate brothers—Wilbraham—was shot, it is true, but no substantial evidence has appeared to point to any person as the assailant. The only conclusion to be reached, then, is that he died by his own hand.

" 'I myself have little doubt that this was so. The poor boy had been greatly depressed since the death of his brother, to whom he had been very closely attached.

" 'Perhaps I ought to add that the tragic death of Mr. Lambourne, one of the School staff, appears to have been quite unconnected with the other events. Mr. Lambourne, as I said at the inquest, was a peculiarly unhappy victim of the War, and had been in a poor state of health for many years. The jury rightly returned an open verdict, but my private opinion, for what it is worth, is that the overdose of veronal which caused his death was taken accidentally and not at all with suicidal intent.

" 'That, gentlemen, is really all I have to say. We at Oakington have gone through a gruelling time; for nearly a year it has seemed as if some malign fate were working against us at every turn. I can only say that the School will try to forget these terrible days as soon as possible, and will strive to do its duty in the future as nobly as it has done in the past.' "

As Revell read, he could almost hear the suave, well-chosen words spoken in the calm, soothing voice of the Head himself. The whole thing, in its evenness, its urbanity, its air of serene reasonableness, was thor-

oughly typical of the man. Yet was it not in some sense
a shade *too* reasonable?

He was not quite reckless enough to suggest as much
to its author. Indeed, at breakfast he congratulated
Roseveare wholeheartedly on the statement, and expressed the belief that it would help a great deal towards the closing of the whole affair. Then, after the
meal, he strolled out in the open air and smoked a
languid cigarette. It was another of those glorious summer days of which the season had already been so generous; there was to be a big cricket-match against
Westerham in the afternoon, and already the life of the
School was noticeably beginning to revolve in a more
normal orbit.

Yes, the affair was closed . . . and yet . . . and yet
in some strange and secret way he could not let it be
closed in his own thoughts. Neither Lambourne's confession nor Guthrie's exposition had given that sense
of finality that ought, he felt, to have been in his own
mind. Too many mysteries remained; too many questions had never been answered. Thus, with a sort of
sickening willingness, he allowed himself to be led back
into the realm of doubt.

The mood persisted for several days, till one afternoon, in a moment of half-sinister idleness, he got out
his notebook and glanced through the pencilled relics
of those many hours he had spent over the Oakington
case. He had made copious notes of various conversations he had had with the chief actors in the Oakington
drama; there were pages, for example, concerning
Guthrie's remarks. Then he came to reports and summaries of talks he had had with Lambourne. Queer to
think that the crimes that Lambourne had discussed so

abstractedly and nonchalantly had all the time been his own!

Lambourne had said (according to Revell's scribbled memoranda):

"I suspected it from the moment the news of the first accident reached me. But then I nearly always do suspect things. I have a morbid mind. . . . Nobody, however clever, should expect to get away with more than one murder. From a technical point of view, the repetition mars the symmetry of the thing. . . . After my years at the War, I find it hard to share the general indignation when someone tries a little unofficial slaughter on his own."

All that, Revell had to admit, was fairly incriminating. Along with Lambourne's bookcase of crime literature it might be held to show him as a person capable of planning and imagining murder.

Again, Lambourne had said:

"If Ellington isn't the murderer, there probably hasn't been a murder at all. . . . I didn't want you to know too much against Ellington—it might have biassed you in deciding whether the accident was faked or not."

Yes, that was certainly corroboration of the fact that Lambourne had, very cleverly and with an appearance of judicial fairness, sought to throw suspicion on Ellington. Revell was gratified to find that, even at such an early stage of the proceedings, he himself had written, apropos of Lambourne: "Is he entirely trustworthy? Is his pose of indifference sincere?"

Once again, Lambourne had said:

"Most people, if careful enough, can commit one murder safely. The temptation is to commit a second.

Even that may be successful. But the third time, by the law of averages, is likely to be unlucky. . . . Once the murderer has got it into his head that he's cleverer than the rest of mankind, he begins to think of murder quite casually. Two successful murders very often lead to a third."

And after saying that, Revell remembered, Lambourne had joked about the possibility of Ellingtons murdering some third person in due course—probably his wife.

Ah well, Revell reflected, there would be no third murder, since the murderer was now dead himself.

Suddenly, seized with a fit of inspiration, he turned to the first blank page and scribbled down:

"The beastly part of this case is the tremendous amount that depends only on what people have *said*. The explanation of my being sent for at first depends on what Roseveare *said*, and on what he *said* Mrs. Ellington *said*. The whole theory of Lambourne as the murderer depends again on what Lambourne *said*, and on what Mrs. Ellington *said* he *said*. There really seems to have been far too much *saying* and not enough discovery of independent evidence."

Then, apparently satisfied for the time being, Revell locked the notebook in a drawer, lit another cigarette, and strolled out into the warming air. Summer at Oakington was really rather delightful, with the clank-clank of the roller over the cricket-pitch and the songs of the birds in the high trees. A pity the buildings were so frightful. Revell, varying the confession of Landor, could say that art he loved, and next to art, nature.

As he passed the front entrance of Ellington's house, he saw, emerging from the porch, Mrs. Ellington with a man whom he did not recognise. She greeted him with a pleasant if rather wistful smile and hastened to introduce him to the stranger. The latter, apparently, was none other than Mr. Geoffrey Lambourne, who had come to Oakington to attend to matters connected with his brother's death. Mrs. Ellington, after a few moments, left the two men together; she seemed glad enough to do so, and Revell could easily understand her motive. The raking over of recent events must have been peculiarly distressing to her.

Geoffrey Lambourne, on further examination, appeared as a short, rather stout man, round-faced and spectacled, not much like his brother and seemingly many years his senior. Revell was interested in his mere identity, and could feel considerable sympathy with him. They took a stroll, at Revell's suggestion, round the Ring, and Lambourne, in a delicate, rather over-sensitive voice told Revell that he was the representative of an English firm in Vienna and had come to England especially to wind up his brother's affairs, interview his solicitors, and so on. "It's all been a little curious, his death, don't you think?" he said. The faintly quizzical understatement, spoken in such a quiet tone under that blazing sky, made Revell suddenly shiver.

"Very curious," he answered, guardedly. "But then, I think your brother was in many ways a very curious man."

"May I ask if you knew him well, Mr. Revell?"

"Oh, not very well. But we liked each other's company, I think."

Mr. Geoffrey Lambourne nodded. "He liked yours, at any rate. Several of his letters to me contained mentions of you."

"Really? I had no idea he would ever think me

worth writing about. I certainly liked him—he had a wry sense of humour that rather appealed to me." (Certainly, Revell reflected, he *had* had a wry sense of humour.) "I suppose you were very much attached to him?"

"I was." The simplicity of the admission held its own pathetic dignity. "We were the sole survivors of our family—both bachelors too, and likely to remain so." He blinked gently as he entered a patch of open sunlight. "Max was the only human being in the world I had to care about, and I—or so I had imagined—occupied a similar place in his affections."

Revell was quick to notice the pluperfect tense of this last remark. "So you *had* imagined?" he echoed.

The other nodded. "Yes, exactly. But I had better tell you, if you are interested, just what happened when I arrived in England."

"Yes, please do."

"I had been wired for, you understand, by the solicitor who acts for us both. I was not in time for the inquest, but I was able in Paris to buy English newspapers that reported it. I am glad, by the way, that the jury returned an open verdict, for I am perfectly certain that my brother was not the sort to take his life deliberately. The veronal habit was a surprise to me, but I can hardly blame him, poor fellow—he was, as your Headmaster said, a most tragic victim of the War. But I must tell you what happened at my visit to the solicitor. I had naturally expected that my brother's possessions, small though they might be both in quantity and value, would pass to me—in fact, we had both made wills in each other's favour some dozen years ago. Judge of my surprise when the solicitor informed me that my brother, greatly against his persuasions, had made a later will, dated only last year, leaving everything he had to à complete stranger."

"Indeed?"

The other coughed deprecatingly. "Please do not suppose that the bequest itself troubles me. I am not badly off, and in any case, my brother left nothing but his books, a few pounds in the bank, and his term's salary payable up to the date of his death. What does —or perhaps I had better say, *did*—perturb me a little was the discovery that he knew anyone whom he cared for sufficiently to put me in, so to speak, a second place. Or rather," he added, with a slight smile, "no place at all. In this second will of his, I was not even so much as mentioned."

Revell was itching to learn the name of this mysterious beneficiary, but he felt that Geoffrey Lambourne was the kind of man who told his tale better when left alone. He therefore contented himself with a sympathetic murmur.

"Yes," continued Lambourne, "I was a little hurt at first, I confess. And when I further learned that it was a woman, I was perhaps even annoyed."

"A woman?"

"Yes. The woman who introduced us just now. Mrs. Ellington."

"Good Lord, you don't say so?"

"You are surprised, Mr. Revell?"

"Well, yes, I must admit I am. Though really not so much, perhaps, on second thoughts. At least, I can think of a reason for it."

"So can I—a very obvious one."

"You mean that your brother was in love with her?"

"It wouldn't surprise me, having seen her."

Revell smiled. "Yes, she's an exceedingly attractive

woman, I admit. Your brother certainly admired her, but I don't imagine there was ever anything like a real affair between them. Mrs. Ellington sympathised with him a great deal—they had many tastes in common—far more, no doubt, than she had with her husband, who isn't the most suitable man for her to have married. Whenever your brother struck his bad patches she was able to help him in many ways—she had been a nurse, you know. I really think that's all it came to."

"You like her, then?"

"Yes, I do. Very much."

"Thank you, Mr. Revell. You have told me just what I wanted to know. Mrs. Ellington, whom I liked, I must say, as soon as I met her, was far too modest to explain things as you have done. I can see now exactly why my brother made his will as he did, and I'm no longer troubled about it in the least. Mrs. Ellington I certainly don't blame at all—she says that the bequest came as a complete surprise to her, which I can well believe. Perhaps as an embarrassment as well, for by the look of him, Mr. Ellington is not a man to deduce a good motive when one not so good is equally handy. I note, by the way, that *you* don't care for him, either?"

"We're rather different types, I'm afraid."

They had completed the first round of the Ring, and it was Lambourne this time who suggested a second circuit. Revell agreed, offering the other a cigarette. "It's very decent of you to tell me all this," he said, lighting one for himself. "I haven't been here long enough to have become really intimate with your brother, but perhaps I knew him as well as any of the others did."

"Better, I am sure. You knew, of course, about his War experiences?"

"You mean about his—er—his court-martial and all that?"

Lambourne, however, showed by a sudden clouding over his normally benignant countenance that he had not meant any such thing. When he replied there was even a mild ring of indignation in his tones. "Good heavens, Mr. Revell, am I to understand that the story of his one single lapse followed him here? I am sorry to hear it—I had no idea of it at all. I still do not believe that he committed suicide, but if ever there could have been a reason for his doing so, it would have been the raking up of that sad affair."

"It didn't follow him here," Revell answered, with a feeling of having badly put his foot in it. "So far as I know, not a soul at Oakington knew about it except me. I'll be frank with you and tell you how I got to know. You've heard, of course, of the two boys whose deaths here during the past year have caused such a sensation in the papers?" The other nodded. "Well, a detective from Scotland Yard was here recently looking up all our pasts and so on. He took me into his confidence a bit and told me of the affair."

"He had no business to," was the quick response. "It was a thing that ought to have been forgotten long ago. And in any case, after all these years, I don't feel that the slightest real disgrace attaches to my brother. He was, behind that attitude of cynicism that so many people misunderstood, one of the bravest and sincerest men who ever lived. He was among the first to enlist when the War broke out, and for two years he waged a constant battle, not so much against the Germans, as against a far more terrible foe—his own nerves. You may think this is high-flown language—but I assure you I'm only telling the simple truth. My brother fought a long and terrible battle, till at last his nerve gave way. He was court-martialled. He would doubtless have been shot but for the pleading of an officer who understood him a little. And afterwards he went back to the trenches and never gave way again till a particularly bad head-smash caused him to be sent home. In all, he fought for nearly three years, was wounded four times, and also badly gassed. I defy anyone to call that the record of a coward!"

And Mr. Geoffrey Lambourne looked, for the moment, as if he really were capable of defiance.

"I should say not!" Revell answered. "I think it's one of the pluckiest records I ever heard of."

The other warmed to his sympathy. "I knew you would think so. My brother wrote to me that he felt you as a kindred spirit. The trouble with him was always that he was too imaginative, too sensitive to things that other people hardly felt at all. He often worried over other people's troubles far more than they did themselves. They never knew it, of course. He hid everything behind that mask of cynicism. But Mrs. Ellington saw beneath it, apparently. Perhaps you did, also. Was he comfortable here—in his work, I mean?"

"I think so. Oh yes, I'm pretty sure he was." For a moment Revell had a wild idea that he would tell Geoffrey Lambourne the whole amazing story of his brother's confession. Nothing but vague caution prevented him; it would be safer, he felt, on second thoughts, to let the whole unpleasant business remain as it was. There was no knowing what Geoffrey would do if he were told, and whatever he might choose to do could hardly lead to anything but further trouble.

Lambourne, still with quietly smouldering indignation, was continuing. "You know I rather wonder if this other business—the deaths of the two boys—was worrying him at all. I see one of the jurymen at the inquest suggested it, too. It was just the sort of thing that *would* have worried Max. Since the War he had always been deeply interested in crime—often, in fact, I've told him frankly that he was getting morbid about it. He once told me that there wasn't a crime I could think of in which he couldn't to some extent sympathise with the criminal. I remember inventing the most horrible and ruffianly affair, more out of amusement than anything else, but when I had finished he replied quite seriously: 'Yes, I can quite conceive circumstances in which a good man might be driven to do a thing like that.' Over-imaginativeness again, of course."

Revell was finding all this extraordinarily interesting.

"Yes, he even told *me* once, apropos of some murder case, that after being in the War he could never manage to be very indignant over a little private and unofficial slaughter."

Lambourne nodded. "That was just the sort of thing he *would* say. But really, of course, it was a grotesque perversion of the real state of affairs. My brother was deeply indignant over murder; but he felt that the state, after organising murder on a wholesale scale for four years, had no right to be. And he hated what he called the legal torture of criminals. He not only hated it—it upset him whenever he thought about it, which was very often. I recollect at the time of the Thompson-Bywaters case, he was positively ill through worrying over it. I was with him on the night before Mrs. Thompson was executed—we were sharing a room at a hotel—he couldn't sleep a wink, and was in such a state of collapse by the morning that I had to send for a doctor. 'If

I could save that woman with my own life, I would,' he told me, and I quite believed him. Whenever he conceived a sympathy for anyone, even though he might never let them know it, he was ready to sacrifice himself in almost incredible ways. And it was the irony of ironies that most people thought him sarcastic and unfriendly and perhaps even callous!"

They had reached the end of the second circuit and were now once again within sight of the entrance of Ellington's house. Mrs. Ellington, as it chanced, came cycling along the drive towards them, and as she approached she dismounted and smiled at Revell. "I hope you've been giving me a good character," she began. "Mr. Lambourne came here hating me pretty badly, so I hope you haven't let me down."

Geoffrey Lambourne made haste to reply. "Not at all, not at all. On the contrary, Mr. Revell has told me how you have on so many occasions helped my brother. I am deeply grateful to you, and I think he did quite right to put you before me in his thought and feelings. I, after all, was a thousand miles away, but you were on the spot."

"Oh no," she answered, embarrassedly. "I did very little. I really don't deserve all your praise. But I'm glad you don't hate me now, anyway."

She smiled again and left them, whereupon Lambourne turned once more to Revell. "A charming woman," he remarked, when she was well out of earshot. "I can guess how my brother felt towards her— it wasn't his way to feel things by halves. And there had never been any woman in his life before." The school-bell began to clang, and he hurriedly consulted his watch. "Good heavens, we've been talking for nearly an hour—I mustn't keep you any longer. I have to return to London this evening—this is really a very hurried visit. But perhaps we may meet again someday. Good-bye."

When Revell sank into an easy chair in the Head's deserted drawing-room, his mind began at first to function with curious slowness, as if it were recovering after the numbness of a blow.

Geoffrey Lambourne's story only, of course, added to the already long enough list of things that people had *said*. Yet, on reflecting carefully, Revell was amazed to find how strangely it fitted in. Guthrie's character study of Max Lambourne had been based on only half a story; Geoffrey Lambourne had now supplied the other half, which would have made the character study entirely different. Guthrie, for example, had mentioned the court-martial episode, but it was Geoffrey Lambourne who, by explaining it, had made it appear in a totally different light. Nothing that Geoffrey had said really contradicted Guthrie's evidence, yet somehow, after hearing Geoffrey, Guthrie's whole idea of Max Lambourne seemed fundamentally absurd.

The confession was, of course, the snag. After all, if a man behaved suspiciously, as Lambourne had done, and if afterwards he confessed to the crime of which he had been suspected, there was usually no reason to disbelieve him. Guthrie, by accepting Lambourne's confession as *bona-fide*, had only acted as most reasonable persons would have done. That suspicion should wrongly point to a man, and that his confession, when made, should be false, was really too much to credit.

And yet . . . and yet . . . could it be that . . . ? Once again Revell found himself theorising wildly without evidence. It was no use trying not to; he could not help it. And the mainspring of his theorising was nothing less than a conviction, strong enough to be proof against all logic, that Max Lambourne had not and could not have committed the murders at all.

Then why on earth had he confessed to them? And suddenly, like a bubble born and swelling on the surface of troubled water, a theory vividly complete darted across Revell's mental vision. Supposing Lambourne had confessed to save someone else . . . ?

Even as the idea came to him, the cautious and critical second self that watched over his actions bade him pause and think where he was going. How scornfully, in his more normal mood of cynicism, would he have rejected such a motive! How he would have laughed at it if he had met with it in a play or a novel! Fantastic self-sacrifice had never appealed to him even ethically, and he had always regarded Sidney Carton's last moments as those of a bore who must also have been a bit of a prig. Yet now, in perfect seriousness, he was casting Max Lambourne for the same unlikely rôle! Was it possible?

Ten minutes of profound thinking convinced him that it was. The theory gained on him; he saw details rising up at every step, like fragments of a new scene when one approaches it on a misty day. The murders, he argued, had been committed by someone else. Lambourne, with a shrewdness quite in consonance with his abilities and with his study of crime, had guessed from the beginning the identity of the culprit. His story about laying the false clue of the cricket-bat was true; in his own queer, tortuous way he had done his best to unmask the murderer. Later, however, he had got into a mess; he had imagined that Guthrie suspected him (and perhaps the detective did), and he had been greatly upset by the severity of Guthrie's cross-examination. Even though he might have known that Guthrie could prove nothing, he would have worried desperately over the matter; in fact, as Geoffrey Lambourne had said, it was just the sort of thing he could not endure.

Then suddenly (so Revell's theory continued), he had realised how the whole terrible business might react on Mrs. Ellington. The detective, in course of time, might subject *her* to the same savage questioning. Even if he did eventually arrive at the right conclusion and arrest Ellington, there could be nothing but unhappiness in store for Mrs. Ellington. For though she might not care for her husband a great deal, to see him tried and convicted for murder would be a frightful ordeal. And an ordeal, too, from which he (Lambourne) would save her if he could. Most likely he had not reached his final decision until that last evening when she had visited him. Her kindness then, her solicitude for his health, and his own deep love for her, might all have combined to give him a vision of that simple, ultimate sacrifice which would ensure her peace of mind. After all, what did it matter? He had no family to disgrace; his health was bad; he would probably not live long in any case. He had no future to which he or any other human being could look forward hopefully; he was doomed, in some sense, as much as any convicted criminal. Why not, indeed, cut the Gordian knot that entangled his own miserable affairs, and those of Oakington itself? If he had said of Mrs. Thompson, a stranger, that he would save her with his own life if he could, would he not be far more likely to feel the same impulse of self-sacrifice towards Mrs. Ellington, whom he loved?

Revell had to check himself from thinking too eloquently. But it really was remarkable how easily the de-

tails fitted in. Lambourne's motives for the two murders, as recounted by Mrs. Ellington, had been more
than a little fantastic; but that was quite natural if they
had been merely a last-minute improvisation by Lambourne himself. The overdose of veronal, too, took on
another aspect when viewed in this light; Revell was
now convinced, with Guthrie, that it had been suicide.
To confess to a crime one hadn't committed was surely
enough; to stand trial and go to the scaffold for it was
well beyond most human endurance. Revell could picture the scene in Lambourne's room on that fatal
night—could picture Mrs. Ellington soothing him, as
she believed, to sleep, after receiving his promise that
he would repeat his confession to the detective on the
morrow. But doubtless he had not been really asleep,
but merely closing his eyes, happy with her so close to
him and well satisfied with the neatness of his plan. And
then, when at length she had gone, he had—perhaps with
a last cynical smile—reached out for the bottle and
played his final act in the rather incomprehensible
drama of life.

Revell jotted down the whole of this new theory
without its emotional trimmings, and then considered
it as critically as he could. It seemed to him to have few
flaws. Of two theories, both equally unprovable, he
considered it rather more credible than the other. Both
were intricate, both were perhaps fantastic; but his was
psychologically in character, whereas the other was not.

But of course the greatest and most important differ-
ence between the new theory and the old one was that
while the former was a final and definite closure of the
whole affair, the latter opened it wider than ever. For if
Lambourne had not committed the two murders, then
someone else had; and that someone else was still, pre-

sumably, alive and at Oakington. And suddenly, with a fresh and more sinister thrill, Revell re-read his earlier memorandum of one of Max Lambourne's aphorisms— "two successful murders very often lead to a third."

A third? Was it possible, then, that at that very moment somewhere within those sham Gothic walls the murderer was already contemplating the final item of his triple bill?

CHAPTER X

MORE THEORIES

AN INTER-SCHOOL cricket-match on a blazing midsummer afternoon is decidedly not an occasion to encourage morbid introspection, and it must be admitted that Revell's latest theory did not seem quite so probable as he languidly listened to the plick-plock of the Oakington cricketers from a deck-chair by the side of the pavilion. He was supposed to be watching them, but in reality his eyes were half-closed and he could see nothing but sunlight and the brim of his Panama. From time to time, obedient to a warning murmur about him, he would cautiously open one eye and ejaculate a tired cry of "Well played, sir!" or "Oh, jolly well hit, sir!" It amused him to be a ritualist on such occasions.

It was true that his theory did not seem quite so fundamentally probable under that canopy of blue sky and sunshine. To begin with, it was several days old, and he had almost pondered it out of existence. Indeed, after so much prolonged reflection, he had now at odd moments considerable difficulty in believing that there had been any murders, or even deaths at all, and that Lambourne, Ellington, Guthrie, and the rest of them could have been any more substantial than creatures of a dyspeptic dream. Only his own mysterious presence at an Oakington School cricket-match kept him a little anchored to reality. Why *was* he at Oakington, anyway? Oh yes, the boy Marshall and so on. . . . He found himself strangely transfixed between sleep and wakefulness, while something subconsciously authoritative warned him to be careful. He had had the thing too much on his mind; he was in danger of becoming obsessed with it. Perhaps Roseveare and Guthrie were right; it was better to forget. Yes, better to forget. Better by far he should forget and smile than that he should remember and go mad. . . . Ah, well played, sir! Very pretty— *very* pretty! . . .

Gradually he became aware that some object of fair size intervened between his eyes and the Oakington eleven. And that object, under closer examination, revealed itself as the front portion of a pair of trousers. Furthermore, on tilting his hat-brim a little upwards, he perceived that the trousers were occupied, as it were, and surmounted by an Eton jacket and a face which, in a vague sort of way, he seemed to remember.

"Excuse me, sir, but could I and my friend see you for a minute or two?"

"See me?" He stared sleepily. "Why yes, of course, if you particularly want to."

The boy nodded with extraordinary gravity. "I'm Jones Tertius, sir—you spoke to me when you came here last year. And this is my friend Mottram."

A second Eton jacket obtruded into the line of vision, but by this time Revell was three-quarters awake. "Oh, you're Jones, are you? Jones—*Jones?* Good Lord, yes— I remember, of course." The final quarter of complete consciousness returned to him with a rush. "Delighted to see you again, Jones—and your friend, too. Can I help you at all?"

"Well, you see, sir, we thought—or at least Mottram thought——"

"Stop a minute. Is it anything particularly private?"

"Well, perhaps it is, sir, in a way."

"Then let's take a stroll where we shan't be interrupted." He rose out of his deck-chair and unostentatiously piloted the two boys beyond the pavilion throng. "Looks as if we shall win, eh?" he commented. "That batsman's got a fine stroke—what's the chap's name?"

"Teviot, sir," replied Mottram.

"Ah yes, Teviot—he had a brother here in my time, I think." Not that Revell cared two straws about Teviot and his brother, but it was the sort of conversation that the Head's secretary might legitimately be overheard having with two juniors.

When the three of them were well out of earshot of the crowd, Revell changed the subject abruptly. "Now then, Jones, you and your friend can talk to me as much as you like."

Jones flushed and seemed rather nervous. "It's like this, sir," he began. "We thought—or rather, it wasn't me who thought at first, sir, but Mottram— It was he who had the idea—and he—he asked me—and—" His breath or perhaps his nerve gave way at that point, and Revell, who liked and understood youngsters better than he admitted, gave his arm a friendly squeeze.

"Well," he said sympathetically, "since Mottram seems to have done all the thinking, perhaps it wouldn't be a bad idea if he did the telling, eh?"

Jones looked greatly relieved; it was clearly only his good manners as an earlier acquaintance that had constrained him to act as spokesman. Mottram, on the other hand, as soon as the signal was given, began to talk with a suddenness that reminded Revell of a B.B.C. announcer late with his programme and trying to save an odd minute over the reading of the news items. "Jones told me," he rattled off, "about you questioning him about Marshall Secundus, sir, and when you came here again just after Marshall Primus was killed, I thought you were probably a detective, sir."

"Oh, you *did*, did you?" The truth, or partly the truth, in a single sentence! Mottram was clearly a force to be reckoned with. "Well, it was an ingenious theory, but that's all, I'm afraid. You know now, of course, that I'm merely Doctor Roseveare's secretary."

"Yes, sir, but I thought perhaps that was only a sort of blind—detectives often do that sort of thing when they're working on a case."

"Do they, by Jove? You seem to know a lot about detectives and their ways."

"Yes, sir. My father's a detective."

"Oh, I see. That accounts for it." (And he snobbishly thought: Good heavens, does the modern detective, not content with graduating at Oxford, send his sons to a boarding-school?) "Anyhow," he added, "I'm not a detective, either in disguise or otherwise, so I'm afraid you're wrong."

"I'm sorry, sir."

"Oh, it doesn't matter, I assure you. And I'm quite interested in the affair about the Marshall boys, and if you do happen to know anything of special interest about it, I'd be glad to hear what it is."

"It wasn't about the two boys, sir—it was about Mr. Lambourne."

"Mr. Lambourne, eh?"

"Yes, sir. You see, I thought that perhaps as the two

boys may have been murdered, Mr. Lambourne may have been murdered as well."

Revell had the presence of mind to be severe. "Mr. Lambourne murdered? My dear fellow, you're talking through your hat, or you would be, if you'd got one on! And really, though I daresay you mean well, it's not altogether proper of you to go about spreading ideas of that kind! Didn't you read the Head's remarks in the newspapers a little while ago? I'm sure you did. He said that probably there hadn't been any murders at all. And now, apart from taking no notice of that, you're calmly suggesting that the death of Mr. Lambourne was another murder! I'm ashamed of you, Mottram. You're obviously an intelligent person—I'm sure your opinions must count a good deal amongst your friends, and it's just your kind of person who ought to squash these absurd rumours, not invent them!"

Revell thought that was rather well spoken. But Mottram was not to be intimidated. "I'm sorry, sir, I didn't think you would be annoyed. But I haven't spread any rumours. I haven't talked to anybody about this except Jones. And I *do* think the two Marshalls were murdered, anyhow, and so do a lot of other people, my father says."

"But, my dear boy, leaving the two Marshalls out of it for the time being, what possible reason can you have for thinking that Mr. Lambourne was murdered?"

"I don't say he was, sir. I only say that if the two Marshalls were, he might have been as well."

"*Might have been!* And how much do you suppose that counts without any evidence?"

"Oh yes, I know, sir." He seemed for a moment to be slightly uncomfortable. Then summoning fresh courage, he went on: "The fact is, sir, there *is* something we happen to know that Jones thought you might be interested in. Of course it doesn't matter, sir, if you'd rather we didn't bother you with it."

Revell laughed. "Now you're coming to earth. I'm willing enough to hear facts, but I really must decline to listen to wild theories without a shadow of foundation!" (And he successfully contrived to look indignant as he said it!)

"It's about the night that Mr. Lambourne—died—sir. You remember that at the inquest Mrs. Ellington was supposed to have been the last person to see him. She said that she left him soon after eleven o'clock."

"Yes, I remember."

"Well, sir, somebody went to see him later than that."

Revell controlled his inward excitement. "You'd better tell me how you know and all about it."

"Yes, sir. We thought you'd be interested." There was just a suggestion of a snigger on Mottram's face. "You see, sir, Jones and I were matched against each other in the School chess tournament, and as we were rather late in playing off the game we asked Mr. Lambourne during the afternoon if we could stay up after lights-out and play it off in the Common Room. It's better, you know, to have everything quiet when you're playing chess."

"Doubtless. But it wouldn't have been much of an excuse for staying up late when I was a boy here."

"Ah yes, sir, but we asked Mr. Lambourne. He often gave us permission for things that no one else would."

"I see. Well, go on. He told you you could stay up, I suppose."

"Yes, sir. We began to play about ten, and I won about a quarter past eleven. That was earlier than we'd expected, so we thought we wouldn't go up to the dormitory immediately. We put the light out and sat bv the window, you see——"

"In the dark?" Revell interrupted.

"There was moonlight, sir."

"But surely you wouldn't sit there doing nothing, even if there was moonlight?"

"Well, sir, I suppose it doesn't matter if you *do* know —we were having a smoke."

"A *smoke*?" He laughed. "The old game, I see—I used to do it myself. But not at your age—it's really too early." He tried to look fatherly. "However, go on with the story."

"About a quarter to twelve, sir, just when we were thinking it was time to go to bed, we heard footsteps along the corridor coming towards the Common Room door—it sounded like somebody in slippers. Of course we got an awful wind-up, thinking somebody in the rooms above might have smelt something, but the footsteps went right past the door and down to the end of the corridor. After they'd gone by I went to the door and opened it an inch or so to see who it was, and it was Dr. Roseveare, sir, in his dressing-gown. Of course, as you know, sir, there's only one place he could have been going to—there's nothing beyond the Common Room except Mr. Lambourne's room and the store-cupboards."

"Well, what happened after that?"

"I don't know, sir. We waited a bit, till we thought he'd be safely in Mr. Lambourne's room—then we scooted off to bed. But you see, sir, what it means—that the Head must have been there later than anybody else!"

"Oh yes, I quite see that, Mottram." He felt he must at all costs minimise the importance of the affair, and he also did not much care for Mottram, in whom he recognised an unpleasantly exact replica of the sort of youngster he himself had been at such an age. "Interesting to know all this, of course, but it no more proves Mr. Lambourne was murdered than it proves Queen Anne was murdered. 'Fraid you won't successfully follow in your father's footsteps, Mottram, if you let yourself jump to such wild conclusions." And to show that the matter had made only the slightest of impressions on him, he resumed his chatter about the cricket and led the two boys gently back to the pavilion.

But he knew that it was, or might be, tremendously important. Mrs. Ellington, according to her evidence, had left Lambourne at a little after eleven. The Head, in his dressing-gown, had visited him at a quarter to twelve, and had returned at some later time unknown. Why? What could have been the need for a visit at such an hour? And, most of all, why had Roseveare, when questioned by Guthrie, told a direct lie by stating that he had not seen Lambourne after nine o'clock?

That night, as Revell smoked a cigarette in bed, he found himself thinking, incredulously at first, of Mottram's impudent suggestion that Lambourne had been murdered. Then suddenly, as if a window had been opened in a hitherto closed room, he thought—Good God, suppose the little devil were right? Suppose Lambourne had known too much, and the real criminal, whoever he was, had visited him that night and dosed him, somehow or other, with the veronal tablets? Was it possible? It did not invalidate the self-sacrifice motive, though of course it might be found to supersede it. And it most certainly recalled Lambourne's axiom that two successful murders often led to a third. What, then, if the so-probable third had already been committed, and Lambourne, by the bitterest of ironies, had been its victim?

So, for a little time, Revell permitted himself to suspect the Head. Roseveare had, all along, behaved with a certain suspiciousness; he possessed, too, more perhaps than anyone else at Oakington, the kind of brain that could plan deeply and craftily. Unfortunately, apart from the one item of his late and unacknowledged visit to Lambourne, there was not a tittle of evidence against him. There was not even a possible motive. Why on earth should a headmaster murder two of his boys and thereby ruin the reputation of his school?

To which the answer came, in due course, that Roseveare need by no means have murdered the boys at all. Supposing that Ellington had done that, that Lambourne had discovered proof, and that Roseveare, to avoid the worst sort of scandal, had politely snuffed out the too-clever investigator? *There* was a motive, at any rate, and a fairly likely one. Was the theory possible, then?

When Revell reached that point in his reflections, he dashed his head desperately against the pillows and made up his mind that he would die rather than formulate any further theory. He had theorised and theorised and theorised, and each theory fitted in so beautifully until the next one came along, and at the end of it all he was hardly an inch nearer any provable solution. It would certainly drive him completely mad if he did not give it up; it was a sort of mental debauchery that sapped his energies and made him feel as impotent as a Euclid theorem in the hands of a relativist mathematician. Henceforth, he decided, with many vows, he would merely observe. He would observe Ellington,

Mrs. Ellington, Roseveare, Daggat, Brownley, Jones Tertius, Mottram, the School House cat—every living thing, in fact, in that extraordinary conglomeration of mysteries that was placed between Nottingham High School and Oundle in the Public Schools' Year-Book. He would be the angel in the house—the recording angel, at any rate, in School House.

CHAPTER XI

AMOROUS INTERLUDE

So it began—the strangest idyll, glowing
    Fitfully nearer to his young heart's core,
And also, on the woman's side, o'erflowing
    With sharp and febrile ardours that are more
Than ever likely to make sudden showing
    After ten years of marriage to a bore,
Breeding repressions such as Doctor Freud did
    Well to tell us how are best avoided.

So wrote Revell towards midnight in his room in School House on the seventh of July, 1928. As more befitting his secretarial position, he had ceased to lodge at the Head's house and had been allotted instead the room opposite Ellington's adjacent to the junior dormitory. The change suited him well, since he had more time to himself and could feel himself less under the immediate surveillance of Doctor Roseveare.

It was his first completed stanza for a month, and he was rather proud of it. (It would need a preliminary one, of course, closing up his hero's previous adventure and introducing a new one, but that could be done later. One of the advantages of the *Don Juan* idea was that the hero could do anything he or his creator liked so long as he kept within the rhymed Iambic pentameter.)

Revell had been observing for exactly a fortnight, and he had kept his vow—he had not permitted himself a single new theory. The restriction had at first been irksome, but after a time he had grown almost completely satisfied to be merely a watcher, a noter-down of unconsidered trifles. Such as, for example, that Ellington was getting more ill-tempered and morose than ever; that his wife bore her burden with a patience which must, sooner or later, break down; that the Head, too, was showing signs of the abnormal strain of recent affairs; that Mottram was cheeky and needed a thrashing; that the new master appointed in place of Lambourne was an amusing youngster named Pulteney, fresh from Cambridge; and that house-matches were less of a bore to watch when Pulteney and himself had previously arranged an intricate series of shilling bets upon the number of runs made by each of the twenty-two players.

And also, of course (for it deserves a paragraph to itself), that Mrs. Ellington was an exceedingly charming woman. He had thought so all along, but the revelation had not come to him with full intensity till he took on his rôle of Sunday and week-day observer. He saw her quite often—by chance that was just pleasantly flavoured with the doubt as to whether both of them had not been looking out for each other a little. They talked a good deal about matters which had nothing to do with the School and its affairs—of books, plays, pictures, and so on; she knew very little, but had a lively intelligence, and it delighted Revell to instruct her. She hardly ever mentioned her husband, but it was impossible to ignore the ever-present tragedy of her married life; Ellington was at worst churlish and at best boring. Revell, as his own friendship with her developed and as his feelings for her increased in warmth, could well imagine the relationship that had existed between herself and Lambourne. How she must have enjoyed Lambourne's clever chatter after her husband's surly silences; and how he, in turn, must have ached for the woman who had borne, so uncomplainingly, the first decade of a probable life-sentence.

To Revell, naturally, the chief count against Ellington was that he was a double murderer. Yet it was strange how one could accept even the most horrible situation after a time; and there were certainly moments when Revell almost forgot about the murders and hated Ellington most of all for some minor but exasperating piece of rudeness towards his wife.

Once, however, he made an interesting and rather revealing experiment (though, true to his vow, he did not allow himself to dogmatise from it). He was dining with the Head and allowed the conversation to turn on the new-comer, Pulteney. He said he liked him, and spoke approvingly of his discipline, both in form and in the house. Roseveare cordially agreed, and Revell added: "To be quite frank, that seemed rather the weak spot in Lambourne, admirable as he was in other ways—he sometimes let the kids have too much of their own way."

Roseveare again agreed, and Revell, who had carefully planned his own moves in the conversation, continued: "A rather amusing example of his slack ways came under my notice quite recently, in fact. I remember it particularly because it happened on the night before he was found dead—I'd decided to chaff him about it the next day, poor fellow. I was taking a stroll about the quad. latish in the evening—perhaps it would be half-past eleven or so—when, as I came near School House, I thought I heard voices in the Common Room. Naturally I went to investigate, and what d'you suppose it was? Two juniors playing chess! Of course it was no business of mine, especially as they said Lambourne had given 'em permission, so I just left 'em there, and Heaven alone knows when they *did* go to bed. But chess, mind you—at getting on for midnight!"

He saw that Roseveare had gone very slightly pale and that his knuckles were whitening as he clenched them on the table. "Who were the ruffians—purely as a matter of curiosity?" he queried, with an effort to appear casual.

But Revell had expected the question, and was not to be caught so easily. "Didn't ask 'em, I'm afraid, and probably wouldn't know 'em even if I saw 'em again. You can guess they had the lights pretty low."

And then he changed the subject. He was quite satisfied; he had made another observation.

In his talks with Mrs. Ellington he never mentioned the murders. It was easy not to, now that the affair had practically died out of the newspapers; and, of course, the fact that in her eyes Lambourne was the proved culprit while he himself believed so differently, acted as a simple barrier to discussion between them. Sometimes, though not often, she mentioned Lambourne in some other connexion, and Revell was pleased to note how generous and fair-minded she was; her belief in his guilt had not closed up all the wells of her pity for him.

She was, Revell thought, entirely and deliciously adorable. Sometimes, as they took tea together, or as they chatted during some chance meeting in the lane, he almost caught himself wanting to kiss her. Her deli-

cate smallness appealed so mutely for protection, and
her dark eyes, that were sad as a rule when they first
met, brightened so noticeably during their moments
together that he could not but feel that she, as well as
he, was attracted. It more than gratified him; it almost,
when he grasped the full significance of it, intoxicated
him. Oakington was a dark forest and he himself was a
knight of chivalry faced with the task of rescuing a
particularly enchanting damsel from the maw of a particularly nauseating ogre. More and more, as those days
of July slipped by, his aim became rescue as well as
retribution; and though he dreaded the moment when
she would learn the truth, he looked forward to the
equally inevitable moment when she would realise how
and from what he might have saved her.

They came to calling each other by their Christian
names. Hers was Rosamund. He made absurd puns about
it; once, when she came cycling along the drive on a
rainy afternoon, he called out "Sic Transit Gloria Rosa-
mundi", which he thought not bad. She smiled, dismounted, and answered: "I'm going to have a real transit very soon. Tom's arranged that we shall leave England on the tenth of August. Just think of it—only a
fortnight after Term ends for all the shopping I shall
have to do!"

"You're going away so soon?" He was almost bewildered.

"Yes. We shall be on our plantation or whatever it is
by the time the Autumn Term begins here. It's a terrible rush, but of course if we're going to go, there's not
much point in delaying over it."

Revell nodded, still dazedly. He was amazed to discover what a personal blow it was to him. Disappoint-
ment and then indignation succeeded. "But, Rosamund,

what an awful life for you! Have you really thought what it will mean? Some God-forsaken back-block in the middle of Africa—no theatres, no books, no shops——"

"Oh, but we shall have a car," she interrupted, "and every three months or so I shall drive the two hundred miles for a week's shopping in Nairobi. And Mudie's will probably send out a box of books now and again, including yours as fast as they come out, Colin. And there are several other people living within twenty miles or so."

"God—I don't know how you can bear to think of it all."

"But I don't think of it. I just live on from day to day." She stared mutely at the front tyre of her bicycle. "What else is there to do?"

"I know." It was pouring with rain, but neither of them moved. "I shall be sorry not to see you again," he said at last.

"Yes. And I too. We have been good friends." And she added, with a lessening of reserve that only emphasised the reticence of her entire attitude hitherto: "I believe you understand a great deal more than I could ever tell you. Perhaps we shall meet again at the concert tonight? Will you go?"

"If *you* go. Rather. I'll keep a seat for you."

She smiled and mounted her machine, and he went back to his room in a state of curiously mingled joy and misery. She had spoken to him perhaps more intimately than ever before, yet it was all clouded over by the imminence of her departure. He had never guessed that it could matter so much to him. Just over three weeks and she would be *en route* with her husband for Africa. Revell perceived, with a feeling of sheer panic, that there was no time to be lost. The unmasking of Ellington would have to take place during those three weeks, or else never at all. And his own observations, though so far significant were hardly yet of a kind to be acted upon.

The departure was itself, of course, a suspicious thing. Why such enormous hurry to get away from Oakington? Did it not seem as if Ellington wished to put as great a distance as possible between himself and the scene of his crimes?

Meanwhile, all the more intensely in the face of their possible separation so soon, Revell looked forward to the concert. It was a terminal affair, held in the Memorial Hall, and attended by the whole school. A few of Oakington's most promising musicians took part, and this native talent was helped out by visiting artists from London who might or might not be worth hearing. Revell, whose appreciation of music was fastidious, would never have thought of going but for Mrs. Ellington; yet for her sake he would cheerfully endure, if not fire and water, at least Liszt's Second Rhapsody bungled by a nervously ambitious schoolboy.

She joined him just before the concert began and smilingly thanked him for keeping a seat for her. (Ellington, of course, was not with her; he was entirely unmusical.) During the first half of the programme, made up of various items by the boys, Revell hardly exchanged a word with her, but when the interval came they chatted a little. It had always been their habit to pretend, to themselves, at any rate, that they were only left together by some astonishing accident of fate; thus Revell, observing the convention, gave the necessary opening. "I suppose Mr. Ellington couldn't manage to come?"

And she answered: "No, he doesn't care for concerts much. He's gone to Easthampton on business and won't be back till the last train."

The second half of the programme consisted simply of the Kreutzer Sonata, played by a visiting pianist and violinist of considerable talent. Revell, at any rate, with Mrs. Ellington by his side, was in a mood to be impressed. The Kreutzer had always been a favourite of his, and to hear it now gave him an extraordinary sensation of having Heaven on his side. During the tranquil adagio movement he was calmed, mellowed, made ready for the triumphant ecstasy to which the final presto movement raised him. When the last chord had been struck he was left full of speechless emotion. Only after they had fussed their way out through the crowd and were standing together in the bright starshine did he find words, and then merely to suggest a stroll.

She agreed.

They set out for the conventional circuit of the Ring. There was no moon, but a sky pale with stars, and the beauty of it threw enchantment even over the architectural monstrosities of the skyline. Oakington was going to bed; ten o'clock chimed from the School clock; light after light disappeared from those rows of windows that were the dormitories. The smell of the trees and the mown grass was in the air; an owl hooted into the blue-black silence.

He began, with the Kreutzer Sonata still dreamily in his ears: "D'you know, Rosamund, I'm beginning to find myself in a queer situation. I—I rather think—I'm falling in love with you."

"Are you?" She did not seem particularly surprised, but there was a tremor of something else in her voice.

"Yes, I'm afraid so. Do you mind?"

"Why should I mind something so—so—something so—" She hesitated, and then suddenly seemed to shake herself into another mood. "Really, Colin, I don't quite know what I'm talking about, and neither do you, I think. I don't mind, of course—in fact, I feel rather thrilled about it—but it's all rather futile and pointless in a way, don't you think?"

"Yes, but—" He tried to protest, but there was no need, for with immense astonishment he found her in his arms and her lips approaching his. "Colin," she whispered, "Colin—just once—and then never again—just once——"

He kissed her. It went to his head like rare wine; he began to chatter wildly in his enthusiasm. Gone now was his caution in mentioning Ellington; he spoke of him quite openly as a man whom she did not and could not love. "Oh, why *did* you marry him, Rosamund? I've always wondered. He's so utterly the opposite of you in every way—do you think everyone hasn't noticed it? Rosamund, you hate him, I know—you *must* do—it's impossible to think of you spending all the rest of your life with him. And in Kenya, of all places. Rosamund, you simply *can't* do it!"

"I can. I shall just have to."

"Not if you were to run away from him."

"But I couldn't do that."

"Why not?"

And he had a swift vision of Rosamund and himself sharing some art-and-crafty studio in Chelsea, himself writing highbrow novels and Rosamund painting futurist pictures or making terra-cotta statuettes or casting horoscopes or keeping a hat shop or employing her time in some such task that possessed the conventional amount of unconventionality. His own four or five pounds a week plus, say, half as much from her, would easily permit them to sustain an idyllic existence on love, art, gin, and tinned sardines. Delightful prospect! Was he game for it? He believed he was, and with rising enthusiasm in his voice, rapidly sketched out to her the bare outlines of such a future.

"You're a dear boy," she said, when he had finished. "I believe I should be perfectly happy with you like that, too. But of course you don't really mean it. It's the Kreutzer Sonata gone to your head, that's all. What a pity I'm not a designing woman, or I might take you at your word!"

"*Do!*" he cried, eagerly. "I only wish you would!"

She laughed. "Suppose I do, then? When shall we go to your little Chelsea studio? To-night? There's the last train to town at eleven, you know. Or perhaps to-morrow would give us more time to pack. And I could leave the conventional note on the dressing-table for Tom. . . . Ah, I can see from your eyes that you don't really mean what you've been saying. Never mind—I'm not offended. I love you for your romantic impulsiveness."

"But I *do* mean it," he retorted, stung a little. "I mean every word of it. And at the end of the Term——"

"Why wait till then?"

"I—I don't know—except that it would give us time to —to prepare things. And there would be less scandal here, too. After all, there's been enough lately."

That seemed to bring a cloud within sight of them both. "True," she admitted. "It's been the most dreadful of years—when I look back on it all—" She shivered a little. "The only bright spot was when you came here. You're such an unlikely sort of person to be a headmaster's secretary. Whatever made you give up that wonderful life in London to come to Oakington?"

"Just a change of atmosphere."

"Yes, I should think so." She was silent for a while, and then added, in a different voice: "No, Colin, on second thoughts I don't know that I'd want to go away with you. You wouldn't treat me as I'd want to be treated. You'd think me too small—too scatter-brained, I suppose—to be trusted with your intimate secrets. You don't *really* trust me, do you?"

"Trust you? Why, of course I do!"

"Then why didn't you tell me the truth about why you came here? Do you think I really believe you only came for a change of atmosphere? Besides, you don't do an hour's secretarial work in a week. No, my dear Colin, you're a clever boy, and you're having some clever game of some kind, though I'm not quite certain what it is. And I shouldn't wonder if you've only been making love to me with some hidden purpose."

"Rosamund, that's not true!" He was sincerely indignant that she should think him capable of such a thing. "I assure you——"

"You assure me that you came here from London merely for a change of atmosphere, and that the Head lets you stay here as his secretary and do no work?" She suddenly began to cry. "I'm sorry," she whispered, "but I can't help it. I believed you for a moment—just while you were kissing me—but—but now——"

"No, really—" He tried to take her in his arms again, but she eluded him. "Really, you mustn't do that. . . . Rosamund. . . . It isn't that I've been really deceiving you—it's'—oh, dash it all, if there's no other way of convincing you, I'll tell you everything——"

"Not if you'd rather not. Not unless you're sure you thoroughly trust me."

"Of course I trust you. It never had anything to do

with that. It was merely—oh, Rosamund, didn't you say yourself how dreadful the past year had been? Well, I knew that, and I wanted to save you from being dragged into any more of it."

"*More of it?*" Her voice was incredulous. "But surely —surely it's all over now? I had hoped——"

"Yes, I know. So had I—so had everybody. But I'm rather afraid it isn't—or at any rate, may not be—*quite* over yet."

"I don't think I understand at all," she said, in a slow, chilled voice. "Tell me the whole truth, Colin, however terrible it is."

But that, of course, was just what he could not do; he could not tell her how he suspected her husband. So he told her merely that in his opinion the murderer had not been Lambourne. She was astonished, bewildered— the revelation disturbed, he could see, the whole foundations of her recent life. "Not Mr. Lambourne?" she echoed. "But, Colin, he confessed to me!"

"I know he did, but it wasn't true."

"Then why—why should he confess?"

"He might have wanted to save someone else."

She was bewildered for a long time. He could not be too explicit with her lest he made it clear who, in his opinion, *had* committed the murders. In fact, his whole story was far less convincing than it ought to have been, by reason of the large suppressions he had perforce to make. Yet, in the end, she seemed dubiously persuaded. Woman-like, she went straight to the crux of the matter. "But, Colin, if Mr. Lambourne didn't do it, then who did?"

"Yes, of course. And that's just what I don't know for certain, though I've got suspicions."

"Won't you tell me?"

"It wouldn't be fair. They may be quite unfounded. Far better not talk about it till the suspicions become certainties."

"But supposing they never do?"

"They probably will. Criminals always give themselves away if you watch them long enough."

"Do you really think that?"

"I'm sure of it."

"But—how horrible it all is—it may be somebody we all know—somebody we meet every day——"

"Quite possibly." He nodded gravely. He felt that years hence, when he came to write his reminiscences as a crime-investigator, he would begin a chapter with the sentence: "Of all the mysteries that it has fallen to my lot to unravel, that of the Oakington murders was undoubtedly the most horrible. . . ."

She clung to his arm with a timid gesture that made him feel superbly protective. "Colin, let's go in now—I think I'm a little scared after all this. It's getting late, too—Tom will soon be back."

From the way she spoke her husband's name he knew that he had avoided giving her the slightest inkling as to where his suspicions lay.

On the way back to the School they talked in a new mood of seriousness. "So you see," he explained, "what it all means. There were only three people in the world who knew that Lambourne had confessed to you—Detective Guthrie, me, and yourself. But there are only two—yourself and me—who know that Lambourne's confession was false."

"And there is only *one* who knows—or has an idea—who really is the murderer."

He half-smiled. "Perhaps."

"Mr. Guthrie believed that Mr. Lambourne had done it?"

"Oh yes. As he was so often careful to tell me, it was facts *he* was bothered about, not theories. The fact that Lambourne had confessed to you was enough for him. Perhaps it ought to have been enough for me, too, but—well, it wasn't."

"So you're doing this altogether on your own?"

"Altogether." He felt a strong pride rising in him. "I believe that somewhere on these premises there is a person who has committed the most devilish crimes, and if the police are satisfied to give the matter up as a bad job, then I am not."

"You're brave, Colin."

"No, it isn't that. It's more, to be quite frank, a sort of damnable conceit that I've got."

"You think you'll get the murderer, then, in the end?"

"Yes, I do. I've certain evidence already, and I hope to get more very soon."

She shuddered. "It all sounds so terribly ruthless. Oh, let's hurry—I seem to see people hiding behind every tree."

He left her at the door of her house and climbed to his own room in a state of strange excitement. He had kissed her, and she was the first married woman he had ever kissed. He perceived that he had passed a definite milestone in life.

But the incident was not repeated. Indeed, there came no suitable opportunity. When first they met again after the night of the concert, she warned him that they must be more discreet. "Because I have an idea Tom guesses how I feel towards you," she explained, and the confession helped to soften the restrictions it foreshadowed. Revell, too, now that the Kreutzer Sonata mood had worn off, was less inclined to be reckless; he saw at any rate that to have Ellington jealous of him would only complicate the final and more important issue.

The matter, however, led to a short but rather revealing conversation. He agreed that the very last thing he desired was to make things more difficult for her than they were.

"It isn't that," she answered. "I'm not thinking of myself at all—so far as I'm concerned I wouldn't much care what happened. I'm thinking of you."

"*Me?*"

"Yes."

"But *I* don't care, either—not personally. A writer isn't supposed to have much of a reputation, you know."

She smiled. "I wasn't thinking of your reputation. It's more a matter of your personal safety. Oh, I know you'll think that's absurd and melodramatic, but it isn't. You don't know Tom as I do."

The obvious corollary that neither did she know Tom as he did, struck at him with sinister intensity. "But surely you don't mean to say that I should be in actual physical danger from him?"

"You might be," she answered. "It's a frightful thing to have to confess about one's husband, but it's true. He'd do nearly anything in a fit of jealousy. And I think—already—he's a little jealous of you. That's why we must be careful."

So they saw far less of each other during that final fortnight of the Term. It was just as well, Revell admitted to himself, for there had been more than a whisper of talk among the masters, and even the Head had come to know that his secretary and the wife of one of his housemasters had struck up a rather close friendship. As end of Term approached, however, the scandal-mongers were baffled, for Revell and Mrs. Ellington entirely ceased their habit of openly chatting for half-an-hour on the edge of the quadrangle within sight of all Oakington. Once or twice she called on him in his room in the evening, but stayed only for a moment or so, finding him busy on what he had already come to think of as "the case." He had never, in fact, been so intent upon anything in his life. So much, he knew, depended on whether, during the few days that still intervened before the departure of the Ellingtons, he could manage to discover some last fragment of conclusive evidence. It was maddening to be so morally certain of Ellington's guilt and to have collected such a mass of suspicious probabilities against him, yet to lack just the one single thread of hard fact that would knit the whole into a presentable indictment. As each day passed and still that fact eluded his most strenuous search, Revell became fidgety to the point of panic. Hour after hour in his room in School House he sat at his desk before the window pondering over the pencilled entries in his notebook in the hope that somehow or other an avenue of swift investigation might suggest itself. He even sent to his Islington lodgings for his portable typewriter and laboriously typed out the contents of his notebook on quarto sheets; he thought that their added clarity in such a form might well reward him for his trouble.

End of Term came; Oakington dispersed to its homes; the School itself took on that air of dreary desolation that always hangs about deserted buildings. On the last evening before the break-up, Ellington, in the presence of the whole school assembled in the Hall, had been presented with a large and opulent-looking cowhide valise. Doctor Roseveare's speech had naturally been a perfect model for such occasions. He had mentioned Ellington's years of faithful service, had hinted vaguely at recent ill-health and at a decision to assist recovery by living the freer, more invigorating life of the Colonies. "And so, remembering what a lot of good wishes he will have to take with him, we thought we would give him this bag to carry them in!" Oh, very pretty—*very* pretty, Revell had murmured to himself.

Revell's position at the School, now that Term was over, was becoming somewhat anomalous, but Roseveare eased it considerably by suggesting that he should stay on a few days if it convenienced him at all. Revell accepted the offer with relief, and in his own room that night addressed himself to a last, frenzied attempt at solving the Oakington problem. First of all he typed out, in concise form, the sum-total of his reasons for suspecting Ellington. They were as follows:

(1) He had strong motive for both crimes.

(2) He has no alibi for the time when the second murder was committed, and probably none for the time of the first, either.

(3) The revolver with which the second murder was committed belonged to him.

(4) He is, according to his wife, a violent man.

(5) His plans to leave England almost immediately.

Fairly impressive, Revell thought, as he looked it over. And then, rather suddenly, he thought of something else that should, he upbraided himself, have struck him long before. It was a chilly evening for the time of the year, and he had donned a dressing-gown for warmth while he sat at his writing-desk. That reminded him of the dressing-gown that Wilbraham Marshall had worn on the night of the murder. Thus, with amazing swiftness, the sequence of argument developed. The boy, Revell assumed, had been shot whilst standing on the edge of the bath. He would, therefore, since the bath was empty, have been wearing his dressing-gown. Almost certainly it would have been stained with blood; ergo, the murderer, if he wished to leave an impression of an accidental dive, would have had to remove the soiled dressing-gown and leave another, unsoiled, on the side of the bath. Doubtless the former had been destroyed, but the latter, included presumably amongst the boy's other possessions, might well yield valuable clues. Whose was it, for example, and how had it been obtained?

The idea seemed so promising, and the urgency of the whole matter had lately been driving Revell into such agonies of fretfulness, that he allowed himself the relief of feeling that he had now really and definitely scored. The dressing-gown ought, somehow or other, to implicate Ellington. How, of course, had yet to be discovered, and there was distinctly no time to waste. He did not even at first know where the dressing-gown was; but a seemingly casual chat with Brownley drew the information that it had been taken charge of by Detective Guthrie along with other belongings of the dead boy.

Revell was slightly chagrined by that, for Guthrie was perhaps the last person he wished to drag back into the affair. Guthrie, in his opinion had bungled the case altogether and thrown it up far too readily; he had also, Revell considered, treated a youthful amateur with a patronage and condescension quite unjustified by their respective degrees of success. Yet there was nothing else

for it; the clue of the dressing-gown must not be overlooked. So Revell, after much cogitation, there and then
composed the following:

My dear Guthrie,
    I am still interesting myself somewhat in various as-
pects of recent unhappy events here. A point has occurred to me in connexion with the dressing-gown left
in the swimming-bath on the night of the tragedy. I
believe you took charge of it, and if it is still in your
possession, would it be permissible for me to see it, at
some time and place to suit your convenience, but preferably as soon as possible?
Yours faithfully,
Colin Revell.

He was rather proud of that letter; it seemed to con-
ceal the significance of the matter and to suggest rather
a painstaking research student busily gathering material
for a thesis. Guthrie would probably laugh at the amateur who continued to bother with a case long after it
was finished, but that could not be helped.

Revell had just signed the letter and sealed it in an
addressed envelope when Mrs. Ellington chanced to
call with a few books that he had lent her from time
to time. (They were Brett Young's *Tragic Bride*; Edith
Wharton's *Ethan Frome*; and the play edition of *Young
Woodley*—all of which he had had to send for specially
from his rooms in Islington. But it had been part of her
education, of course, and therefore worth the trouble.)
"We've already begun to pack some of our things," she
explained, "and I didn't want these of yours to get mixed
up with the rest."

He invited her to sit down, but she declined. "Really,
no, I mustn't stay—it's too late. And besides, you're
busy." She approached his desk and looked over his

shoulder. "What—a letter to Mr. Guthrie?" Her exclamation of astonishment gratified him, though, as a matter of fact, he would rather she had not known about the letter. "Colin—do you mean—does this mean—that at last—at last—you've discovered who did it?"

He swung round and faced her startled eyes. "Not perhaps all that, Rosamund," he answered, but with a triumph he could not disguise. "All the same, things are coming to a bit of a climax. My letter to Guthrie may— if I'm lucky—round off the whole thing."

"You mean that it will prove who did it?"

"It may *lead* to a final proof."

"But the School is broken up—everybody's away."

He answered cautiously: "Yes, I know—it's a pity it cóuldn't have happened earlier." He had to go very carefully over this extremely slippery ground, or she would assuredly begin to suspect the truth. "Still, it's an advantage that everything's been kept so secret. Guthrie's method of filling the School with policemen isn't perhaps the best, after all."

She nodded. "It's terrible, though." He saw with deep pity the strain that was put upon her; he smiled and, changing the subject, asked how she felt about going away so soon.

"I'm trying my best to be thrilled," she answered, valiantly. "It seems almost impossible to believe that I shall soon be seeing Paris, Marseilles, Suez, the Red Sea, and so many other places. I hate the thought of the life at the end of it all, but I daresay I shall manage to enjoy the journey."

"Unfortunately the journey will only last three weeks, whereas the life after it——"

"Oh yes, but please don't remind me of it."

He felt he could all the better remind her of it because in his own mind he was telling himself: "She will never see those places—at least, not with Ellington. By the day planned for the departure, Ellington will be under arrest. It will be a bitter ordeal for her, but perhaps less bitter than the one she is fearing now."

They chatted on for a time, more intimately than since the night of the concert, till at last, with the chiming of the School clock, she exclaimed: "Oh, how thoughtless I've been—I've made you miss the post with that important letter! Really, Colin, I'm ever so sorry! Do forgive me!"

He had missed it right enough; the last collection from the village post-office was made at ten-fifteen, and it had just chimed the half-hour. A pity; it would mean perhaps a day's delay, and a day that could ill be spared. Her face, however, so anxious and self-reproachful, made him take an easier view of the matter. After all, he could go out and post the letter early in the morning in time for the first collection. He comforted her by saying so, and assured her that it was not her fault at all. Besides, it would reach Guthrie sometime on the morrow. "And as soon as he gets it," he added, "the wheels ought to be set in motion, and maybe within twenty-four hours—" He shrugged his shoulders; he could not forbear a little boastfulness in front of her. "It's been a fearful job," he said, with the air of a veteran detective, and he rejoiced to see the strange look of wonder in her eyes.

Suddenly, standing near the window, she stepped back with a startled exclamation. "Oh, Colin, I must hurry back. I've just seen Tom at the front door and he looked up and saw me here. Isn't it awful to have to run away like a guilty schoolboy? But I must. So good night."

But for the compelling thought of what was so soon to happen, he would have refused to let her go. He would have said: "No, you are doing no harm here and here you shall stay. And if your husband fancies he has any grievance, then let him come here and talk to me about it. . . ." That, undoubtedly, would have been magnificent, but, in the circumstances, it would hardly have been the right kind of war. So, with inward indignation and a final handshake of sympathy and understanding, he opened the door for her and heard her light footsteps die away along the corridor.

CHAPTER XII

ALMOST THE FOURTH OAKINGTON TRAGEDY

It was getting on for eleven, but he was far too excited for sleep; the dressing-gown clue and her visit to him had combined to fill his mind with surging anticipations. What, he speculated, would happen to her after her husband's arrest? How would she take it? Was there anywhere she could go, or anyone who would look after her? It would be a frightful position for a woman to be in, but was it any more frightful than the position she was in, all unknowingly, at the moment? He wondered if definite suspicion of her husband had ever crossed her mind. Some little thing that he had said or done—some odd happening or coincidence that had seemed trivial enough at the time, but which she might have remembered since—had she ever envisaged the terrible possibility? He rather believed that she hadn't, despite Roseveare's queer story of her behaviour after the dormitory affair. It was a pity, in a way; it would have made it easier for her when the crisis did come.

She would have to leave Oakington of course. How would she manage during the trial? If she came to London, as she would probably have to, he could make things as pleasant for her as possible. And then afterwards—at an altogether decent interval afterwards—was it also possible . . . ? Revell was not wholly mercenary (no more so, that is, than most young men of his age and income), but he could not help a thrill at the thought that she would inherit (presumably) all the money that Ellington had inherited from the two boys. She would be a tolerably rich woman, in fact. Would she, then, with an income of a hundred pounds a week or so, be attracted by a vagabond life in a Chelsea studio? Very well, if not, he would have to be adaptable. For her sake he would cheerfully become a country gentleman; he would even hunt foxes and attend agricultural shows if it were positively demanded of him. With her, anyhow, he would have a thrilling and joyous existence; he was confident of that.

Pleasant dreams; and they passed the time very satisfactorily until midnight. Cigarette after cigarette he smoked in his chair by the empty firegrate, yet still the tide of excited anticipation flowed in his brain without abatement. There was no chance of sleep yet, he knew—not that he particularly wanted to sleep, for his thoughts were quite enjoyable enough to be savoured for another hour or so. And an additional pleasure was the fact that, for the time being, he could do no more at "the case"; until Guthrie replied, the affair was beyond his control. He was, in a way, heartily sick of pondering over the ghoulish details of the murders, and now that he could lawfully put them out of his mind for the time being, he felt as buoyant as a schoolboy excused homework.

Shortly after midnight he left the easy chair and uncovered his typewriter at the desk in front of the window. He would, he decided, compose a stanza of his epic before going to bed. And the stanza, naturally enough, would be about his hero's affair with a pretty woman unfortunately married to a man as nearly as possible like Ellington. This woman, as nearly as possible like Mrs. Ellington, had just had a clandestine meeting with her lover (a youth as nearly as possible like Revell), and when she got back to her own home she discovered that:

"Her husband was in bed; his huddled torso
    Upwards and downwards in his slumber heaved;
It jarred on her; she wished he didn't snore so;
    And then besides, she was a trifle peeved
To think——"

To think what? She had really so many things to be peeved about (or aggrieved about, for that matter—the rhyme would suit equally well), but just what, out of so many? He pondered, with his fingers poised above the typewriter keys. Then suddenly, facing him from the uncurtained window as he looked up, he saw something that made his heart miss a beat and the blood tingle sharply through all the veins of his body.

It was, or appeared to be, the barrel of a revolver placed right up against the outside of the window-pane and pointing directly at his eyes. It was at the right-hand side of the pane, close up to the wooden window-frame, and it was impossible in the darkness to see how it was fixed or held in position. Revell, at the first instant of seeing it, had stared incredulously; he half-thought himself dreaming. Then, as his wits returned to him more completely, he jerked his chair backwards and stood up; and at that moment, with his eyes still fixed upon it, the strange phenomenon disappeared.

Was he mad? Had he been overworking his brain till the danger-point of hallucination had been reached? He would not have been surprised, for the apparition at the window had not been plain enough to be sworn to. Quickly, with sharpening determination to discover what, if anything, had happened, he went to the window and threw it wide open. There was nothing to be seen except the black and starless night. The very emptiness and innocence of it seemed more than ever to point to the theory of hallucination. But Revell was desperately anxious to take no chances, and every second increased his excitement. Inevitably his brain linked the matter with the entire chapter of Oakington horrors; and, if the apparition had been real at all, he was quick to realise that it could signify only one thing. An attempt had been made on his life. Not a moment ago the revolver had been there; now it was gone, but its owner could not be far away—must, in fact, be quite close. And with a growing perception that every second counted, Revell dashed into the corridor.

First he turned to the left, into the dark and empty dormitory. He pressed the switch that should have illuminated it, but no light appeared. The same old trick of the broken fuse? It was natural, perhaps, that he should think so at first, but he remembered, a second later, that Brownley had been in the dormitories during the day removing all the globes and shades for a terminal clean. Nevertheless, though it was almost pitch dark and he could see nothing, he strode down the central gangway

between the two long tiers of beds. It was not the best
thing to have done, as he realised as soon as he reached
the end wall, for he heard a sharp movement at the
doorway where he had entered and a rush of footsteps
along the corridor past his room.

He raced back; his blood was up. The revolver at the
window now became an indisputable fact, for he had
heard the assailant escaping. Revell chased wildly after
him, oblivious of the probability that the fellow still had
his revolver with him. At the landing where the stairs
led down to the lower floors, Revell halted! it seemed
likely that the fugitive had taken the obvious line of
escape. But then, in the almost total darkness to which
his eyes were becoming accustomed, he noticed that the
small door, usually closed and locked, which admitted
to the stairs leading up to the disused sick-rooms, was
very slightly ajar. It was as if someone had tried to
bang it behind him but had given it just too little a
push. Revell, listening with his ear to the opening, fancied he heard faint sounds above; that settled it; he
pushed the door wide open and began to climb.

The ancient sick-rooms, musty from long disuse, sent
their own peculiar smell down the stairs to greet him.
He had no light, not even a box of matches; his quarry,
too, was by that time hidden, perhaps, and able to listen
carefully to the sounds of the pursuit. Revell thought
of all that in a vague sort of way, but it hardly affected
his attitude towards the immediate future. He was only
conscious that at last, at long last, Ellington had played
into his hands. The man had been deuced clever with
his earlier affairs, but this last one, engendered probably
out of sudden sex-jealousy of another man, had made
him over-reach himself. That was how Revell phrased
it to himself, and he was full of an avenging fury. Some-

one had actually tried to murder him, to shoot him in cold blood as he sat at his typewriter; it was a monstrous thing, and he experienced though a hundred times more intensely, the feeling that constrains so many Englishmen to write to the *Times*.

At the top of the stairs he found himself panting for breath. He knew the plan of those old rooms as well as anybody; he had spent many well-remembered days in them as a boy. A corridor went off to the right, and from it the various small rooms opened off, divided from each other and from the corridor by matchboard partitions. To the left were lavatories, a kitchen, and the room where Murchiston had been wont to examine the tongues of an earlier generation of Oakingtonians. Revell tried the handle of one of the doors; it was locked. Then, almost as if Providence had given him a sign (Daggat would certainly have thought so), he heard a faint sound along the corridor to the right.

But now the need for caution began to occur to him. He was in total darkness; he had no flashlight or weapon; the pursued might at any moment turn the beam of a torch upon him and fire. It was not a pleasant thought that somewhere in the darkness a few yards away from him a person, possibly a homicidal maniac, crouched in a corner knowing that he had been traced at last. The danger of people who have already committed several murders is that nothing very much worse can happen to them if they are convicted of an extra one; Revell realised this, and the implication was by no means comforting. Those sick-rooms, too, were eerie places to be in; there was a stale smell of drugs and disinfectant still lingering about them after a decade of disuse. The boards, he recollected, had been torn up in some of them; if he were not careful he might pitch head foremost to the floor. And then, presented with such an opportunity, what might not his assailant do?

Revell paused; his heart was beating like a pumping-engine; perspiration, also, began to stream down his forehead and face. The joists creaked under his feet, and a breath of tainted air wafted by him, as if in alarm at being so unusually disturbed. Decidedly he was in an awkward position—alone with a maniac on a disused floor of an empty school. Courage, that had flowed so strongly in him at first, began to ebb away with every second. And then, with a sudden freezing sensation at the base of his spine, he heard a sound from the far end of the corridor—a faint creaking of the joists, as though someone were beginning to move again after a stillness. Supposing the murderer were now to reverse the rôles and become the pursuer instead of the pursued? A thrill of fear clutched at Revell's heart, and involuntarily he took a step back. He was at the head of the stairs now; he had only to dash down and he would be quite safe. It looked a craven thing to do, perhaps, but really, it was only common sense; no one could blame him; there had been two and perhaps three Oakington murders already—why make a possible fourth? Besides, he could lie in wait at the bottom, summon help, or do something or other. He was just preparing for a cautious downward retreat when something happened that stiffened every hair of his head. It was a sound from below like the careful closing of a door.

Trapped? It looked as if he might be, anyhow, and he silently cursed himself for having been such a reckless fool. Meanwhile he was enveloped by a feeling of slow paralysis, and as he stood there with his back pressed against the wall he knew well enough that he was in deadliest fear as well as danger. The joists still creaked along the corridor to the right—was it only his imagination that made the sound of the creaking seem nearer? But there was something even more horrible to come, for a few seconds later he heard a faint but perfectly identifiable sound from below—the tap of a footstep climbing the stairs.

He licked the perspiration as it streamed down over his lips. What could he do, trapped between an enfilading terror on the right and an ascending one from below? There was no inch of room to escape; he was sheerly cornered, and whatever movement he made could only decrease the distance between himself and one or other of his pursuers. For he was convinced, by now, that they *were* his pursuers; and like a horrible nightmare there came the sudden vision of a possibility that had never before occurred to him, though it was simple enough, by all standards—the possibility that the Oakington murders had been the work, not of one person only, but of *two*! And the two now were after *him*!

If only he could have flashed a light in either direction he would not have cared so much, though the darkness, he knew, hid him from them as effectively as it hid them from him. But the terror lay in not knowing who, or even in some sense *what* was coming; better even to be a target for revolver-practice than to wait in total darkness for something unknown and terrible to lay hands on him.

The footsteps on the stairs were climbing towards him. He was certain of it, though he felt rather than heard their approach. They were soft, stealthy footsteps, creeping up towards him through the blackness. He was sure that in another moment he would either turn sick or scream at the top of his voice or else hurl himself desperately downwards against whatever horror might be ascending. All he did, however, was to close his eyes, as if to shut out the very perception of darkness. The footsteps were quite near to him now; whatever belonged to them could not be more than a few yards away. Yet still no light! He felt that he *must* break down, *must* ultimately secure the blessed relief of unconsciousness, *must*—and yet somehow could not. Then, to his utmost horror, he felt a hand reaching out of the darkness and cautiously roving over his hand, his arm, his shoulder, his neck. He opened his mouth to scream, but the hand suddenly closed over it, while a hoarse voice whispered in his ear: "Follow me down, you fool, and for God's sake be quiet!"

He never knew exactly what happened just after that. The next he clearly remembered was being in his own room, in his own easy chair, with Guthrie offering him brandy out of a flask. Yes, *Guthrie*.

"Feeling better, eh?" the detective said, in a kindly voice.

Memory came back to him with a rush. "Yes—oh yes, I'm all right—but up there—in the sick-rooms—there's someone hiding——"

"Don't get excited—I know all about it. I turned the key in the lock at the bottom of the stairs as we came down."

Turned the key in the lock! Why on earth hadn't he himself thought of something so absurdly simple? He stammered: "But—but—aren't you going to—to arrest him?"

"All in good time—no need for you to worry. A little bit of a wait will do our friend up there no harm. First of all, as soon as you feel ready for it, I'd like to know just a few details of this latest development."

Revell was still dazed; he stared at Guthrie in vague astonishment. "I don't understand," he gasped. "I don't understand why you are here—I don't—I don't think—I understand—anything."

"No?" Guthrie's voice was quietly sympathetic. "All right, then, it doesn't matter. You've had a pretty fair shock—I'm not surprised it's taken a bit of the wind out of you. But you were chasing somebody, weren't you?"

Revell jerked out: "Somebody tried to shoot me— through that window—I ran after him—and he went up to the sick-rooms."

"You *saw* him try to shoot you?"

"I saw the revolver and I knew who he was." After which, in slow staccato phrases, he recounted the whole incident.

For the next few moments Guthrie behaved like an altogether different man. Usually calm and imperturbable in manner, he became suddenly agile and excited; he sprang to the window, opened it wide, and gave the sill and framework a most minute examination. When he turned round again his lips were tight with anger. "A pretty trick, Revell," he said, bitterly. "Well worthy of the others. Come and look here." And as Revell staggered to his feet and approached the window, the detective took his arm with a sudden friendliness that was again unusual. "I'm damned glad you're still alive, anyhow. It's only by amazing luck that you are. The difficulty, you see, was to shoot without being seen —to take aim, that is, without the criminal having to put a head round the corner. You were typing, you say, just before you noticed the revolver pointing at you?"

"Yes."

"Sitting here at this desk?"

"Yes."

"You've often been in the same position before, I suppose?"

"Yes, fairly often."

"I see." He led Revell close to the window. "Notice these two nails on the inside of the window embrasure. They're new—that was rather careless, for it would have been just as easy to find rusty ones. But it was a devilish neat idea, all the same. For if you place the barrel of a revolver plumb against the brickwork and at the same time lying across these two nails, it will aim directly at the head of anyone sitting as you were at the desk here. The assassin had only to lean out of the end dormitory window next door, hold the revolver in position, and shoot as soon as the sound of your typewriter began. Simple, but rather desperate when you come to ponder over it. Our friend must have rather badly wanted you out of the way."

"It was jealousy," Revell answered. "His wife told me he was like that. And he saw her here with me a little while ago."

"Oh?" Guthrie raised his eyebrows slightly. Then he wandered about the room with apparent casualness, picking up first one thing and then another. At last the writing-desk and its contents attracted his attention. "Hullo, what's this—a letter for me? I suppose I may open it." Revell watched him half-dreamily, still too bewildered to attempt any interference. He saw the detective read the letter, slip it into its envelope, and put it into his pocket without remark.

"I still don't quite understand why you are here," Revell said at length.

"No? Ah well, never mind—all in good time, as I said before. You can thank your lucky star I *was* here, anyhow. Have a smoke—it'll calm your nerves." He lit his

own pipe and puffed vigorously. "The Oakington murderer is, of course, upstairs. I daresay you guessed as
much. There's no chance of escape—the windows are
too far from the ground and barred as well. And here,
by the way, is the revolver that nearly did for you. I
found it on the stairs on the way up. The murderer must
have been in a deuce of a hurry to drop it." He produced from his hip-pocket a villainous-looking long-
barrelled weapon. "This is what is called a Colt Point
22 Police Positive. Not a nice thing to be plugged with,
by any means. Yes, my lad, you've been damned
lucky." He turned to the bookshelves at his elbow, ab-
stracted an A.B.C. guide, and began languorously to
search the pages. "Ah, there's a train to town in half
an hour from now—the night mail from Easthampton.
I should catch it, if I were you."

Revell faced this new suggestion with fresh bewilderment. "But—but *why?*"

"Oh well, you've had enough fun for one night,
surely. Leave me the job of putting the bracelets on
our friend. You'll be able to read all about it in the
papers tomorrow."

Revell suddenly realised the drift of the other's remarks. "Mr. Guthrie," he answered, with flushing
cheeks, "you needn't think you can take me in as easily
as that! I can see what you're after. You've bungled
this case pretty badly up to now, yet you want to come
in for all the credit just as if you hadn't. *I* tracked
down the Oakington murderer, not you, and though I
don't mind you coming in with me on it, I'm damn well
going to see that you don't shove me out! After sweat-
ing over the business long after you'd given it up as a
bad job, don't you think I deserve to be in at the finish?"

Guthrie nodded quite equably. "All right, if that's

how you look at it." He shrugged his broad shoulders; Revell was rather surprised that he should give in so easily. "Well, if we *are* going to do the job together, we'd better get it done, that's all. Do you feel equal to any possible unpleasantness?"

"Of course," answered Revell, valiantly. "We shall be armed, anyhow."

"Oh, I wasn't so much thinking of that. Still, you can carry this affair with you, if you like. It isn't loaded now, so you can wave it about if you feel inclined. Anyhow, let's go."

He led the way out into the corridor, and a moment later, after unlocking the door at the foot, they were climbing the stairs to the floor above, but this time with Guthrie's powerful electric torch illuminating the way. Revell's heart was beginning to beat fast again, but Guthrie appeared quite calm. "This was where we first met, wasn't it?" he whispered, as they reached the top. "Romantic spot, eh?" He turned to the right, with Revell following him.

There were five rooms in a row, each with the door closed. Guthrie opened the first, flashed his torch round, and closed the door again. "Nothing there," he said.

The next three rooms were similarly searched; since they were completely bare of furniture it did not take more than a rapid flash of the torch into all the corners. They knew then, of course, as they had perhaps expected from the beginning, that their quest would end at the fifth room. As Guthrie opened the door of it a strange sound came from within—a sound as of a dry, coughing sob. And a second later the rays of the torch lit up, in the furthest corner, the small huddled figure of Mrs. Ellington.

CHAPTER XIII

LUNCH FOR TWO IN SOHO

Two DAYS later, at the hour of ten in the morning, Colin Revell sat up in bed at his Islington lodgings and gloomily surveyed the sunlight streaming in at the sides of the window-blind. He had slept badly—had had troubled, nightmarish dreams that had wakened him from time to time in a sickly glow of perspiration. Now, as his full consciousness returned, the nightmare horrors vanished, but memories took their place—and memories that were hardly to be preferred.

With a yawn of misery he jolted himself out of bed and wound up the paper blind. Islington greeted him with its familiar frowsiness; it was a Friday, and innumerable vendors were pushing their hand-carts towards the Cattle Market. The sun shone mistily out of a sky that was like a curtain of soiled muslin stretched just above the house-tops. Why *did* one live in such a place? Why, in fact, did one live at all? For in his mind's eye he was seeing the cool green lawns of Oakington. Fate had decreed that he should at last sigh wistfully for his Alma Mater.

Mrs. Hewston's tap on the door-panel reminded him of more earthly things. "Are you gettin' up, sir?" she called out, in that tone of sing-song commiseration which Revell found hardest of all to endure.

"Yes," he answered, curtly.

"I do 'ope you're feelin' better, sir."

"Oh yes, Mrs. Hewston, thanks—there's really nothing at all the matter with me."

"That's what you *say*, sir, but it don't seem true, reelly. Any'ow, I'll put the breakfast out for you, sir."

"All right."

She went down again and busied herself with the preparation of the inevitable ham-and-eggs. She was indeed a good deal mystified by her lodger's condition. As she informed her neighbour across the garden fence: " 'E don't 'ardly seem the same person since 'e come back from that school. 'E don't eat, and 'e don't sleep ('cos me bein' a light sleeper and 'is room bein' over mine, I can 'ear 'im movin' about at all hours of the night), and 'e don't read 'is paper—in fact, 'e don't seem to take no interest in anything. Sort of listless, like. It's my belief them murders 'as thoroughly got on 'is nerves. But you'd think 'e'd be more satisfied now, wouldn't you, seein' they've found out as 'ow the woman done them after all?"

"After all" was typical of Mrs. Hewston. It conveyed, without exactly saying so, the impression that all along in her own mind she had suspected the truth. Which was certainly not the case.

Meanwhile, after a wash, but without his customary bath and shave, Revell descended to his ground-floor sitting-room. The thought of ham-and-eggs, by now a little chilled under their cover, was hardly cheering. He turned to the sideboard and brought out a gin-bottle. Before opening it he went to his desk for a ruler and measured the height of the liquid—five and a half inches, and when he had gone to bed it had been six. Mrs. Hewston again, he reflected, without malice, without even irritation. She always did, and she always would, and what the hell did it matter, anyway?

What did anything matter, in fact? He mixed himself a stiff gin-and-tonic and drank it off at a gulp. Then he sat heavily in his chair beside the empty firegrate and closed his eyes. His typewriter, still locked, faced him from the corner where he had dumped it down two days before, and the manuscript of his unfinished epic lay mixed up with a heap of unopened letters on his writing-desk.

But behind his closed eyes there was no relief. Indeed, thoughts and images only crowded more impetuously; he lived again through those frightful moments at the top of the sick-room staircase, felt again that fearful brain-splitting shock when Guthrie had shone his torch through the doorway of the fifth room. What had happened after that was still, as it had been at the time, a vague nightmare in his mind. The woman's wild shriek of defiance, her tigerish attack, Guthrie's ruthless but calm retaliation, and that horrible procession of the three of them up to the moment of his collapse. He still saw her blazing, hunted eyes, and still heard her hoarse screaming. Guthrie, no doubt, had grown used to such scenes, but for him, Revell, they were a memory that would always horrify.

God—how awful it was. And to think that she, whom he had believed the most charming and innocent creature that ever breathed. . . . Oh, damn it all, there was nothing for it but another drink. He rose, and in doing so, noticed the streamer headline on the front page of his morning newspaper. "Mrs. Ellington in Court—Sensational Evidence"—it shouted. The ghouls! He threw the paper across the room where he could not see it. But of course that was really quite useless—the whole business was altogether impossible to escape. Every placard would contain one or other of those fateful words—"Ellington" and "Oakington." . . . Oh yes, there was decidedly nothing for it but another drink.

But while mixing it he heard foosteps and voices outside his room, and in a few moments Mrs. Hewston opened the door with the information, given in the same tone of graveyard sympathy, that a gentleman had called to see him. And before he could give any reply, the nondescript and average figure of Detective Guthrie came into view and, after a friendly nod of dismissal to Mrs. Hewston, stepped past her into the room.

"Well, my lad," he began, with a robust cheerfulness that jarred exquisitely on every one of Revell's nerves, "I thought I'd pay you a morning call. Your landlady's been giving me an awful account of you, but of course I know what landladies are. Nothing much wrong really, I suppose, eh?"

"Oh no." Revell managed a dismal smile. "Have a drink?"

"No thanks. I don't drink in the morning, and neither should you, by the way. Now I come to look at you, though, you do seem a bit dickey. Only natural, of course, after the shock of Wednesday's little affair."

Revell abandoned the mixing of his drink and reestablished himself in the armchair, motioning Guthrie to take the one opposite. The detective did so.

"As a matter of fact," he went on, "I came chiefly to tell you that, for the present, at any rate, I don't think we shall need your evidence. I quite appreciate your scruples in the matter, and it's just possible we may be able to do without you altogether, even at the Assizes. I'll do my best for you, anyhow. We shan't, of course, take up the matter of that attempted attack on you. Too many counts on the indictment never help the prosecution. So you needn't fear you're going to have a lot of limelight turned on you."

Revell nodded. "Thanks. That's good of you."

"Oh, don't thank me—it was all decided at the Yard, but I was very glad, of course, for your sake." His gaze roved round the room. "Look here, don't let me interrupt your breakfast."

"You're not doing—I didn't intend to have any."

"Oh, nonsense, man—you must *eat*."

"*Je n'en vois pas la nécessité.*"

"Oh, don't be funny." Guthrie lifted the cover and peered at the neglected ham-and-eggs. "I must admit it doesn't look very tempting. But Revell, you know, you mustn't let this Oakington business upset you too much. It *is* upsetting, I know—even to a hardened old sleuth like me. I've only arrested three women for murder in twenty years, and I can't say I've grown used to the experience."

"Oh, I shall be all right soon."

"Of course you will. Cheer up, anyhow, and don't take gin for breakfast if you want to live to a decent old age." He stared at the other doubtfully for a moment and then, as if seized with a sudden idea, continued: "Look here, come to lunch with me in town—we'll go to some quiet little place where we can chat, if you like. There's a French restaurant I know near Leicester Square—you'll have an appetite for the food there when you see it, I'm certain. Go up and dress and I'll wait for you down here."

Revell opened his mouth to decline, but the other anticipated him. "Go along now—I won't listen to any refusal. Got a newspaper, by the way, that I can look at while you're getting ready?"

Revell pointed to the newspaper on the floor. "Thanks," replied the detective genially, as he picked it up. "I say, what a splash these papers are making of

the affair! By Jove, it reads well! Run along and take
your time—I shall be quite happy here."

Over an hour later—shortly after noon, to be precise
—Revell and the detective stepped out of a taxi in a
narrow Soho street. Revell's spirits were, if anything, a
shade less doleful. To begin with, he had put on a new
brown suit that his tailor had just finished for him, and
he was distinctly aware that he looked well in it. London, too, was less gloomy than Islington, and even beyond his misery there were the beginnings of hunger.

In the small ante-room to the restaurant the detective
broke his rule and drank a cocktail. Revell stood a second one, and after that the two repaired to a table and
composed what Revell had to admit was a really credit-
able lunch. *Petite Marmite, Sole Mornay, Poulet en Cas-
serole, Canapé Macmahon*—each in turn tempted him
and won. He ate; he enjoyed. And a large bottle of
Liebfraumilch still further improved his attitude towards the world in general.

During the meal he spoke little, but Guthrie kept up
an entertaining flow of talk just faintly tinged with
"shop." Revell found him quite amusing to listen to; indeed, he was rather surprised to find him possessed of
such conversational powers.

At Guthrie's suggestion they took coffee and liqueurs
in a small room at the rear of the restaurant. They had
lunched so early that they had the room to themselves;
it was a sort of lounge, fitted up with tile-topped tables
and deep armchairs. There, in relaxed attitudes, they
made themselves thoroughly comfortable, while good
black coffee, excellent old brandy, and a cigarette, made
even Revell feel that life was partially worth living.

"Good place, this," he commented. "I must come here again."

Guthrie nodded. "Yes, they give you good food and don't worry you with trimmings. Hang your own hat and coat up on the hooks—not an army of retainers to collect sixpences from you. And this lounge place here I've always liked—you're not the first person I've brought, I can assure you. Some pretty queer secrets have been told here."

"Are you going to tell me any?"

Guthrie smiled. "I'm not sure, yet. Are you busy this afternoon, by the way?"

Revell shook his head. "I've nothing on that can't be let go, anyhow." He hadn't, as a matter of fact, anything on at all, and he felt far too drunk to think of bothering about it, even if it had existed.

"Good. *I'm* quite free too, as it happens. I thought, as we may not meet again for some time, you might care to hear a bit about the case. Don't hesitate to say so, though if you'd rather not."

"I'd like to hear about it—I think."

"Yes, and I'd rather you did, too. You're a clever chap, Revell, and you've a clever brain, but I'm not at all sure that if you didn't learn the truth you wouldn't go rearing up some new gigantic theory of your own." He laughed. "Joking apart, you had some ingenious ideas about this Oakington affair. *Too* ingenious, some of them, unfortunately. Yet the real truth, when I managed to get at it, was just as extraordinary. You'll have a pretty good retort when I've finished, Revell—you'll be able to say that nothing you imagined was really any more unlikely than what *did* happen."

Guthrie paused, puffed at his pipe for a few seconds, and then went on: "I could easily, if I wanted to, pose as a Heaven-sent Sherlock in this affair, but I'm not going to. I'd rather be frank—after all, I shall get quite enough credit in the newspapers. They'll boom me no end, which will be very gratifying, of course, but the plain truth is—and I don't mind admitting it to you— that except for spotting the culprit I haven't been particularly right about things. Of course the main thing is to get your man—or woman, even—but I do feel, all the same, rather like a boy who's got the answer right and parts of the sum wrong. By the way, if you're going to listen to the full yarn, I must just put through a telephone call first, if you don't mind—shan't be a minute."

When he came back, after the interlude, he resumed: "Yes, I was fairly wrong as well as fairly right. I was wrong, for instance, about the death of the first boy. I was wrong about Lambourne's death, too. Of course, when I say I was right in this and wrong in that, I only mean that my preconceived theories do or do not tally with the woman's confession. You can say, if you like, that there's no earthly reason why she should be believed now any more than before, and naturally I can't deny it. She's the most consummately clever liar I've ever come across, and quite capable of hoodwinking us to the end if she had anything to gain by it. The point is that she hasn't. We've got her, anyhow, so I can't see why she should stuff us up with a lot of unnecessary yarning."

"Did she volunteer a confession, then?" Revell's voice trembled a little in the varying throes of brandy and memory.

"More or less. I gave her the usual warning, of course, but she began to talk, all the same. She seemed rather to like telling us how clever she'd been. Not unusual, you know, with the superior sort of criminal."

"And how was she? I mean—how did she seem to take it all—the arrest and so on?"

"Oh, not so badly. After the big scene she just caved in—they often do. We took down all she said in shorthand, worked it up into a statement, had it typed, and then got her to sign it. She was quite calm by then. You'd have been astonished—she read it over and put her name at the end as quietly as if had been a cheque for a new hat."

He continued: "Let's clear up a few side-issues first of all. There was Roseveare, to begin with. I admit I began by suspecting him—not tremendously, but on general principles. There was, and perhaps is, something just faintly fishy about him. Sort of man who *could* be crooked, if he wanted to—you know what I mean? He's certainly as cunning as an old fox, but he has his charm."

"*I* rather liked him, anyhow."

"So did I—so did everybody. He *was* likeable. Just the opposite with Ellington, of course. You remember how thrilled we were to discover that Ellington and Roseveare were old pals, as you might say? You, I recollect, hatched a wild theory about something sticky in Roseveare's past that Ellington was blackmailing him about. There wasn't the slightest evidence of any such thing, of course, but you thought it possible—just because you didn't like Ellington. That was part of the whole trouble—nobody *did* like Ellington, and most people were more than willing to believe the worst about him. As a matter of fact, his feeling for Roseveare was marvellously different from what you thought. Roseveare had befriended him in the past, and Ellington had followed him about in sheer gratitude ever since. As faithful as an old mastiff—and about as savage, too."

"Why on earth did his wife marry him, I wonder?"

"Why did he marry her, for that matter? She wasn't too much good, even in those days. There was a scandal over her at the hospital where she was a nurse—I soon found *that* out. She wasn't even technically faithful to Ellington, and it was *that*, I think—some affair that she had with someone—that made him come back to England and ask Roseveare for a job."

"Decent of Roseveare to give him one."

"Oh yes. And it increased, of course, Ellington's gratitude. Mrs. Ellington, too, was pleased, and the first thing she did at Oakington was what more than one woman had done before her—she fell in love with the Head."

"Seriously?"

"The only serious affair she's ever had in her life—so she says. She seems rather proud of it. And I daresay Roseveare, behind his coy and innocent manner, wasn't wholly unsusceptible—in fact, I rather think he was just a little bit of a fool over her. Not much, mind you—and only for a time. He thought she was rather a tragic figure—the poor little colonial girl married to a man who didn't understand her and had brought her back from the great open spaces—all that sort of thing. Ellington hadn't told Roseveare anything against her—he was a man of honour to that extent. So the friendship prospered, and while everything was going on so nicely, Robert Marshall met his death by the accidental fall of a gas-fitting in the dormitory."

"*Accidental?*"

"Yes. *She* says it was, and I always rather thought so

myself. There was never any definite evidence to the contrary, and the murder theory was very far-fetched. Incidentally, I found after careful inquiry amongst some of the boys that there *had* been horseplay in the dormitory—swinging on the gas-brackets and so on, though of course after the boy's death they were all very terrified about admitting it. Yes, I think we'll agree that it was an accident, though a deuced queer one, in view of what it led up to."

He went on, leaning forward a little: "We come now to Lambourne. I needn't say much about him except that he must have the credit or discredit of laying the spark to the train of gunpowder. Really, I'm getting quite eloquent—you must stop me if I fly too high. Anyhow, to return to sober fact, Lambourne in the course of conversation with Mrs. Ellington shortly after the accident, remarked upon the cleverness of such a method of committing murder. He treated her, indeed, to a complete lecture on murder as a fine art—you can imagine him doing it, I daresay. And thus the great idea was born in her mind.

"It certainly *was* great, from her standpoint. She wanted three things—first, to be rid of her husband—second, to have money—and third, to marry Roseveare. Doubtless she assumed that if she managed the first two, the third would follow pretty easily. And after a good deal of careful thought she hit on a plan of campaign which was so diabolically unusual that I excuse you all the theories you ever had in your life, since the real thing was as astounding as any of them. Lambourne, as I said, put murder into her mind, but the elaboration of the idea was wholly hers. And briefly, it was as follows. She would kill the second brother in such a way that guilt would inevitably fall on her husband. But first of all, before doing that, she had another little scheme in hand. About a week after the accident she went to Roseveare and pretended—she was a superb actress, remember—to be upset and hysterical. When Roseveare asked her what was the matter, she began to talk wildly and hysterically about the accident and her husband's connexion with it—hinting that he had been up in the disused sick-rooms a good deal of late, that there was more in the accident than had happened, and so on. Roseveare naturally pooh-poohed the matter, which of course she had expected him to. She knew that as things stood then, the idea was absurd, but she also knew (and this was the diabolical cleverness of her) that if the second brother died by another apparent accident, those wild hints of hers about her husband's connexion with the first affair would recur to Roseveare with terrible significance.

"Here, however, we come to the first example of the lady's weak spot—and that was a tendency to have moments of sheer panic. Roseveare, it seems, had after all been slightly impressed by her hysterical suspicions (she must have acted too well), and had sent for a young man named Colin Revell to look into the matter unofficially. The whole explanation he gave you, by the way, is probably the exact truth. But Mrs. Ellington for some reason had one of her panicky moments when Lambourne told her that someone was already on the track—so she immediately went to Roseveare and told him that she'd been a very naughty and hysterical woman to think such horrid things about her husband, that she hadn't really meant any of them, and that she was very, very sorry! Roseveare believed her only too willingly and dismissed his young inquiry agent at the earliest possible moment. Extraordinary, really, that she should have worried about you at all, Revell. What *had* she to fear? Nothing—yet for all that, your arrival upset her nerve for the time being. I should think you ought to feel rather proud of that."

Revell made no comment, and Guthrie proceeded: "Well, now we pass to the actual murder, and I expect you're thinking it's about time we did. Mrs. Ellington, after you'd gone back, soon regained her lost courage and began to plan her 'murder by accident.' She must have made her detailed plans very quickly and almost at the last minute. She knew that Wilbraham was a swimmer and very often went to the baths on the warm evenings. On the particular day decided upon she contrived, by an apparently casual suggestion to her husband, to have the bath suddenly emptied. (She frankly admitted her responsibility for this, which was a distinctly clever touch.) Then, soon after ten in the evening, when the boy came down to the baths all ready for a swim, she met him, seemingly by accident, and entered with him on some pretext or other. That wouldn't be difficult—they were cousins, remember, and on fairly intimate terms. It wasn't more than half dark, and when they got into the main building a surprise awaited them—the bath was empty. And I'll warrant you she acted that surprise jolly well."

Guthrie's voice had become a little husky; he poured himself out the remains of the now cold coffee and drank it. Then he went on: "Most of this I'm glad to say I deduced. Afterwards, however, I wasn't so lucky. My notion was that she'd suddenly shot the boy while the two of them were standing on the edge of the bath, and had then bashed his head about to disguise the bullet-wound. A pretty awful thing for a woman to do, when you come to think about it, and I'm not really surprised that Mrs. Ellington decided on something much more artistic. She wanted the boy's head to be bashed in completely, and she came to the really brilliant conclusion that the best way to achieve this would be to make him actually fall from that top diving-platform. She did it (I've only her word for it, of course, but it sounds quite credible) by larking about with him for a time and then challenging him for a race up to the top. There are two ladders, you know, approaching the platform from either side, so conditions were quite good for a race. The two reached the top, and there, in the gathering twilight, she whipped out her revolver and shot him so that he fell head foremost on to the tiled floor sixty feet below. There was no need to bash his head in."

Revell shuddered involuntarily. "She had nerve," he muttered.

"Up to a point, yes, but beyond that—however, I shall come to that later on. She had nerve enough to go to the fuse-box and cut the fuses, and to unstrap the boy's wrist-watch (it hadn't been injured in the fall) and climb back with it to the top diving-platform. Oh, and you remember the note you wrote me about the dressing-gown? You thought it might have led to a clue, but I'm afraid I'd given it my fullest attention long before, and there was no clue in it at all. The dressing-gown and slippers found by the side of the bath the next morning were simply the boy's ordinary dressing-gown and slippers, and no amount of perseverance could deduce anything else from 'em. The beauty of it was, you see, that before going up the ladder to the platform, the boy took off his dressing-gown—it's an awkward garment to be wearing in a climbing-race. And, of course, that suited the lady admirably, though I wouldn't say she absolutely foresaw it. Probably she had some alternative plan if circumstances had arisen differently. Anyhow, as it was, there were only the boy's slippers to be removed after the murder, and they hadn't any blood on them.

"I'd better clear up one other small point while I'm about it. I daresay it may have struck you as rather remarkable that nobody heard the shot. One reason, of course, was the fact that the swimming-baths are a fair distance away from the other School buildings. But the chief reason, I think, was that everyone assumed that the affair had happened so much later than it did. You, for instance, went about asking people if they had heard anything during the night—they hadn't, of course. But when I asked them what they had heard during the evening I got quite a lot of interesting answers. Several people, for example, thought they had heard something between ten and eleven o'clock, but there'd been so many noises of all kinds during the day that they hadn't taken much notice. Mrs. Ellington had chosen her time well. Even at Oakington most people are awake at ten-thirty on a midsummer evening, and, though it may seem a paradox, there is always less chance of a noise being noticed when most people are awake than when they are asleep. That night, also, as it happened, workmen had been busy until dusk knocking platforms and grandstands together in readiness for the Oakington Jubilee celebrations, so there was an additional reason for a noise passing unnoticed. I'm not denying that she took a risk, of course. But then, all murderers must do that.

"Now," he continued, after a short pause, "we can turn to what happened immediately after the murder. Mrs. Ellington, of course, went home and to bed. And here comes another factor in the situation. Ellington was a very jealous man, and suspected his wife with Lambourne. That night—the night of the murder, that is—he fancied she had been to visit him. He didn't tax her with it—that wasn't his way—but he brooded and went out to walk his feelings off a little. Meanwhile Lambourne, thinking to have a swim, had gone down to the baths and had found the body there. I don't doubt that it was a fearful shock to him and that he really did do exactly what he said he did. His story, improbable enough in itself, has a certain ring of possibility in it when you think of the man who told it. He suspected murder instantly, but whereas other men would have raised an alarm and declared their suspicions, Lambourne's less straightforward brain accepted the challenge, as it were, and set about to trump the other fellow's card. Believing that Ellington had bashed the boy's head in and taken away the weapon, he fabricated, just as he confessed, the evidence of the cricket-bat. Then he took his stroll and met Ellington. It must have been a dashed queer meeting—Lambourne thinking Ellington had just committed murder, and Ellington thinking Lambourne had just been carrying on with his wife. . . ."

He smiled slightly and continued: "I think you know how *I* came into it all. Somebody sent Colonel Graham, the boy's guardian, an anonymous letter, which he brought to us along with newspaper cuttings of the two inquests. He had suspicions, rather naturally, and I went off to Oakington by the next train to see what I could find out at first-hand.

"You mustn't imagine that Graham's misgivings were taken at their face value. Coincidences do happen, often enough—in fact, they're far less unusual than the murder of two boys by a schoolmaster. Until I found independent evidence of some kind, there was really no case against anybody. To begin with, I spent a few days scouting round the place as a perfect stranger. The first thing to do, if possible, was to interview the writer of the anonymous letter, but it had been typewritten and had a London postmark, so *that* wasn't a very promising line of investigation. I don't know now who wrote it, but I strongly suspect Lambourne. . . . You see, then, my difficulty when I arrived at Oakington. I had nothing at all to go on but the coincidence of the two apparent accidents and an anonymous letter that might or might not be some malicious hoax. All the usual clues that one looks for after a murder had been cleared away beyond hope of discovery. It was really enough to make any detective hold up his hands in despair. Then, just in the nick of time, came the finding of the cricket-bat.

"By then, as you know, there were all sorts of rumours about the place and it was pretty generally known that Scotland Yard was on the job. Two of my men, plain-clothes chaps, of course, found the bat during a casual stroll about the grounds. They weren't looking for anything—they just tumbled across it. It struck me at the time that the thing must have been very badly hidden, and why, after all, should it have been hidden at all and not destroyed? Still, it was evidence, and it enabled us to get a Home Office order for the exhumation of the body, and that, of course, led to the discovery of something that was a complete surprise to us—the bullet in the boy's brain.

"All this must have startled Mrs. Ellington pretty considerably, for her detailed plans to have her husband suspected had been on rather different lines. You see now, perhaps, why I was so secretive about what it was that my men had discovered? Mrs. Ellington knew it couldn't have been the revolver, for she had hidden that carefully. She didn't know, of course, anything about Lambourne's faked cricket-bat clue. All she did know was that *something* had been discovered, *somewhere*, and *somehow*, and she must have spent awful moments wondering whether she had dropped a handkerchief or a spot of face-powder or some other incriminating trace in the swimming-bath. It's not a ·bad plan to give people these awful moments, and it certainly worked with Mrs. Ellington. You said just now that she had nerve, and I agreed that she had, but only up to a point. That's the whole truth of the matter, and I'm rather proud that, having noticed it, I made use of it all along.

"Not, of course, that I suspected her at first. On the contrary, there was a fairly strong case against Ellington himself—the cricket-bat clue, the missing revolver clue, his obvious motive—oh yes, I daresay we might have got a conviction. Only, to me, at any rate, the case seemed too strong—as well as in some ways too weak. We had found the cricket-bat a little too easily. The missing revolver had been confessed to by Ellington himself. The motive—well, it was obvious enough, but wasn't it, in a sort of way, *too* obvious? All this may sound rather vague, but then it *was* only a vague feeling, at the time. I'm quite certain that if Mrs. Ellington's plans hadn't gone astray we should have been provided with some much more convincing clues to implicate her husband—clues that were neither too far-fetched nor too obvious. She was clever enough to get inside the skin of a detective, as it were, and see things with just his critical mind. She was much cleverer than Lambourne—she would never have left such a schoolboyish signpost as a blood-stained cricket-bat lying under a bush. As for what she *would* have left us, if she had had a chance, I can't tell you. But I'll wager it would have pointed to her husband in some subtle and rather indirect way.

"For days, as a matter of fact, I felt like arresting Ellington—on suspicion, at any rate. And yet, in a way, I never felt any enthusiasm about it—subconsciously, even then, I must have known he wasn't guilty."

Guthrie smiled. "We detectives deal in evidence, of course, not in subconscious intuitions. Anyhow, before long, the case against Ellington was decidedly weakened by Brownley's statement that on the fatal night he had seem Lambourne walking towards the Ring with a cricket-bat. I had already, in a way, been rather favourably impressed by Ellington. I didn't like him, and I don't like him, but I didn't think he 'was the 'killer' type and I certainly doubted his ability to plan anything very astute. So, you see, my suspicions veered a a little towards Lambourne. It wasn't easy to think of a motive in his case, but then he was such a queer person that he might well have had a queer enough reason. I did, I admit, think for a time that he might have killed the boy to throw suspicion on Ellington. And it was then that Mrs. Ellington got into her second panic. (Her first, you remember, was when you first arrived at Roseveare's summons.)

"I had questioned Lambourne pretty stiffly, and had got out of him the story of what he really did on the night of the murder. I don't know that I actually disbelieved him, but he evidently thought I did, and was sufficiently upset by it all. What happened after that was in a way superbly logical. He had one of his periodic nerve attacks, Mrs. Ellington ministered to him as on former occasions, and the next day he was found dead of an overdose of veronal. Whereupon Mrs. Ellington volunteered the information that on the previous evening he had made a full confession of murder to her, and had promised to make the same over again to me in the morning. All perfectly feasible and not really improbable, when you come to think about it. Her story and her way of telling it were both admirably convincing. It wasn't legal evidence, of course, but it was moral evidence of a rather unshakeable character. There was really nothing for me to do after listening to it but to shrug my shoulders and shake the dust of Oakington from my feet for ever. Which I did. Or rather, to be more accurate, appeared to do."

Revell leaned forward excitedly. "You mean that you didn't believe her?" he exclaimed.

"Believe her? Not only did I not believe her, but by the time she had got to the end of her yarn I knew for certain that she had murdered the boy herself."

"Good God!"

"Yes, I was certain of it. And it was a single word that told me—a single word of two letters and one syllable—a word that we all use perhaps a hundred times a day. I don't suppose you'll remember it—the really significant things in life are often the least memorable. It was when she was describing how Lambourne had confessed. She did it all so perfectly—except for just that one word. She told how Lambourne and the boy had walked along by the side of the bath as far as the diving-platform, how Lambourne had waited till the boy was standing on the edge facing the empty bath with the platform just above him, and how Lambourne

then had sprung back and shot up at the boy from behind. Revell, when I heard her say that, I had to use all
the self-control I possess—for it told me, as clearly as a
vision from Heaven, that the woman had done it!"

"I'm afraid I don't quite follow the argument."

"No? I'm not surprised—it was a thing I might easily
have missed myself if I hadn't been lucky. Repeated at
second-hand, as I did it just now, I don't suppose it did
exactly leap out at you. But I assure you, Revell, it was
convincing enough to me. That little word 'up' was the
one morsel of truth that the woman couldn't help letting escape."

"The word 'up'? How? I don't remember——"

"Not even now? I'll say it again then. In recounting
Lambourne's confession, she told us that he had 'shot
up at the boy from behind.' Now d'you get it? Why
on earth should she have used that word 'up'? Lambourne's rather a tall fellow—he wouldn't have needed
to shoot up at all, for the boy was only of medium
height. But Mrs. Ellington herself was exceptionally little—hardly five feet, I should say—and for her it would
have had to be a distinctly upward shot. Unconsciously,
while describing Lambourne's supposed movements,
she had had her own in mind, and that one little word,
to anyone who noticed it, was as eloquent as a signed
confession."

He paused and then went on: "Of course you can
laugh if you like and say that it was a preposterously
vast conclusion to draw from a preposterously minute
premise. I quite agree, and I was fully aware of it at
the time. No one knew better than I did that it wouldn't
stand for a minute before a judge and jury. To begin
with, there was no one to swear that she had said it—

and there were a hundred other ways in which a clever counsel could have ridiculed it to pieces. I simply had to pack up and go, although I was perfectly sure that she had committed murder and had managed to palm it off on a poor devil of a suicide.

"And even that wasn't quite so hellish as the real truth, as it happened. Here, again, I depend on nothing but her own statement, but she told this part of it so proudly that it may well be true. It's frightful enough, in all conscience, for, according to her, Lambourne's death was neither suicide nor accident, but murder. And it was she who murdered him!"

Revell stared speechlessly.

"Yes. And the way she managed it was perhaps the most astonishing part of the whole business. She'd got into a panic, you see, with all the inquiries being made, and she had the idea that if someone only confessed everything would be all over. So, knowing that Lambourne was hopelessly in love with her, she went to him and told him nothing less than the whole truth. Yes, it wasn't *he* who confessed to *her*, but she who confessed to *him*. And at the end of it all, working upon his hysteria, she suggested a suicide-pact between them—that they should both make their exit together from a horrible world. She played on Lambourne's shattered nerves like a virtuoso, and in the end, no doubt by making love to him pretty daringly, she had her way. Roseveare, as it happened, came along just then—just a sudden idea to see if Lambourne was asleep, that was all—he listened a few minutes outside the door, heard a bit of the love-making, and walked away in disgust. I gather he had suspected Mrs. Ellington of that sort of thing before."

"Did he tell you all this?"

"Yes—explained it fully after the inquest on Lambourne. His one idea, of course, was and had been all along to avoid any more scandal to.the School."

"Yet he lied to you about that second visit of his to Lambourne's room."

"No, he didn't. It was the fault of my too-precise question. I asked him when he last saw Lambourne, and he answered—quite truthfully—nine o'clock. He didn't see him after that, though he heard him talking."

"It was pretty cool of him, though, to say nothing about it at the inquest."

"No doubt. But, as he told me, he couldn't see how the purely private scandal of an affair between Lambourne and Mrs. Ellington could affect the matter. Anyhow, as he frankly admitted, it was his aim to let the inquest go as smoothly as possible."

Revell nodded. "He's a cool customer, though. The curious thing is that two boys happened to see him as he paid that second visit to Lambourne's room—they were playing chess in the Common Room. They told me about it, and I naturally wondered what on earth the Head had been up to. . . . But please go on—don't let me interrupt the exposition."

"There's not a very great deal to go on to, now. Of course Mrs. Ellington didn't keep her share of the compact. Lambourne took his overdose, but she only pretended to take hers, and the result we all know. But I do hold that it was a rather magnificent improvisation on a theme suggested by mere panic."

"She was a marvellous woman," said Revell slowly.

"In many ways, yes. But for that one tiny slip I might never have suspected her. Even then, if she had kept

her head, I could have proved nothing. She had me on
toast, if she had only known. She had *you*, too, but in
a rather different way, and that's why I didn't make
much of a confidant of you in the matter. In fact I was
very glad for you to think that I'd really been taken in
by it all."

"Oh you were, were you?"

But Guthrie did not immediately reply to the rather
disgruntled remark. He stared for some moments at his
finger-nails and then resumed: "Time's getting on,
Revell—I arranged to meet a friend here this afternoon."
He put a steadying hand on Revell's arm as the latter
moved to get up. "No, no—that wasn't a hint for you
to go—not at all. As a matter of fact, I rather want you
to meet my friend. He should be here any minute now."
He took out his watch, compared it with the clock on
the far side of the room, and lit his pipe again. "Yes,"
he went on, reflectively, "that was a wonderful theory
of yours about Lambourne confessing to save some
other person. The sort of thing, you know, that would
never have occurred to a practical-minded fellow like
myself. But my friend's different. He's more like you—
a bit complicated in the attic. Ah, here he comes, by
Jove."

Guthrie rose to his feet with a welcoming smile, and
Revell, turning round, was astonished to see the benign,
spectacled face of Mr. Geoffrey Lambourne.

CHAPTER XIV

ENTER THIRD (AND LAST)
DETECTIVE

FOR A moment Revell was too bewildered to speak. Then at last, taking the stranger's proffered hand, he managed to gasp: "Mr. Lambourne? But—but—I thought you'd gone back to Vienna?"

Guthrie placed a chair for the stranger to sit between them. "Of course, you've met before, you two—I can see that," he remarked, pleasantly. "I think perhaps we'd better blow our little gaff and have done with it. This isn't really Mr. Geoffrey Lambourne at all—in fact, so far as I know, there isn't any such person in the world. It's my friend and colleague Detective Cannell, of the Yard."

Revell found this rather more bewildering than ever. "But surely I met you at Oakington—" he stammered, staring blankly across the table at the round and absurdly cheerful face of the mystery man.

The latter nodded. "Quite right, Mr. Revell," he said, in that same quiet, soothing voice that Revell had liked instinctively on the occasion of their first meeting. "I *was* Mr. Geoffrey Lambourne for the time being, it is true. I gather that you haven't explained things yet, Guthrie?" he added, turning to his friend.

"Not altogether," Guthrie answered. "The first part took longer than I had expected. I'm terribly hoarse, by the way—I wish you'd do the rest."

"Very well." And the other turned to Revell with a smile. "We owe you a considerable apology, Mr.

242

Revell, but we hope you'll forgive us when you've heard all the details. You may wonder why we trouble to tell you about it now, but the truth is that we both dislike deceiving innocent people, and even when it has to be done we prefer, if possible, to undeceive them afterwards. Yes, that's so—we have a conscience, though you mightn't think so. You see we rather liked you, Mr. Revell, as well, and that made us regret having to make use of you in the way we did. So now, if we can, we shall make amends. You'll drink another brandy with me, I'm sure?"

Revell hardly acquiesced, but the other took his silence for acceptance and gave the order. Then he went on: "Let's see, now, Guthrie, how much does our young friend know?"

"I got as far as Lambourne's supposed confession and my own supposed retirement from the case," replied Guthrie.

"Ah, yes. I'm afraid the plain truth, Mr. Revell, whether Guthrie told it you or not, is that he was pretty badly stumped by this Oakington case. Here was a woman whose husband inherited a large sum of money by the deaths of two boys. The first boy was killed accidentally—therefore she thought to herself— what a fine idea if I kill the other boy and my old man gets hanged for the murder! Nothing left then but the money, which will just suit me . . . that was her idea, wasn't it? But Guthrie, try as he would, couldn't find a shadow of evidence against her. So he came to me, in the end—and not for the first time, let me say. He talked—oh, how he did talk!—all one evening and nearly all one night about the case—we both examined it from every possible angle—we theorised and wrangled and argued—and what did we discover at the end of it all?"

He paused dramatically. Then, in scarcely more than a whisper, he answered: "Nothing."

The waiter came with the brandies and the little interruption gave Cannell time to raise steam, as it were. "Nothing at all, Mr. Revell, I do assure you. That blessed woman had committed the almost perfect crime. There wasn't a ha'porth of legal evidence against her. That little word 'up' that Guthrie has probably told you about—how a counsel would have sneered at it! 'It is the sort of clue you read about in detective-stories,' he would have said. Or else he would have denied that she'd ever used the word. Or else he would have called as witnesses the doctors who performed the autopsy and asked them if from their examination of the body they believed that the shot had been fired in an upward direction. And of course, since the head was so injured that the course of the bullet was quite untraceable, they would have had to reply that there was no evidence of direction at all.

"We also knew just a little bit of scandal about the lady's past, but it wouldn't have helped us in a court of law. No, the fact is, there was simply *nothing* against her that could be proved. And, if you want the truth, there isn't much now. But for that signed statement of hers, I don't know what we could be sure of getting her on—even an attempted murderous assault upon you would want some pretty hard proving. It may interest you to know, by the way, that the weapon that nearly killed you belonged to her husband. He had bought it quite recently in preparation for his life in Kenya."

"And if you *had* been killed," put in Guthrie, "it seems quite possible that Ellington might have been hanged for it. There was method even in that woman's madness."

The other detective resumed: "Ah yes—she had an extraordinary talent for improvisation. If only her nerve had equalled it—if only she had sat tight—laughed at you, Mr. Revell—put out her tongue at you—shrugged her pretty little shoulders and told you, metaphorically, of course, to go to hell! A man might have done it, if ever a man had had her type of genius to begin with. But her nerve was only a woman's. We broke down that nerve—you, me, and Guthrie between us—and that's about all we did do."

Revell shook his head despairingly. "I still don't quite see how you come into this affair, Mr. Cannell. What made you appear at Oakington as Mr. Geoffrey Lambourne?"

"Ah, quite right—that's what I must explain to you. You see, when Guthrie and I found ourselves completely at a deadlock in this case, we decided to use a little guile. We knew there was no hope of a frontal attack, so we planned what the military tacticians call an enveloping movement. And with your unconscious assistance we succeeded."

"I still don't quite follow."

"You will in a moment. The details of the plan were my own, but the conception—the broad outline—was agreed to by both Guthrie and myself. Briefly, our idea was to stand by, unknown to the lady, and watch what happened in a particular set of circumstances. To that end I composed the unique and original character of Geoffrey Lambourne, visited Oakington, saw our heroine, and found her particularly charming. But it was you whom I wanted to see most of all. I wanted to tell you all about my poor, imaginary brother. I must say I was rather proud of the way I carried it through, especially afterwards, when I noted its effect upon you."

"You mean that it was all a pack of lies that you told me?"

"By no means. It was an impersonation founded to a large extent upon the truth. Lambourne really had left a will in Mrs. Ellington's favour, and I'm pretty certain it was for the obvious reason. In fact, though I never met the fellow, I wouldn't mind betting that my own interpretation of him was a good deal more accurate than Guthrie's."

Guthrie interposed: "Quite probably. I never pretend to do that sort of thing. Psychological jerry-building doesn't appeal to me temperamentally, though I admit it has its uses."

Cannell went on: "You see, Mr. Revell, the chief reason for not believing Lambourne guilty was the obvious fact that he wasn't at all the sort of man to do such a thing. Not much of a reason for a chap like Guthrie, but you and I, perhaps, are human enough to let it weigh. At any rate, by telling you the sort of man Lambourne was, I very successfully convinced you that he couldn't have been the criminal, didn't I?"

"You mean that you wanted me to reach that conclusion?"

"Oh, much more than that. I wanted you to begin an entirely new attempt to solve the Oakington riddle on your own. You did so. And all the time I wanted you to become more and more friendly with the pretty lady. You did that, too. I wouldn't have minded if you'd even begun to suspect her a little—in fact, part of my Geoffrey Lambourne impersonation was aimed to lead you gently in that direction. But it didn't work—and, anyhow, everything else went according to plan, so that one little point hardly mattered. The great thing was that sooner or later she should get to know that you

were investigating the case on your own, and that the
whole thing wasn't finished with, as she had supposed.
I guessed she'd play Delilah to your Samson, and a particularly fascinating Delilah, too. Guthrie's not so sure
—her style of looks doesn't appeal to him. He and I,
of course, were watching all the time. We had our eye
on her as she became more and more worried lest her
earnest younger lover should stumble accidentally on
the truth. Rather refined torture for her, when you
come to think of it, but not more than she thoroughly
deserved. Night after night she knew that you were sitting up in your room, pondering over the problem to
which she alone was the answer. You saw her looking
pale and worried, and you thought in your innocence
that her husband was the cause of it. But he wasn't—it
was you yourself."

"Which was what you had intended?"

"Precisely. We knew her weak spot, and when you
know that about your enemy, the battle's half won. Her
weak spot was *fear*. Even when she was in an absolutely
secure position, she couldn't put away from her the terror of being discovered. Twice, under the stress of this
fear, she had given way to panic, and Guthrie and I
were quite certain she would do it a third time. We
were watching and waiting for it, and in the end—
though not in the way we had foreseen—it came."

Revell gulped down what was left of his brandy.
"But I don't like it," he cried, thickly. "I'm beginning
to see your game, and I don't like it a bit. It seems to
me like damned, dirty work. Why couldn't you have
stayed on at Oakington and watched her openly? If
she was so terrified of me, surely she'd have been still
more terrified of you?"

Cannell shook his head. "Think—we were detectives,"

he said quietly. "We had absolutely no *locus standi* at Oakington except as servants of the law. If we had stayed, we should have had to arrest somebody—we should have had to make out a case—and there *was* no case. Don't forget that. How could two detectives foist themselves indefinitely on a public-school merely to terrify someone against whom there wasn't a shadow of legal evidence? Impossible, my dear boy, and I'm sure you can see it was. It was a clear case for private enter-prise—for the gifted amateur—and particularly for the amateur who was an Old Boy of the School and whom the Headmaster could appoint as a temporary secretary without attracting undue attention."

"Good heavens—you mean that Roseveare was in the game, too?"

"He helped us, yes. It was necessary."

Revell glared at his two companions with eyes that grew more angry with every second. "I see," he ex-claimed, not too coherently, for he had drunk quite enough. "I was a decoy, eh? You couldn't get any evi-dence yourself, so you used me to pull the irons out of the fire for you!" His face was flushed; the drink he had taken gave his rage a certain dream-like quality of which he was curiously aware as he continued. "I sup-pose, since you couldn't prove the other murder, you rather hoped she'd murder me to give you a chance of proving that?"

Cannell shook his head sadly. "My dear Revell, that is unjust to us. We had no idea you were in personal danger—we had no idea that her third moment of panic would take the form it did."

"It was your letter to me that sent things off with a bang," interposed Guthrie. "Fortunately I was keeping an eye on your room that night—I'd seen her in it with you a bit before the thing happened. Then when I saw some vague person leaning out of the dormitory window towards yours I guessed something was wrong and I raced up as quick as I could. You owe your life to that bit of spying, Revell."

"And after all," said Cannell, "you weren't hurt—though it was only by the greatest of good fortune, I know——"

A slow, dull pain was tearing through Revell's head. "Not hurt, eh? *Not hurt?* To be fooled all the time—to —to have you two prying and spying—oh, damnation—it's more than I can stand—I'm going—I'm going—" He lurched up from his chair, spilling the remains of the coffee and upsetting the brandy glasses. His head throbbed; there was a monstrous dark blur before his eyes; he had been a fool, he reflected, to have that second brandy.

The two detectives were helping him, one on either side. There was a halt in the restaurant, where Guthrie paid the bill, even for the cocktail that Revell was supposed to have stood him, for Revell was far beyond rememberance of such a detail. He was, in fact, barely sober enough to walk the dozen yards or so across the restaurant to the street-door.

Out on the pavement, while a uniformed porter went for a taxi, he heard Guthrie saying: "By the way, Revell, this Oakington affair's going to make the devil of a stir when it comes on at the Assizes, you know. A Fleet Street friend of mine asked me this morning if I'd do a few articles about it after the trial, but of course I had to refuse—not professional, you know. But I mentioned you—cracked you up no end—said you were absolutely in the thick of it all and knew the dame from A to Z. So I wouldn't be surprised if you hear something pretty soon. 'Mrs. Ellington as I Knew Her'—that sort of thing, you know. And if you take my advice, you won't accept a penny under a hundred quid for the job—they'll give it you if you stand out firm enough."

And he heard Cannell saying: "Don't think too hardly of us. We did the only thing that was to be done, and in the only way it could be done. You helped us tremendously—it all, in the end, depended on you."

He felt them shaking his hand and hoisting him into a taxi; he heard the door bang to; then, with a sideways lurch as the cab started, his head and face lolled on to the unpleasantly-tasting cushions.

He was in a drowsy coma when the cab pulled in at the Islington kerbside. The driver left his perch, opened the door, and with cheerful good humour wakened him and helped him out. "It's all right, sir," he said, as Revell began to fumble in his pockets. "You don't owe me nothin'. The other gentlemen made that all right. Shall I ring the bell, sir, or do you think you can manage? ... Very good, sir, thank you. Mind the step. . . ."

Two minutes later Revell was safely sprawled in his favourite armchair. Mrs. Hewston was out, enjoying her weekly pilgrimage to the grave of the late Mr. Hewston. There was no occupant of the house save the large cat that purred a welcome about his legs.

He was calmer now, and inclined to vary his self-pity with a touch of cynicism. Yes, it had all been the very devil of a business, but a hundred quid for a series of articles was good money, and there was the Head's cheque for twenty-five, too—not ungenerous for three weeks of pretended secretaryship. . . . Mrs. Ellington as he knew her, eh? Well, well, perhaps he could make it readable. He could describe her dark, lustrous eyes, her pert little nose, the queer little romp of laughter that she had sometimes, her soft yielding kiss . . . ah, no, no, he could hardly go as far as that. Not in newspaper articles, at any rate; but it might be worked into his epic poem, somehow.

She was, and he still thought so, the most charming, the cleverest, and altogether the most devilish female he had ever known, and he knew that in later life he would always thrill at the thought that he had almost been murdered by her. What a brain she had had, and what a personality, and what powers of acting and imagination! If only she had turned such qualities to good account instead of bad—if, for example, she had used them to run a West-End beauty parlour or to stand for Parliament. . . .

But he felt himself becoming trite; such reflections, perhaps, were best left to provincial J.P.'s. Later in the day, when he was less drunk, he came to the sudden and startling decision that he would, after all, join that New Guinea expedition. He would write his Mrs. Ellington articles beforehand, and then, gorged with gold, set out for the great open spaces where a man could live a man's life and all that sort of thing. What was more, the youthful hero of his epic poem, surfeited with the tribulations of the world, should join a precisely similar expedition and for a precisely similar reason. He and his author had both, for the time being, done with civilisation. More particularly, even, they had done with women. Women were . . .

Needless, however, to follow the matter into too intense detail. Time, the Great Healer, with the help of a strong gin-and-tonic, had restored considerable ravages by midnight; indeed, it was round about then that Revell completed a stanza which expressed, through the narrative experience of his hero, what he believed to be the exact truth of the matter. He thought of Mrs. Ellington, no longer with bitterness, but with a tranquil, almost an ennobling sadness of mind and heart. . . .

" . . . And when he thought of her, a strange emotion
    Linked her mind with lands he might explore;
She was the mystic continent and ocean,
    The far-flung island and the distant shore;
And in a dream he drank the magic potion,
    Sweeter than wine, that made his spirit soar
Till he was Cook, Columbus, and Cabot,
    Frobisher, Livingstone—in fact, the lot!"

A CATALOGUE OF
SELECTED DOVER BOOKS
IN ALL FIELDS OF INTEREST

A CATALOGUE OF SELECTED DOVER
BOOKS IN ALL FIELDS OF INTEREST

RACKHAM'S COLOR ILLUSTRATIONS FOR WAGNER'S RING. Rackham's finest mature work—all 64 full-color watercolors in a faithful and lush interpretation of the *Ring*. Full-sized plates on coated stock of the paintings used by opera companies for authentic staging of Wagner. Captions aid in following complete Ring cycle. Introduction. 64 illustrations plus vignettes. 72pp. 8⅝ x 11¼. 23779-6 Pa. $6.00

CONTEMPORARY POLISH POSTERS IN FULL COLOR, edited by Joseph Czestochowski. 46 full-color examples of brilliant school of Polish graphic design, selected from world's first museum (near Warsaw) dedicated to poster art. Posters on circuses, films, plays, concerts all show cosmopolitan influences, free imagination. Introduction. 48pp. 9⅜ x 12¼. 23780-X Pa. $6.00

GRAPHIC WORKS OF EDVARD MUNCH, Edvard Munch. 90 haunting, evocative prints by first major Expressionist artist and one of the greatest graphic artists of his time: *The Scream, Anxiety, Death Chamber, The Kiss, Madonna*, etc. Introduction by Alfred Werner. 90pp. 9 x 12. 23765-6 Pa. $5.00

THE GOLDEN AGE OF THE POSTER, Hayward and Blanche Cirker. 70 extraordinary posters in full colors, from Maitres de l'Affiche, Mucha, Lautrec, Bradley, Cheret, Beardsley, many others. Total of 78pp. 9⅜ x 12¼. 22753-7 Pa. $5.95

THE NOTEBOOKS OF LEONARDO DA VINCI, edited by J. P. Richter. Extracts from manuscripts reveal great genius; on painting, sculpture, anatomy, sciences, geography, etc. Both Italian and English. 186 ms. pages reproduced, plus 500 additional drawings, including studies for *Last Supper*, Sforza monument, etc. 860pp. 7⅞ x 10¾. (Available in U.S. only) 22572-0, 22573-9 Pa., Two-vol. set $15.90

THE CODEX NUTTALL, as first edited by Zelia Nuttall. Only inexpensive edition, in full color, of a pre-Columbian Mexican (Mixtec) book. 88 color plates show kings, gods, heroes, temples, sacrifices. New explanatory, historical introduction by Arthur G. Miller. 96pp. 11⅜ x 8½. (Available in U.S. only) 23168-2 Pa. $7.50

UNE SEMAINE DE BONTÉ, A SURREALISTIC NOVEL IN COLLAGE, Max Ernst. Masterpiece created out of 19th-century periodical illustrations, explores worlds of terror and surprise. Some consider this Ernst's greatest work. 208pp. 8⅛ x 11. 23252-2 Pa. $5.00

DRAWINGS OF WILLIAM BLAKE, William Blake. 92 plates from Book of Job, *Divine Comedy, Paradise Lost,* visionary heads, mythological figures, Laocoon, etc. Selection, introduction, commentary by Sir Geoffrey Keynes. 178pp. 8⅛ x 11. 22303-5 Pa. $4.00

ENGRAVINGS OF HOGARTH, William Hogarth. 101 of Hogarth's greatest works: *Rake's Progress, Harlot's Progress, Illustrations for Hudibras, Before and After, Beer Street and Gin Lane,* many more. Full commentary. 256pp. 11 x 13¾. 22479-1 Pa. $7.95

DAUMIER: 120 GREAT LITHOGRAPHS, Honore Daumier. Wide-ranging collection of lithographs by the greatest caricaturist of the 19th century. Concentrates on eternally popular series on lawyers, on married life, on liberated women, etc. Selection, introduction, and notes on plates by Charles F. Ramus. Total of 158pp. 9⅜ x 12¼. 23512-2 Pa. $5.50

DRAWINGS OF MUCHA, Alphonse Maria Mucha. Work reveals drafts-man of highest caliber: studies for famous posters and paintings, render-ings for book illustrations and ads, etc. 70 works, 9 in color; including 6 items not drawings. Introduction. List of illustrations. 72pp. 9⅜ x 12¼. (Available in U.S. only) 23672-2 Pa. $4.00

GIOVANNI BATTISTA PIRANESI: DRAWINGS IN THE PIERPONT MORGAN LIBRARY, Giovanni Battista Piranesi. For first time ever all of Morgan Library's collection, world's largest. 167 illustrations of rare Piranesi drawings—archeological, architectural, decorative and visionary. Essay, detailed list of drawings, chronology, captions. Edited by Felice Stampfle. 144pp. 9⅜ x 12¼. 23714-1 Pa. $7.50

NEW YORK ETCHINGS (1905-1949), John Sloan. All of important American artist's N.Y. life etchings. 67 works include some of his best art; also lively historical record—Greenwich Village, tenement scenes. Edited by Sloan's widow. Introduction and captions. 79pp. 8⅜ x 11¼. 23651-X Pa. $4.00

CHINESE PAINTING AND CALLIGRAPHY: A PICTORIAL SURVEY, Wan-go Weng. 69 fine examples from John M. Crawford's matchless private collection: landscapes, birds, flowers, human figures, etc., plus calligraphy. Every basic form included: hanging scrolls, handscrolls, album leaves, fans, etc. 109 illustrations. Introduction. Captions. 192pp. 8⅞ x 11¾. 23707-9 Pa. $7.95

DRAWINGS OF REMBRANDT, edited by Seymour Slive. Updated Lipp-mann, Hofstede de Groot edition, with definitive scholarly apparatus. All portraits, biblical sketches, landscapes, nudes, Oriental figures, classical studies, together with selection of work by followers. 550 illustrations. Total of 630pp. 9⅛ x 12¼. 21485-0, 21486-9 Pa., Two-vol. set $14.00

THE DISASTERS OF WAR, Francisco Goya. 83 etchings record horrors of Napoleonic wars in Spain and war in general. Reprint of 1st edition, plus 3 additional plates. Introduction by Philip Hofer. 97pp. 9⅜ x 8¼. 21872-4 Pa. $3.75

THE EARLY WORK OF AUBREY BEARDSLEY, Aubrey Beardsley. 157 plates, 2 in color: *Manon Lescaut, Madame Bovary, Morte Darthur, Salome,* other. Introduction by H. Marillier. 182pp. 8⅛ x 11. 21816-3 Pa. $4.50

THE LATER WORK OF AUBREY BEARDSLEY, Aubrey Beardsley. Exotic masterpieces of full maturity: *Venus and Tannhauser, Lysistrata, Rape of the Lock, Volpone,* Savoy material, etc. 174 plates, 2 in color. 186pp. 8⅛ x 11. 21817-1 Pa. $4.50

THOMAS NAST'S CHRISTMAS DRAWINGS, Thomas Nast. Almost all Christmas drawings by creator of image of Santa Claus as we know it, and one of America's foremost illustrators and political cartoonists. 66 illustrations. 3 illustrations in color on covers. 96pp. 8⅜ x 11¼. 23660-9 Pa. $3.50

THE DORÉ ILLUSTRATIONS FOR DANTE'S DIVINE COMEDY, Gustave Doré. All 135 plates from Inferno, Purgatory, Paradise; fantastic tortures, infernal landscapes, celestial wonders. Each plate with appropriate (translated) verses. 141pp. 9 x 12. 23231-X Pa. $4.50

DORÉ'S ILLUSTRATIONS FOR RABELAIS, Gustave Doré. 252 striking illustrations of *Gargantua and Pantagruel* books by foremost 19th-century illustrator. Including 60 plates, 192 delightful smaller illustrations. 153pp. 9 x 12. 23656-0 Pa. $5.00

LONDON: A PILGRIMAGE, Gustave Doré, Blanchard Jerrold. Squalor, riches, misery, beauty of mid-Victorian metropolis; 55 wonderful plates, 125 other illustrations, full social, cultural text by Jerrold. 191pp. of text. 9⅜ x 12¼. 22306-X Pa. $6.00

THE RIME OF THE ANCIENT MARINER, Gustave Doré, S. T. Coleridge. Dore's finest work, 34 plates capture moods, subtleties of poem. Full text. Introduction by Millicent Rose. 77pp. 9¼ x 12. 22305-1 Pa. $3.00

THE DORE BIBLE ILLUSTRATIONS, Gustave Doré. All wonderful, detailed plates: Adam and Eve, Flood, Babylon, Life of Jesus, etc. Brief King James text with each plate. Introduction by Millicent Rose. 241 plates. 241pp. 9 x 12. 23004-X Pa. $5.00

THE COMPLETE ENGRAVINGS, ETCHINGS AND DRYPOINTS OF ALBRECHT DURER. "Knight, Death and Devil"; "Melencolia," and more—all Dürer's known works in all three media, including 6 works formerly attributed to him. 120 plates. 235pp. 8⅜ x 11¼. 22851-7 Pa. $6.50

MAXIMILIAN'S TRIUMPHAL ARCH, Albrecht Dürer and others. Incredible monument of woodcut art: 8 foot high elaborate arch—heraldic figures, humans, battle scenes, fantastic elements—that you can assemble yourself. Printed on one side, layout for assembly. 143pp. 11 x 16. 21451-6 Pa. $5.00

CATALOGUE OF DOVER BOOKS

THE COMPLETE WOODCUTS OF ALBRECHT DURER, edited by
Dr. W. Kurth. 346 in all: "Old Testament," "St. Jerome," "Passion,"
"Life of Virgin," Apocalypse," many others. Introduction by Campbell
Dodgson. 285pp. 8½ x 12¼.   21097-9 Pa. $6.95

DRAWINGS OF ALBRECHT DURER, edited by Heinrich Wölfflin. 81
plates show development from youth to full style. Many favorites; many
new. Introduction by Alfred Werner. 96pp. 8⅛ x 11.   22352-3 Pa. $4.00

THE HUMAN FIGURE, Albrecht Dürer. Experiments in various tech-
niques—stereometric, progressive proportional, and others. Also life studies
that rank among finest ever done. Complete reprinting of Dresden Sketch-
book. 170 plates. 355pp. 8⅜ x 11¼.   21042-1 Pa. $6.95

OF THE JUST SHAPING OF LETTERS, Albrecht Dürer. Renaissance
artist explains design of Roman majuscules by geometry, also Gothic lower
and capitals. Grolier Club edition. 43pp. 7⅞ x 10¾   21306-4 Pa. $2.50

TEN BOOKS ON ARCHITECTURE, Vitruvius. The most important book
ever written on architecture. Early Roman aesthetics, technology, classical
orders, site selection, all other aspects. Stands behind everything since.
Morgan translation. 331pp. 5⅜ x 8½.   20645-9 Pa. $3.75

THE FOUR BOOKS OF ARCHITECTURE, Andrea Palladio. 16th-century
classic responsible for Palladian movement and style. Covers classical architectural remains, Renaissance revivals, classical orders, etc. 1738 Ware
English edition. Introduction by A. Placzek. 216 plates. 110pp. of text.
9½ x 12¾.   21308-0 Pa. $7.50

HORIZONS, Norman Bel Geddes. Great industrialist stage designer, "father
of streamlining," on application of aesthetics to transportation, amusement,
architecture, etc. 1932 prophetic account; function, theory, specific projects.
222 illustrations. 312pp. 7⅞ x 10¾.   23514-9 Pa. $6.95

FRANK LLOYD WRIGHT'S FALLINGWATER, Donald Hoffmann. Full,
illustrated story of conception and building of Wright's masterwork at
Bear Run, Pa. 100 photographs of site, construction, and details of completed structure. 112pp. 9¼ x 10.   23671-4 Pa. $5.00

THE ELEMENTS OF DRAWING, John Ruskin. Timeless classic by great
Viltorian; starts with basic ideas, works through more difficult. Many
practical exercises. 48 illustrations. Introduction by Lawrence Campbell.
228pp. 5⅜ x 8½.   22730-8 Pa. $2.75

GIST OF ART, John Sloan. Greatest modern American teacher, Art Students League, offers innumerable hints, instructions, guided comments to
help you in painting. Not a formal course. 46 illustrations. Introduction
by Helen Sloan. 200pp. 5⅜ x 8½.   23435-5 Pa. $3.50

THE ANATOMY OF THE HORSE, George Stubbs. Often considered the great masterpiece of animal anatomy. Full reproduction of 1766 edition, plus prospectus; original text and modernized text. 36 plates. Introduction by Eleanor Garvey. 121pp. 11 x 14¾.   23402-9 Pa. $6.00

BRIDGMAN'S LIFE DRAWING, George B. Bridgman. More than 500 illustrative drawings and text teach you to abstract the body into its major masses, use light and shade, proportion; as well as specific areas of anatomy, of which Bridgman is master. 192pp. 6½ x 9¼. (Available in U.S. only)
22710-3 Pa. $2.50

ART NOUVEAU DESIGNS IN COLOR, Alphonse Mucha, Maurice Verneuil, Georges Auriol. Full-color reproduction of *Combinaisons orne-mentales* (c. 1900) by Art Nouveau masters. Floral, animal, geometric, interlacings, swashes—borders, frames, spots—all incredibly beautiful. 60 plates, hundreds of designs. 9⅜ x 8-1/16.   22885-1 Pa. $4.00

FULL-COLOR FLORAL DESIGNS IN THE ART NOUVEAU STYLE, E. A. Seguy. 166 motifs, on 40 plates, from *Les fleurs et leurs applications decoratives* (1902): borders, circular designs, repeats, allovers, "spots." All in authentic Art Nouveau colors. 48pp. 9⅜ x 12¼.
23439-8 Pa. $5.00

A DIDEROT PICTORIAL ENCYCLOPEDIA OF TRADES AND IN-DUSTRY, edited by Charles C. Gillispie. 485 most interesting plates from the great French Encyclopedia of the 18th century show hundreds of working figures, artifacts, process, land and cityscapes; glassmaking, paper-making, metal extraction, construction, weaving, making furniture, clothing, wigs, dozens of other activities. Plates fully explained. 920pp. 9 x 12.
22284-5, 22285-3 Clothbd., Two-vol. set $40.00

HANDBOOK OF EARLY ADVERTISING ART, Clarence P. Hornung. Largest collection of copyright-free early and antique advertising art ever compiled. Over 6,000 illustrations, from Franklin's time to the 1890's for special effects, novelty. Valuable source, almost inexhaustible.
Pictorial Volume. Agriculture, the zodiac, animals, autos, birds, Christmas, fire engines, flowers, trees, musical instruments, ships, games and sports, much more. Arranged by subject matter and use. 237 plates. 288pp. 9 x 12.
20122-8 Clothbd. $13.50

Typographical Volume. Roman and Gothic faces ranging from 10 point to 300 point, "Barnum," German and Old English faces, script, logotypes, scrolls and flourishes, 1115 ornamental initials, 67 complete alphabets, more. 310 plates. 320pp. 9 x 12.   20123-6 Clothbd. $13.50

CALLIGRAPHY (CALLIGRAPHIA LATINA), J. G. Schwandner. High point of 18th-century ornamental calligraphy. Very ornate initials, scrolls, borders, cherubs, birds, lettered examples. 172pp. 9 x 13.
20475-8 Pa. $6.00

ART FORMS IN NATURE, Ernst Haeckel. Multitude of strangely beautiful natural forms: Radiolaria, Foraminifera, jellyfishes, fungi, turtles, bats, etc. All 100 plates of the 19th-century evolutionist's *Kunstformen der Natur* (1904). 100pp. 9⅜ x 12¼.   22987-4 Pa. $4.50

CHILDREN: A PICTORIAL ARCHIVE FROM NINETEENTH-CENTURY SOURCES, edited by Carol Belanger Grafton. 242 rare, copyright-free wood engravings for artists and designers. Widest such selection available. All illustrations in line. 119pp. 8⅜ x 11¼.
23694-3 Pa. $3.50

WOMEN: A PICTORIAL ARCHIVE FROM NINETEENTH-CENTURY SOURCES, edited by Jim Harter. 391 copyright-free wood engravings for artists and designers selected from rare periodicals. Most extensive such collection available. All illustrations in line. 128pp. 9 x 12.
23703-6 Pa. $4.00

ARABIC ART IN COLOR, Prisse d'Avennes. From the greatest ornamentalists of all time—50 plates in color, rarely seen outside the Near East, rich in suggestion and stimulus. Includes 4 plates on covers. 46pp. 9⅜ x 12¼.   23658-7 Pa. $6.00

AUTHENTIC ALGERIAN CARPET DESIGNS AND MOTIFS, edited by June Beveridge. Algerian carpets are world famous. Dozens of geometrical motifs are charted on grids, color-coded, for weavers, needleworkers, craftsmen, designers. 53 illustrations plus 4 in color. 48pp. 8¼ x 11. (Available in U.S. only)   23650-1 Pa. $1.75

DICTIONARY OF AMERICAN PORTRAITS, edited by Hayward and Blanche Cirker. 4000 important Americans, earliest times to 1905, mostly in clear line. Politicians, writers, soldiers, scientists, inventors, industrialists, Indians, Blacks, women, outlaws, etc. Identificatory information. 756pp. 9¼ x 12¾.   21823-6 Clothbd. $40.00

HOW THE OTHER HALF LIVES, Jacob A. Riis. Journalistic record of filth, degradation, upward drive in New York immigrant slums, shops, around 1900. New edition includes 100 original Riis photos, monuments of early photography. 233pp. 10 x 7⅞.   22012-5 Pa. $6.00

NEW YORK IN THE THIRTIES, Berenice Abbott. Noted photographer's fascinating study of city shows new buildings that have become famous and old sights that have disappeared forever. Insightful commentary. 97 photographs. 97pp. 11⅜ x 10.   22967-X Pa. $4.50

MEN AT WORK, Lewis W. Hine. Famous photographic studies of construction workers, railroad men, factory workers and coal miners. New supplement of 18 photos on Empire State building construction. New introduction by Jonathan L. Doherty. Total of 69 photos. 63pp. 8 x 10¾.
23475-4 Pa. $3.00

THE DEPRESSION YEARS AS PHOTOGRAPHED BY ARTHUR ROTH-STEIN, Arthur Rothstein. First collection devoted entirely to the work of outstanding 1930s photographer: famous dust storm photo, ragged children, unemployed, etc. 120 photographs. Captions. 119pp. 9¼ x 10¾.
23590-4 Pa. $5.00

CAMERA WORK: A PICTORIAL GUIDE, Alfred Stieglitz. All 559 illustrations and plates from the most important periodical in the history of art photography, Camera Work (1903-17). Presented four to a page, reduced in size but still clear, in strict chronological order, with complete captions. Three indexes. Glossary. Bibliography. 176pp. 8⅜ x 11¼.
23591-2 Pa. $6.95

ALVIN LANGDON COBURN, PHOTOGRAPHER, Alvin L. Coburn. Revealing autobiography by one of greatest photographers of 20th century gives insider's version of Photo-Secession, plus comments on his own work. 77 photographs by Coburn. Edited by Helmut and Alison Gernsheim. 160pp. 8⅛ x 11.
23685-4 Pa. $6.00

NEW YORK IN THE FORTIES, Andreas Feininger. 162 brilliant photographs by the well-known photographer, formerly with Life magazine, show commuters, shoppers, Times Square at night, Harlem nightclub, Lower East Side, etc. Introduction and full captions by John von Hartz. 181pp. 9¼ x 10¾.
23585-8 Pa. $6.00

GREAT NEWS PHOTOS AND THE STORIES BEHIND THEM, John Faber. Dramatic volume of 140 great news photos, 1855 through 1976, and revealing stories behind them, with both historical and technical information. Hindenburg disaster, shooting of Oswald, nomination of Jimmy Carter, etc. 160pp. 8¼ x 11.
23667-6 Pa. $5.00

THE ART OF THE CINEMATOGRAPHER, Leonard Maltin. Survey of American cinematography history and anecdotal interviews with 5 masters—Arthur Miller, Hal Mohr, Hal Rosson, Lucien Ballard, and Conrad Hall. Very large selection of behind-the-scenes production photos. 105 photographs. Filmographies. Index. Originally Behind the Camera. 144pp. 8¼ x 11.
23686-2 Pa. $5.00

DESIGNS FOR THE THREE-CORNERED HAT (LE TRICORNE), Pablo Picasso. 32 fabulously rare drawings—including 31 color illustrations of costumes and accessories—for 1919 production of famous ballet. Edited by Parmenia Migel, who has written new introduction. 48pp. 9⅜ x 12¼. (Available in U.S. only)
23709-5 Pa. $5.00

NOTES OF A FILM DIRECTOR, Sergei Eisenstein. Greatest Russian filmmaker explains montage, making of Alexander Nevsky, aesthetics; comments on self, associates, great rivals (Chaplin), similar material. 78 illustrations. 240pp. 5⅜ x 8½.
22392-2 Pa. $4.50

HOLLYWOOD GLAMOUR PORTRAITS, edited by John Kobal. 145 photos capture the stars from 1926-49, the high point in portrait photography. Gable, Harlow, Bogart, Bacall, Hedy Lamarr, Marlene Dietrich, Robert Montgomery, Marlon Brando, Veronica Lake; 94 stars in all. Full background on photographers, technical aspects, much more. Total of 160pp. 8⅜ x 11¼.   23352-9 Pa. $5.00

THE NEW YORK STAGE: FAMOUS PRODUCTIONS IN PHOTOGRAPHS, edited by Stanley Appelbaum. 148 photographs from Museum of City of New York show 142 plays, 1883-1939. *Peter Pan, The Front Page, Dead End, Our Town,* O'Neill, hundreds of actors and actresses, etc. Full indexes. 154pp. 9½ x 10.   23241-7 Pa. $4.50

MASTERS OF THE DRAMA, John Gassner. Most comprehensive history of the drama, every tradition from Greeks to modern Europe and America, including Orient. Covers 800 dramatists, 2000 plays; biography, plot summaries, criticism, theatre history, etc. 77 illustrations. 890pp. 5⅜ x 8½.
20100-7 Clothbd. $10.00

THE GREAT OPERA STARS IN HISTORIC PHOTOGRAPHS, edited by James Camner. 343 portraits from the 1850s to the 1940s: Tamburini, Mario, Caliapin, Jeritza, Melchior, Melba, Patti, Pinza, Schipa, Caruso, Farrar, Steber, Gobbi, and many more—270 performers in all. Index. 199pp. 8⅜ x 11¼.   23575-0 Pa. $6.50

J. S. BACH, Albert Schweitzer. Great full-length study of Bach, life, background to music, music, by foremost modern scholar. Ernest Newman translation. 650 musical examples. Total of 928pp. 5⅜ x 8½. (Available in U.S. only)   21631-4, 21632-2 Pa., Two-vol. set $9.00

COMPLETE PIANO SONATAS, Ludwig van Beethoven. All sonatas in the fine Schenker edition, with fingering, analytical material. One of best modern editions. Total of 615pp. 9 x 12. (Available in U.S. only)
23134-8, 23135-6 Pa., Two-vol. set $13.00

KEYBOARD MUSIC, J. S. Bach. Bach-Gesellschaft edition. For harpsichord, piano, other keyboard instruments. English Suites, French Suites, Six Partitas, Goldberg Variations, Two-Part Inventions, Three-Part Sinfonias. 312pp. 8⅛ x 11. (Available in U.S. only)   22360-4 Pa. $5.50

FOUR SYMPHONIES IN FULL SCORE, Franz Schubert. Schubert's four most popular symphonies: No. 4 in C Minor ("Tragic"); No. 5 in B-flat Major; No. 8 in B Minor ("Unfinished"); No. 9 in C Major ("Great"). Breitkopf & Hartel edition. Study score. 261pp. 9⅜ x 12¼.
23681-1 Pa. $6.50

THE AUTHENTIC GILBERT & SULLIVAN SONGBOOK, W. S. Gilbert, A. S. Sullivan. Largest selection available; 92 songs, uncut, original keys, in piano rendering approved by Sullivan. Favorites and lesser-known fine numbers. Edited with plot synopses by James Spero. 3 illustrations. 399pp. 9 x 12.   23482-7 Pa. $7.95

PRINCIPLES OF ORCHESTRATION, Nikolay Rimsky-Korsakov. Great classical orchestrator provides fundamentals of tonal resonance, progression of parts, voice and orchestra, tutti effects, much else in major document. 330pp. of musical excerpts. 489pp. 6½ x 9¼.   21266-1 Pa. $6.00

TRISTAN UND ISOLDE, Richard Wagner. Full orchestral score with complete instrumentation. Do not confuse with piano reduction. Commentary by Felix Mottl, great Wagnerian conductor and scholar. Study score. 655pp. 8⅛ x 11.   22915-7 Pa. $12.50

REQUIEM IN FULL SCORE, Giuseppe Verdi. Immensely popular with choral groups and music lovers. Republication of edition published by C. F. Peters, Leipzig, n. d. German frontmaker in English translation. Glossary. Text in Latin. Study score. 204pp. 9⅜ x 12¼.
23682-X Pa. $6.00

COMPLETE CHAMBER MUSIC FOR STRINGS, Felix Mendelssohn. All of Mendelssohn's chamber music: Octet, 2 Quintets, 6 Quartets, and Four Pieces for String Quartet. (Nothing with piano is included). Complete works edition (1874-7). Study score. 283 pp. 9⅜ x 12¼.
23679-X Pa. $6.95

POPULAR SONGS OF NINETEENTH-CENTURY AMERICA, edited by Richard Jackson. 64 most important songs: "Old Oaken Bucket," "Arkansas Traveler," "Yellow Rose of Texas," etc. Authentic original sheet music, full introduction and commentaries. 290pp. 9 x 12.   23270-0 Pa. $6.00

COLLECTED PIANO WORKS, Scott Joplin. Edited by Vera Brodsky Lawrence. Practically all of Joplin's piano works—rags, two-steps, marches, waltzes, etc., 51 works in all. Extensive introduction by Rudi Blesh. Total of 345pp. 9 x 12.   23106-2 Pa. $13.50

BASIC PRINCIPLES OF CLASSICAL BALLET, Agrippina Vaganova. Great Russian theoretician, teacher explains methods for teaching classical ballet; incorporates best from French, Italian, Russian schools. 118 illustrations. 175pp. 5⅜ x 8½.   22036-2 Pa. $2.00

CHINESE CHARACTERS, L. Wieger. Rich analysis of 2300 characters according to traditional systems into primitives. Historical-semantic analysis to phonetics (Classical Mandarin) and radicals. 820pp. 6⅛ x 9¼.
21321-8 Pa. $8.95

EGYPTIAN LANGUAGE: EASY LESSONS IN EGYPTIAN HIERO-GLYPHICS, E. A. Wallis Budge. Foremost Egyptologist offers Egyptian grammar, explanation of hieroglyphics, many reading texts, dictionary of symbols. 246pp. 5 x 7½. (Available in U.S. only)
21394-3 Clothbd. $7.50

AN ETYMOLOGICAL DICTIONARY OF MODERN ENGLISH, Ernest Weekley. Richest, fullest work, by foremost British lexicographer. Detailed word histories. Inexhaustible. Do not confuse this with Concise Etymological Dictionary, which is abridged. Total of 856pp. 6½ x 9¼.
21873-2, 21874-0 Pa., Two-vol. set $10.00

A MAYA GRAMMAR, Alfred M. Tozzer. Practical, useful English-language grammar by the Harvard anthropologist who was one of the three greatest American scholars in the area of Maya culture. Phonetics, grammatical processes, syntax, more. 301pp. 5⅜ x 8½.   23465-7 Pa. $4.00

THE JOURNAL OF HENRY D. THOREAU, edited by Bradford Torrey, F. H. Allen. Complete reprinting of 14 volumes, 1837-61, over two million words; the sourcebooks for *Walden*, etc. Definitive. All original sketches, plus 75 photographs. Introduction by Walter Harding. Total of 1804pp. 8½ x 12¼.   20312-3, 20313-1 Clothbd., Two-vol. set $50.00

CLASSIC GHOST STORIES, Charles Dickens and others. 18 wonderful stories you've wanted to reread: "The Monkey's Paw," "The House and the Brain," "The Upper Berth," "The Signalman," "Dracula's Guest," "The Tapestried Chamber," etc. Dickens, Scott, Mary Shelley, Stoker, etc. 330pp. 5⅜ x 8½.   20735-8 Pa. $3.50

SEVEN SCIENCE FICTION NOVELS, H. G. Wells. Full novels. *First Men in the Moon, Island of Dr. Moreau, War of the Worlds, Food of the Gods, Invisible Man, Time Machine, In the Days of the Comet.* A basic science-fiction library. 1015pp. 5⅜ x 8½. (Available in U.S. only)
20264-X Clothbd. $8.95

ARMADALE, Wilkie Collins. Third great mystery novel by the author of *The Woman in White* and *The Moonstone.* Ingeniously plotted narrative shows an exceptional command of character, incident and mood. Original magazine version with 40 illustrations. 597pp. 5⅜ x 8½.
23429-0 Pa. $5.00

MASTERS OF MYSTERY, H. Douglas Thomson. The first book in English (1931) devoted to history and aesthetics of detective story. Poe, Doyle, LeFanu, Dickens, many others, up to 1930. New introduction and notes by E. F. Bleiler. 288pp. 5⅜ x 8½. (Available in U.S. only)
23606-4 Pa. $4.00

FLATLAND, E. A. Abbott. Science-fiction classic explores life of 2-D being in 3-D world. Read also as introduction to thought about hyperspace. Introduction by Banesh Hoffmann. 16 illustrations. 103pp. 5⅜ x 8½.
20001-9 Pa. $1.50

THREE SUPERNATURAL NOVELS OF THE VICTORIAN PERIOD, edited, with an introduction, by E. F. Bleiler. Reprinted complete and unabridged, three great classics of the supernatural: *The Haunted Hotel* by Wilkie Collins, *The Haunted House at Latchford* by Mrs. J. H. Riddell, and *The Lost Stradivarious* by J. Meade Falkner. 325pp. 5⅜ x 8½.
22571-2 Pa. $4.00

AYESHA: THE RETURN OF "SHE," H. Rider Haggard. Virtuoso sequel featuring the great mythic creation, Ayesha, in an adventure that is fully as good as the first book, *She.* Original magazine version, with 47 original illustrations by Maurice Greiffenhagen. 189pp. 6½ x 9¼.
23649-8 Pa. $3.00

UNCLE SILAS, J. Sheridan LeFanu. Victorian Gothic mystery novel, considered by many best of period, even better than Collins or Dickens. Wonderful psychological terror. Introduction by Frederick Shroyer. 436pp. 5⅜ x 8½. 21715-9 Pa. $4.00

JURGEN, James Branch Cabell. The great erotic fantasy of the 1920's that delighted thousands, shocked thousands more. Full final text, Lane edition with 13 plates by Frank Pape. 346pp. 5⅜ x 8½. 23507-6 Pa. $4.00

THE CLAVERINGS, Anthony Trollope. Major novel, chronicling aspects of British Victorian society, personalities. Reprint of Cornhill serialization, 16 plates by M. Edwards; first reprint of full text. Introduction by Norman Donaldson. 412pp. 5⅜ x 8½. 23464-9 Pa. $5.00

KEPT IN THE DARK, Anthony Trollope. Unusual short novel about Victorian morality and abnormal psychology by the great English author. Probably the first American publication. Frontispiece by Sir John Millais. 92pp. 6½ x 9¼. 23609-9 Pa. $2.50

RALPH THE HEIR, Anthony Trollope. Forgotten tale of illegitimacy, inheritance. Master novel of Trollope's later years. Victorian country estates, clubs, Parliament, fox hunting, world of fully realized characters. Reprint of 1871 edition. 12 illustrations by F. A. Faser. 434pp. of text. 5⅜ x 8½. 23642-0 Pa. $4.50

YEKL and THE IMPORTED BRIDEGROOM AND OTHER STORIES OF THE NEW YORK GHETTO, Abraham Cahan. Film *Hester Street* based on *Yekl* (1896). Novel, other stories among first about Jewish immigrants of N.Y.'s East Side. Highly praised by W. D. Howells—Cahan "a new star of realism." New introduction by Bernard G. Richards. 240pp. 5⅜ x 8½. 22427-9 Pa. $3.50

THE HIGH PLACE, James Branch Cabell. Great fantasy writer's enchanting comedy of disenchantment set in 18th-century France. Considered by some critics to be even better than his famous *Jurgen*. 10 illustrations and numerous vignettes by noted fantasy artist Frank C. Pape. 320pp. 5⅜ x 8½. 23670-6 Pa. $4.00

ALICE'S ADVENTURES UNDER GROUND, Lewis Carroll. Facsimile of ms. Carroll gave Alice Liddell in 1864. Different in many ways from final Alice. Handlettered, illustrated by Carroll. Introduction by Martin Gardner. 128pp. 5⅜ x 8½. 21482-6 Pa. $2.00

FAVORITE ANDREW LANG FAIRY TALE BOOKS IN MANY COLORS, Andrew Lang. The four Lang favorites in a boxed set—the complete *Red, Green, Yellow* and *Blue* Fairy Books. 164 stories; 439 illustrations by Lancelot Speed, Henry Ford and G. P. Jacomb Hood. Total of about 1500pp. 5⅜ x 8½. 23407-X Boxed set, Pa. $14.00

HOUSEHOLD STORIES BY THE BROTHERS GRIMM. All the great Grimm stories: "Rumpelstiltskin," "Snow White," "Hansel and Gretel," etc., with 114 illustrations by Walter Crane. 269pp. 5⅜ x 8½.
21080-4 Pa. $3.00

SLEEPING BEAUTY, illustrated by Arthur Rackham. Perhaps the fullest, most delightful version ever, told by C. S. Evans. Rackham's best work. 49 illustrations. 110pp. 7⅞ x 10¾. 22756-1 Pa. $2.00

AMERICAN FAIRY TALES, L. Frank Baum. Young cowboy lassoes Father Time; dummy in Mr. Floman's department store window comes to life; and 10 other fairy tales. 41 illustrations by N. P. Hall, Harry Kennedy, Ike Morgan, and Ralph Gardner. 209pp. 5⅜ x 8½. 23643-9 Pa. $3.00

THE WONDERFUL WIZARD OF OZ, L. Frank Baum. Facsimile in full color of America's finest children's classic. Introduction by Martin Gardner. 143 illustrations by W. W. Denslow. 267pp. 5⅜ x 8½.
20691-2 Pa. $3.50

THE TALE OF PETER RABBIT, Beatrix Potter. The inimitable Peter's terrifying adventure in Mr. McGregor's garden, with all 27 wonderful, full-color Potter illustrations. 55pp. 4¼ x 5½. (Available in U.S. only)
22827-4 Pa. $1.10

THE STORY OF KING ARTHUR AND HIS KNIGHTS, Howard Pyle. Finest children's version of life of King Arthur. 48 illustrations by Pyle. 131pp. 6⅛ x 9¼. 21445-1 Pa. $4.00

CARUSO'S CARICATURES, Enrico Caruso. Great tenor's remarkable caricatures of self, fellow musicians, composers, others. Toscanini, Puccini, Farrar, etc. Impish, cutting, insightful. 473 illustrations. Preface by M. Sisca. 217pp. 8⅜ x 11¼. 23528-9 Pa. $6.00

PERSONAL NARRATIVE OF A PILGRIMAGE TO ALMADINAH AND MECCAH, Richard Burton. Great travel classic by remarkably colorful personality. Burton, disguised as a Moroccan, visited sacred shrines of Islam, narrowly escaping death. Wonderful observations of Islamic life, customs, personalities. 47 illustrations. Total of 959pp. 5⅜ x 8½.
21217-3, 21218-1 Pa., Two-vol. set $10.00

INCIDENTS OF TRAVEL IN YUCATAN, John L. Stephens. Classic (1843) exploration of jungles of Yucatan, looking for evidences of Maya civilization. Travel adventures, Mexican and Indian culture, etc. Total of 669pp. 5⅜ x 8½. 20926-1, 20927-X Pa., Two-vol. set $6.50

AMERICAN LITERARY AUTOGRAPHS FROM WASHINGTON IRVING TO HENRY JAMES, Herbert Cahoon, et al. Letters, poems, manuscripts of Hawthorne, Thoreau, Twain, Alcott, Whitman, 67 other prominent American authors. Reproductions, full transcripts and commentary. Plus checklist of all American Literary Autographs in The Pierpont Morgan Library. Printed on exceptionally high-quality paper. 136 illustrations. 212pp. 9⅛ x 12¼. 23548-3 Pa. $7.95

CATALOGUE OF DOVER BOOKS

AN AUTOBIOGRAPHY, Margaret Sanger. Exciting personal account of hard-fought battle for woman's right to birth control, against prejudice, church, law. Foremost feminist document. 504pp. 5⅜ x 8½.
20470-7 Pa. $5.50

MY BONDAGE AND MY FREEDOM, Frederick Douglass. Born as a slave, Douglass became outspoken force in antislavery movement. The best of Douglass's autobiographies. Graphic description of slave life. Introduction by P. Foner. 464pp. 5⅜ x 8½.
22457-0 Pa. $5.00

LIVING MY LIFE, Emma Goldman. Candid, no holds barred account by foremost American anarchist: her own life, anarchist movement, famous contemporaries, ideas and their impact. Struggles and confrontations in America, plus deportation to U.S.S.R. Shocking inside account of persecution of anarchists under Lenin. 13 plates. Total of 944pp. 5⅜ x 8½.
22543-7, 22544-5 Pa., Two-vol. set $9.00

LETTERS AND NOTES ON THE MANNERS, CUSTOMS AND CONDITIONS OF THE NORTH AMERICAN INDIANS, George Catlin. Classic account of life among Plains Indians: ceremonies, hunt, warfare, etc. Dover edition reproduces for first time all original paintings. 312 plates. 572pp. of text. 6⅛ x 9¼.
22118-0, 22119-9 Pa.. Two-vol. set $10.00

THE MAYA AND THEIR NEIGHBORS, edited by Clarence L. Hay, others. Synoptic view of Maya civilization in broadest sense, together with Northern, Southern neighbors. Integrates much background, valuable detail not elsewhere. Prepared by greatest scholars: Kroeber, Morley, Thompson, Spinden, Vaillant, many others. Sometimes called Tozzer Memorial Volume. 60 illustrations, linguistic map. 634pp. 5⅜ x 8½.
23510-6 Pa. $7.50

HANDBOOK OF THE INDIANS OF CALIFORNIA, A. L. Kroeber. Foremost American anthropologist offers complete ethnographic study of each group. Monumental classic. 459 illustrations, maps. 995pp. 5⅜ x 8½.
23368-5 Pa. $10.00

SHAKTI AND SHAKTA, Arthur Avalon. First book to give clear, cohesive analysis of Shakta doctrine, Shakta ritual and Kundalini Shakti (yoga). Important work by one of world's foremost students of Shaktic and Tantric thought. 732pp. 5⅜ x 8½. (Available in U.S. only)
23645-5 Pa. $7.95

AN INTRODUCTION TO THE STUDY OF THE MAYA HIEROGLYPHS, Syvanus Griswold Morley. Classic study by one of the truly great figures in hieroglyph research. Still the best introduction for the student for reading Maya hieroglyphs. New introduction by J. Eric S. Thompson. 117 illustrations. 284pp. 5⅜ x 8½.
23108-9 Pa. $4.00

A STUDY OF MAYA ART, Herbert J. Spinden. Landmark classic interprets Maya symbolism, estimates styles, covers ceramics, architecture, murals, stone carvings as artforms. Still a basic book in area. New introduction by J. Eric Thompson. Over 750 illustrations. 341pp. 8⅜ x 11¼.
21235-1 Pa. $6.95

GEOMETRY, RELATIVITY AND THE FOURTH DIMENSION, Rudolf Rucker. Exposition of fourth dimension, means of visualization, concepts of relativity as Flatland characters continue adventures. Popular, easily followed yet accurate, profound. 141 illustrations. 133pp. 5⅜ x 8½.
23400-2 Pa. $2.75

THE ORIGIN OF LIFE, A. I. Oparin. Modern classic in biochemistry, the first rigorous examination of possible evolution of life from nitrocarbon compounds. Non-technical, easily followed. Total of 295pp. 5⅜ x 8½.
60213-3 Pa. $4.00

THE CURVES OF LIFE, Theodore A. Cook. Examination of shells, leaves, horns, human body, art, etc., in *"the* classic reference on how the golden ratio applies to spirals and helices in nature . . . . "—Martin Gardner. 426 illustrations. Total of 512pp. 5⅜ x 8½.
23701-X Pa. $5.95

PLANETS, STARS AND GALAXIES, A. E. Fanning. Comprehensive introductory survey: the sun, solar system, stars, galaxies, universe, cosmology; quasars, radio stars, etc. 24pp. of photographs. 189pp. 5⅜ x 8½. (Available in U.S. only)
21680-2 Pa. $3.00

THE THIRTEEN BOOKS OF EUCLID'S ELEMENTS, translated with introduction and commentary by Sir Thomas L. Heath. Definitive edition. Textual and linguistic notes, mathematical analysis, 2500 years of critical commentary. Do not confuse with abridged school editions. Total of 1414pp. 5⅜ x 8½.
60088-2, 60089-0, 60090-4 Pa., Three-vol. set $18.00

DIALOGUES CONCERNING TWO NEW SCIENCES, Galileo Galilei. Encompassing 30 years of experiment and thought, these dialogues deal with geometric demonstrations of fracture of solid bodies, cohesion, leverage, speed of light and sound, pendulums, falling bodies, accelerated motion, etc. 300pp. 5⅜ x 8½.
60099-8 Pa. $4.00